DARCY'S ANGEL

A Pride and Prejudice Variation

JENNIFER KAY

For Grandma Jean

It only makes sense that this one is for you.

This work is, of course, based on Jane Austen's masterpiece, and I have taken the liberty of adapting some of her original dialogue to meet my version of the story. I do not claim to own that writing, nor do I claim the original plot ideas reproduced in this novel. Any mistakes are my own.

One

Lizzy

October 1806

The carriage rolled to a stop at the gate of an imposing house. From her seat inside the carriage, Elizabeth Bennet looked out at her new home with a calmness she did not feel. The shadow left by the setting sun, which had long since dipped below the rows of close-set houses, darkened the creamy façade of the house to a dull grey. Elizabeth surveyed each of the four stories in turn, carefully noting which of the narrow windows were illuminated as she attempted to block out the feeling that the house would eat her alive.

The person sitting opposite Elizabeth had no such qualms. Catherine Bennet, known to the world as "Kitty," bounced on the hard seat. "Oh, Lizzy, it's so grand," she exclaimed. "I can't believe we get to stay in a place like this!"

Elizabeth turned her gaze away from the house to survey her sister. At thirteen, Kitty was only three years younger than Elizabeth, but the age gap seemed far greater than that. Elizabeth—indeed, all of their family—was used to thinking of herself and her older sister Jane as young ladies, while Kitty and eleven-year-old Lydia still belonged in the nursery. The fifth sister, Mary, fell between Elizabeth and Kitty in age, yet belonged to neither group. It had always been easy to ignore Mary, Elizabeth mused.

She scowled. She could see now how that must have hurt Mary, but what could be done? They had left without saying goodbye to anyone but their father, might never see any of them again. Perhaps one day she would have a chance to make it up to Mary. Just as likely, her sister would be dead within the week.

The thought sent a surge of dread through Elizabeth's body, paralyzing her for a moment while she fought to keep her emotions under control. She would *not* break down. For days, Elizabeth had held back tears by sheer force of will. She told herself it was for Kitty's sake, but the lie fell flat. If Elizabeth gave in to the fears that whispered in her mind, she didn't know if she would ever stop crying.

So she sat up straighter, squaring her shoulders and lifting her chin. When the carriage door opened, Elizabeth accepted the driver's hand and stepped down with as much dignity as she could muster. She waited for Kitty to jump down and took her hand—although she couldn't say if it was to comfort her sister or keep her from bouncing up and down as she surveyed the imposing houses around them.

"It's so fashionable," Kitty breathed as she took in the scene. "Lydia will be so jealous when I write to tell her about it."

The dread morphed into hot anger, and Elizabeth caught herself just before she snapped at her sister. For as long as she could remember, Kitty had dealt with the unpleasant parts of life by pretending they did not exist. Elizabeth understood that. She even wished she could share in her sister's current delusion: they were on an extended vacation to a fashionable part of London for no reason other than their own entertainment. However, that would mean forgetting Jane, sweet, beloved Jane, who might even now be gone forever. It meant pretending not to care about everything in the world that she held most dear, and that was something Elizabeth found abhorrent.

"Hush, Kitty," she said, and walked forward just as the door opened and a woman stepped outside.

So this is Lady Lichfield, Lizzy thought, pushing thoughts of Jane aside as she studied the person who had appeared seemingly from thin air when there was nowhere else to go. She remembered the look on her father's face when he had told her of the plan, the strain in his voice as he said, "You will like Lady Lichfield, Lizzy. She is a solid, dependable lady. It will ease my mind knowing that you and Kitty are with her."

So why have we never heard of her before? Lizzy had wondered then, as she did now. She should have asked her father, should have pushed him for an answer—*any* answer—rather than being swayed by the exhaustion and worry etched across his face. Maybe then she would know what to expect, how to act, as she stood in the fading light on a London street with her sister hovering behind her.

Lady Lichfield descended the stairs that led up to the front door and Elizabeth got a better look at her. She was a tall, slender woman, and with her lack of prior knowledge, Lizzy found it nearly impossible to guess her age. Then, belatedly, she realized that manners took precedence over observations and bobbed a curtsey, tugging on her sister's hand to make sure that Kitty had done the same.

"You must be Miss Elizabeth and Miss Catherine," Lady Lichfield said as they rose. "I am glad to welcome you to London, although I wish we met under different circumstances. My name is Lady Amelia Lee, dowager countess of Lichfield, and this is my home. Please come in; you must be tired after your journey."

Each of the five Bennet sisters had a unique characteristic. Jane was beautiful, Mary studious, Kitty easygoing, and Lydia playful. Lizzy was the witty one, the sister who always had something clever or interesting to say. She reminded herself of that fact as she stood before Lady Lichfield, knowing she needed to speak. Worry made thinking feel as though she was running through honey, unable to perform even the simplest movements with ease. There was also the fact that Lizzy relied on her understanding of situations to poke fun at them, and she currently had no idea what to expect.

What would Jane do? The thought sliced through the fog in her mind, and Lizzy could think again. Jane would smile. She would be polite and make the best of the situation both for herself and whatever sister was present. There was nothing Lizzy could truly do for her elder sister, but she could behave in a manner that would make Jane proud. That thought alone allowed her to raise her head and smile. "Pleased to make your acquaintance, Lady Lichfield. I am Elizabeth, and this is my sister Catherine, although we are generally called Lizzy and Kitty. Thank you for welcoming us to your home."

Behind her, Kitty echoed, "Pleased to make your acquaintance."

Would Jane do anything else? Lizzy didn't think so. She took a hesitant half-step forward, hoping Lady Lichfield would provide a cue, and was relieved when the woman turned back towards the house and went up the stairs to the front door.

They entered a pretty, if simple, entry hall. Nothing was overly grandiose, but everything Lizzy noticed was a finer quality than she was used to at Longbourn. They were introduced briefly to the butler and housekeeper, then Lady Lichfield was leading them down the hall and up a flight of stairs. "I thought you might like seeing your rooms first," the lady said. "You will be able to freshen up after the journey, perhaps rest for a while. Your trunks will be brought up soon if you would like to change. We will dine in an hour, and then perhaps we can get to know each other a bit better over coffee."

"Thank you, that is very considerate," Lizzy said.

Lady Lichfield smiled over her shoulder as she stopped by a door. "I have made sure that there is fresh water in both of your rooms. If you need anything else, Nell will be your maid. She should be—ah, there she is."

A girl around Lizzy's age stepped out of a room and curtseyed. She wore a simple grey dress covered by a crisp white apron, her brown hair pulled back into a simple knot. She was tall and slender with a kind face, and Lizzy felt slightly better knowing that their maid would not be a dragon—assuming that Nell lived up to the first impression, of course.

"Nell is in training to be a ladies' maid, and I think she will do well for you," Lady Lichfield went on. "Nell, this is Miss Elizabeth and Miss Catherine, of Hertfordshire."

Introductions apparently over, she turned to the nearest door, which stood open. "Elizabeth, this will be your room. Catherine, you will be down the hall." Lady Lichfield nodded towards the door. "I hope you will feel at home here. Catherine, if you will follow me?" She led the younger girl down the hallway, leaving Lizzy to enter her room alone.

Beautiful, was Lizzy's first thought when she walked into her new space. The room faced west, and the sunset-colored sky cast a soft light on the entire room, helped along by a candle placed on a small table by the bed. The bed covering was white and trimmed with lace, with two matching pillows at the head. There was a clothespress and a small dressing table, both a dark wood decorated with carvings of flowers and vines. A stand with an ewer and pitcher of water stood next to the dressing table.

It was the room she would have dreamed about at home, Lizzy thought as she sat down gingerly on the bed, turning her attention to the walls. Even the wallpaper was something she might have picked out herself, a dainty blue-and-white flowered pattern, and the two simple pictures on the walls were similarly to her liking. The overall effect was lovely, and Lizzy knew she would appreciate it during the day. It was only at night when Jane's absence would become overbearing, and the room would turn into nothing more than a beautiful prison.

"Will you be needing anything, Miss?" a voice asked from the doorway, and Elizabeth looked up to see Nell.

"No, thank you," Lizzy said. She indicated the pitcher of water. "I believe I'll wash my face, and then I should see how my sister is settling in." And keep Kitty from doing anything embarrassing like jumping on her new bed, she thought, but Lizzy kept that to herself. Nell would learn what Catherine Bennet was like soon enough. There was no need to start off by gossiping with the maid. Especially when every word she said might realistically be repeated to Lady Lichfield—and who knew what that lady might be like once the politeness of new acquaintance wore off?

*

Dinner was a quiet affair. To Lizzy's relief, Kitty managed to act like a proper young lady. There were no exuberant outbursts or pouts, which Lizzy suspected that could largely be attributed to the fact that Lydia was not present to trigger such displays. Lizzy ate little, her stomach tied in knots for reasons she did not fully understand.

You always wanted to go on an adventure, she scolded herself as she forced down yet another bite. *Now that something new is happening, will you really spend all your time feeling sorry for yourself?* Repeating the thought another twenty or so times, she managed to finish an acceptable portion of the food on her plate. Nevertheless, she had never been so relieved as when the plates were cleared away and the party retired to the sitting room for coffee.

"I'm sure you have many questions," Lady Lichfield began once they were all settled. "I will do my best to answer them, although there are some things that I do not know any more than you do. When you will be able to go home, for example." She gave Lizzy a wry smile, as if knowing that was the question she was dying to ask.

Brightening, Lady Lichfield went on, "Now, you said that you are commonly called Kitty and Lizzy, is that correct? Is there anything else I should know about you that might help this transition go smoother?"

Lizzy hesitated at the question. She couldn't imagine her mother asking such a thing of a stranger. In fact, it reminded her of something her Aunt Gardiner might say.

Unlike her Aunt Gardiner, Lizzy could think of nothing she wanted to tell the woman across from her. In fact, one of the questions she very much would have liked to ask was along the lines of "why can't we stay with our aunt and uncle, who also live in London and therefore aren't at risk for catching the disease everyone else at Longbourn has?"

Because there isn't enough room already, and soon there will be another mouth to feed. Because they don't want anyone who might have caught an illness around the babies. Because Aunt Gardiner can't teach us the things that this stranger supposedly can or introduce us to the people Lady Lichfield knows.

Lizzy knew the answers. She just didn't like them.

Realizing that Kitty hadn't spoken up yet, Lizzy looked sharply at her sister. Was it possible that without Lydia to lead her, Kitty actually felt shy? If so, that might be one of the few good things that came out of their separation. Spoiled by her mother and ignored by her father, Lydia ran wild and Lizzy worried what type of lady her youngest sister would be in several years. Removing Kitty from her presence meant that Lydia's poor influence could be countered before Kitty became totally unmanageable as well.

Reining in her thoughts, Lizzy said, "I suppose you should know that I am sixteen, and Kitty is thirteen. I have been 'out' at home for just over a year. Kitty was supposed to attend a recent assembly for the first time, but it was cancelled due to the illness in the community. We have three other sisters. Jane is the oldest at eighteen, Mary falls between Kitty and me at age fifteen, and Lydia is eleven. I presume that you are acquainted with our parents?"

Lady Lichfield's lips turned up, but the smile did not reach her eyes. "I was friends with your father many years ago. I knew of Fanny—your mother—but was never well-acquainted with her. Are you the only two in the family who did not fall ill?"

"Papa isn't ill, either," Kitty said, then hesitated and looked at Lizzy.

"Mama, Jane, and Lydia are all truly ill," Lizzy took up the explanation. "Mary was the first to feel poorly, but she seemed to be recovering when we left. We were not the first family in the neighborhood to fall ill, and when Mary started displaying symptoms Papa ordered that the rest of us should stay away from her as much as possible. Mama and Jane had gone to tend to her before he gave the instructions, but I have no idea why Lydia fell sick when we did not. Papa said that he intended to keep us well, and sent us away as soon as it became clear that the illness was serious. He stayed because he said someone needed to be there to take care of matters."

Lady Lichfield nodded as if it was the response she had been expecting. "Well, your father requested that I keep you in the house for several days and limit your exposure to the household so that you do not spread the sickness, and I intend to do so. However, he also mentioned that you are both healthy girls and he had every hope that you had escaped unscathed, so with luck you will soon be able to experience more of London. I know this may not have been your choice," her eyes lingered on Lizzy, who looked away, "but I believe that we can be happy together for as long as you are here."

"During that time," she went on, "your father asked that I introduce you to society in London as I see fit and teach you those things you may not have had an opportunity to learn at Longbourn." Lady Lichfield paused, as if she was uncertain of how to continue. Finally, she said, "I was a governess before I married Lord Lichfield, and I have lived for many years here in Town. You will go home as the most accomplished girls in all of Hertfordshire. I am sure of it."

Kitty gave a little bounce in her seat, as if she was imagining returning home as the belle of the ball, but Lizzy turned her face so that neither of the others could see her scowl. It would take time to become so accomplished. With Mary already recovering, she had hoped that they might be in Town for as little as a fortnight. Just what had her father told Lady Lichfield, for the woman to speak as if they would be with her for years?

Two

Darcy

October 1806

The Derbyshire wind was biting, but Fitzwilliam Darcy scarcely felt the cold. If he was honest with himself, he didn't truly feel anything. Since his father had slipped out of consciousness three nights prior, Darcy had run on instinct and deeply ingrained habits. Direct the servants. Agree to whatever Parker or Mrs. Reynolds—the more than capable steward and housekeeper—proposed. Respond politely when spoken to. Absolutely do not think about—*no. Just no.* Look after Georgiana.

The last thought jolted Darcy slightly, and he glanced over to where his sister stood. She was eleven, but Georgiana looked no older than eight as she stood next to Mrs. Reynolds, head bowed against the cold wind. The housekeeper put an arm around her and Darcy frowned. He did not object to Mrs. Reynolds' familiar touch—she had long since ceased to be just a servant as far as Darcy was concerned—but it should have been him providing comfort to his sister. With his father's death, he was not just her brother, but her guardian and therefore primary provider and protector as well. Yet here he stood, frozen, wondering how events could have transpired to lead them to this graveside. He should feel grief, he knew that, but the only emotion that cut through the numbness was rage—*No*.

Georgiana raised her tearstained face, large brown eyes searching his for reassurance, and Darcy marveled briefly at the different forms that their grief took. Then again, George Darcy had taught his son quickly that gentlemen concealed their emotions, putting forward a calm mask no matter what feelings surged below the surface. His daughter had instead found solace in her father's arms and a gentle hand to wipe away her tears. And Georgiana did not know the truth about their father's death.

At that thought, the anger threatened to break through Darcy's stoic control. He pushed it back as if it was a physical force and finally managed to move the three strides to Georgiana's side. She came to him readily, tucking herself underneath his arm and burying her face in his side. Over her head, Darcy sensed Mrs. Reynold's gaze, but he forced himself to keep his eyes on the hole in the ground. It would not do to look away from the box holding what remained of his father until the dirt began to fall.

It was later, as they walked together back to Pemberley—*his* house, what a surreal thought—that Georgiana put voice to the question that had lingered in the back of Darcy's mind all day. "What now?"

He didn't answer right away. When their mother and newborn brother died five years ago, Darcy had been away at school and the questions were answered by their father. Now here he was at twenty-three, with the largest estate in Derbyshire to run and a sister dependent on him. She didn't even have a governess since the last one had recently married and their father had not yet filled the position.

The problem wasn't what he *should* do, Darcy realized as he considered. He'd become a master at doing his duty, being the responsible son and brother and student. If the role of landowner seemed daunting at the moment, well, he had capable men in his employ who would guide him so the transition from his father to himself ran smoothly, even seamlessly. They would tell him what his father had done, what was expected, and he would do it. Left to his own devices, such a life might be easy to adopt. Georgiana would be given a new governess, maybe sent away to a school where she could interact with girls from backgrounds like hers, and he would see her over the holidays. Perhaps he would find a wife and thus bring a female companion to Pemberley for his sister. Yes, Darcy could live out his entire life meeting expectations.

Looking down at his sister, who had turned back to stare at the house in front of them, he knew she would be miserable in that life. How could he hand her over to someone else, when she had already lost both her parents at such a young age? No, Georgiana would stay with him, if only for a while. His father would have wanted it that way.

As for Pemberley—like Georgiana, Darcy turned his eyes to their home. More than anything else, Pemberley had always meant George Darcy. His father's presence filled the halls. It had been one of his great passions, and he had scarcely left the estate since Lady Anne died and they no longer removed to London for the Season.

The thought caught in Darcy's mind. This was the time of year they had always departed Pemberley for London, after all. Would it not be better for Georgiana to get away from the silent house and all the memories for a while? She had spent little time at Darcy House in London, and the city was livelier, full of people who might distract them from those who were gone. He usually avoided Town for exactly those reasons, but right now *anything* seemed better than spending silent days in a place where his father couldn't be forgotten for even a moment.

"What would you think about going to London, Georgie?" he asked, answering her question with one of his own.

"I want to stay with you," she said immediately, white face and wide eyes revealing her fear. He'd been right about not sending her away.

"You misunderstand," he said quickly. "We would both go to London—to stay at Darcy House. Parker will take care of Pemberley, and I have some business concerns that will be easier to address from Town. Perhaps we will even see Richard while we are there." His cousin—and technically Georgiana's other guardian, should something happen to Darcy—had recently acquired a commission in the army, making it harder for him to travel to Derbyshire as he had previously done several times a year. Darcy had hoped to see him for the funeral, but didn't know if the hastily-sent letter had even reached him.

Georgiana nodded slowly. "You won't send me away?" she asked.

"No." He would not lie to her, though, so he went on, "I may see if I can find a new governess for you while we are in London, but you will stay with me. You might grow so sick of my company you will long for a school and female companions."

Even as he said it, Darcy knew the attempt at humor had fallen flat, and he did not blame his sister for gasping and taking a renewed grip on his hand. "Never," she said emphatically. "I never want to leave you."

If Richard were present, he would have teased her about falling in love, young as she was, but he was not and Darcy had already proved his ineptitude at lightening the mood. So he did not argue, only gave a single nod and said, "Then it is settled. We will leave for London in three days' time."

*

A letter was waiting for him when he walked into his father's study—no, it was *his* study now. Unable to bring himself to sit behind the desk just yet, Darcy dropped into the small but comfortable chair by the fire and opened the missive, noting wryly that he had inherited yet another duty: corresponding with his mother's sister, Lady Catherine de Bourgh.

Darcy –

My condolences on the death of your father. If he had waited until later in the year to pass I would have attended the funeral, but the roads between Kent and Derbyshire are still questionable, and Anne is feeling poorly in any case.

Darcy broke off reading. Why had she even bothered to write? How ill-mannered of his father to die at an inconvenient time for his sister-in-law, and his cousin Anne was *always* feeling poorly. He turned back to the letter, drumming his fingers on the arm of the chair. The saving grace of Lady Catherine's letters was their length. She could rarely be bothered to pen a lengthy missive, though she expected at least two full pages in reply and would berate him if he fell short.

I do hope that you and Georgiana are coping with the loss. Anne was quite distressed when Sir Lewis passed, bless her soul. For you especially, though, it is important to remember that duty does not cease. Georgiana will be looking to you for guidance, and I ask you to consider her needs in how you act during this time.

Her governess should behave similarly, and you should correct her if you feel necessary. (She does have a new governess, hasn't she? Your father's last letter was quite vague on the point. It is important for girls like Georgiana to have constant, proper attention if they are to become everything that a young lady ought.)

I will see you at Easter.

Your Aunt,

Lady Catherine de Bourgh

Darcy read the letter a second time, then sighed. He leaned forward and tossed it into the fire, then let himself stay there for a moment, hunched over his knees, head in hands. So one ought to show nothing, even in times of great loss. If that was Lady Catherine's belief, it certainly explained her blasé behavior following her husband's death several years before. Darcy remembered Anne's distress—and Lady Catherine's response to it. He could not imagine snapping at Georgiana the way his aunt had corrected her daughter.

Luckily, Darcy's father had also been present to witness the moment and had made his feelings exceedingly clear on the subject, giving Darcy direction on how to act now. "When I pass—don't look that way, Fitzwilliam, it's a fact of life—give me a small funeral and let Georgiana mourn in her own way. The same goes for you, although I doubt crying in a dark room is your style." He'd glanced meaningfully at Anne, weeping into her handkerchief, and the scowling Lady Catherine beside her. "It's a shame to Sir Lewis that his wife can feel so little over his passing." Then, as if sensing he had stepped over an invisible line, George Darcy had returned to silence. Neither Darcy had ever mentioned the day again.

How did you mourn Mother? Darcy wondered now, staring into the fire. He'd never seen his father cry, but it was no secret that his parents had adored each other. The pain his father must have felt at her death would have been considerable—and yet for the most part it had been concealed from his children, the only tells an ashen face and conspicuous absence of laughter or smiles.

But George Darcy hadn't given any sign of envying Lady Catherine her lack of emotion. If anything, he had reacted with pity. Looking back on the scene, Darcy considered his father's words yet again. *Better to love,* they seemed to say, *and know the grief it could bring, than to live your entire life closed off from the world to protect yourself from any feeling at all.*

Darcy frowned. Lady Catherine's note had lacked her usual hint that Anne expected his proposal any day—or perhaps more accurately, his aunt expected the proposal and her daughter did not care to put in the effort it would take to dissuade her mother of the notion. Or had the hint been there and he'd just missed it? Darcy glanced at the half-burned letter and sat back with a sigh. It didn't matter either way. He would never marry Anne, and the memory of his father made him even more convinced that going through life just meeting expectations would not lead to happiness or satisfaction.

Then again… Darcy's eyes strayed to the pile of letters stacked neatly on his father's desk, and he knew that there were some duties and expectations that could not be cast aside. There were more people to consider than Georgiana and himself, something he had never fully realized before. Perhaps running off to London at the drop of a hat was not the wisest decision he had ever made.

But the idea of staying at Pemberley indefinitely made his stomach sink with dread, and Georgiana *did* rank highest on his current list of concerns. So what was to be done?

*

Three hours later, Darcy looked up from the letter in front of him at the sound of a knock on the door. His mouth was dry and a headache was threatening to set in, but that paled next to the enormity of the responsibilities shouldered by the master of Pemberley. His to-do list had grown with each letter. Find Georgiana a governess. Confirm an investment that one of his father's business partners had found. Let that partner—and in fact, a great deal more acquaintances and partners and London society in general—know that George Darcy had passed. See to legal matters. Find out what legal details actually needed to be addressed. And then, thanks to the report from the steward four days past, settle three arguments and deal with one collapsing bridge.

"Enter," Darcy called, hoping his face did not show the despair and hopelessness he felt.

The door opened to reveal Parker, the steward that had been at Pemberley for the past five years. "Mr. Darcy," he said by way of greeting, bowing his head for a moment and then closing the door behind him. "I did not think you would be buried in paperwork quite so soon."

Darcy resisted the urge to shrug. "I needed to know what requires my attention." He hesitated, then decided it might as well be said. "I would like to go to Town with Georgiana. There are things that could be addressed in a timelier manner while I am there, but that would leave all the domestic matters to you. Perhaps you could tell me how my father arranged matters in his absence." *Besides simply not leaving, that is.*

Parker considered before answering. At last he said, hesitantly, "If I may speak frankly, Mr. Darcy—your father—was a very involved landlord, and he took care of day-to-day concerns of which many great men would not have even been aware. However, my previous employer left almost all of the management to his steward, the man who trained me, and I know what is expected. I worked closely with your father these past years, and I do not think your absence would have any negative impacts on the running of the estate." His eyes widened in alarm, and he hurried on, "Of course, I do not mean to suggest—"

Darcy stopped him with a wave of his hand. "You have not offended me. I understand your point."

The unease on Parker's face did not entirely disappear. "You are correct that certain matters could be handled more easily in London," he said quickly. "Your father had planned to send me to Town to look into investment opportunities. If you would rather go, I would be honored to handle the duties here. And you would be able to make decisions and act on the investments without waiting for me to return."

Darcy's sluggish brain finally read the signs in front of him and he realized the source of Parker's worry. A death in the household—especially that of the man or lady of the house—could mean an upheaval in the staff. Did Parker worry that he would be replaced now that the younger Mr. Darcy sat behind the desk? Would he be thinking Darcy wanted to go to London to find himself a new steward? If so, that was one fear he could allay with alacrity.

"That sounds like a splendid plan, Parker. I will worry far less about Pemberley knowing that you and Mrs. Reynolds have it well in hand. When I return we can address what duties I will resume and which you will continue to manage."

He had been right. The lines of worry disappeared from the steward's face and he gave a curt nod. "Very good sir. Oh," Parker went on, putting a hand in his pocket and pulling out a letter. "This just arrived for you."

He handed it over and Darcy surveyed the handwriting. Like Lady Catherine's, the writing on the envelope was instantly recognizable. Lord James Fitzwilliam, the Earl of Matlock, was the de facto head of the family.

Darcy broke the seal and scanned the letter. Unlike his aunt's, it expressed true sympathy for the loss of his father and an apology for missing the funeral without false excuses. Darcy clenched his free hand into a fist where Parker couldn't see in order to keep his face impassive. It ended with a postscript.

> *The countess is pressing me to invite you and our niece to Matlock for as long a stay as you should desire. If you prefer to mourn in private, we will respect your wishes with no further said. Otherwise, send me word of when you will arrive and we shall have your usual rooms prepared. JF*

Darcy considered the invitation for a moment. Lady Margaret was by most accounts a strict, commanding woman, but she was particularly fond of Georgiana. Having had no girls of her own, Darcy had always suspected she doted on his sister to make up for that lack. The fact that Georgiana had lost her own mother at a young age only increased the inclination. And since Lady Margaret could be both warm and sympathetic when she deemed it necessary, Georgiana confided in her as she never would to the high-handed Lady Catherine.

"If I may inquire, when do you plan to depart for Town?" Parker asked, pulling Darcy's attention from his thoughts.

Making a snap decision, he stood. "We depart in three days, but we will not go directly to London. I have just received an invitation from my uncle to stay at Matlock, and I mean to accept."

THREE

Lizzy

October 1806

Lady Lichfield spoke sweetly, but her house was run on different expectations than Longbourn, as Lizzy discovered over the course of her first week in residence. There was no giggling at the breakfast table—or any table—no sleepy girls slumped over with an elbow propping them up. Breakfast was selected from a sideboard, not grabbed from the table itself, and Lizzy would have loved to see Lady Lichfield's expression if Lydia reached across her to grab the jam as she had so often done to Lizzy at Longbourn.

Surprisingly, Kitty only grumbled slightly over the new rules. As they sat down to their sixth breakfast at the house on Hill Street, she sat up straight, one hand holding her toast and the other neatly settled on her lap. There were no loud yawns or proclamations of how she longed to still be in bed. Had she met Kitty for the first time in Lady Lichfield's breakfast room, Elizabeth would have thought her a well-bred, sensible young lady.

As it was, Lizzy found the entire situation disconcerting. Was it really that easy for Kitty to change one of her defining characteristics? Had she only emulated Lydia's exuberance and poor behavior because it was convenient or amusing? Or had Kitty simply decided that her behavior at Longbourn didn't matter whereas it did here in Town?

Lizzy didn't know. But as she watched her sister over the top of her morning drinking chocolate—quite possibly the one positive to living with Lady Lichfield—she felt distinctly that the girl sitting across from her was little more than a stranger. It didn't help the homesickness that had been steadily growing since their arrival. She was the older sister, the one who was supposed to be comforting Kitty. Now it seemed that Kitty didn't need anything of the sort, and somehow that made Lizzy feel even worse.

"Well, girls, I have some news that I think you will like," Lady Lichfield said, pulling Lizzy's attention from her thoughts. "You've been here for almost a week with no signs of illness. A doctor will be stopping by this morning—in fact, he may be here already—but if he is satisfied, I see no reason to keep you locked away when we have a city to explore."

For a moment, Lizzy's heart leapt. She could go for walks again?

But Lady Lichfield had not finished. "I think our first order of business is to find you suitable clothes.

There are several events we will be attending—yes, Kitty, you will go to some of them as well—and you must be dressed to make a good first impression."

Lizzy frowned. She had always loved new clothes, especially since much of her everyday wear had belonged to Jane first. Surely, though, there couldn't be enough events in a fortnight or even a month to justify more than one new dress apiece?

"What sort of events?" Kitty asked eagerly.

"I'll tell you on the way to the shops. If you are finished, Kitty, would you see if the doctor has arrived? He will be in the drawing room."

Kitty bounced up, eager to hurry along their release from the house, and disappeared out the door. The action made her seem more like the sister Lizzy remembered, but Lady Lichfield had servants and efficient ways to summon them. Kitty wasn't needed to see if the doctor was in the house.

"Elizabeth, I feel that something is troubling you," Lady Lichfield said once Kitty had disappeared. So that was the reason!

"You are observant, Lady Lichfield."

The lady raised one eyebrow. "I try to be, but that does not answer my question, so I will be more direct. What is bothering you, Lizzy?"

Lizzy hesitated, but only for a moment. "The neighbors who contracted the illness first were already recovering by the time that Kitty and I left. The longest case I know of lasted three weeks, and that lady has never been strong. It has been two weeks today since Lydia fell ill. I do not see why we need to purchase dresses when we will not be in Town to wear them once they are completed."

Having said her piece, Lizzy tucked her hands into her lap and waited anxiously. Lady Lichfield unnerved her more than Lizzy cared to admit, because she lacked that indolence that Mr. and Mrs. Bennet so often displayed towards their daughters' conduct. After sixteen years of determining her own behavior, Elizabeth was suddenly second-guessing her own sensibilities.

Lady Lichfield pursed her lips. "I have been debating sharing this with you, and I think that doing so might put you at ease or at least provide you with some answers. It is clear your father respects your intelligence, and I can't imagine he would protest overmuch." Reaching into her pocket, Lady Lichfield pulled out a letter and handed it over.

Lady Lichfield,

No doubt you have been wondering when I would write, but then, you know I have always been a poor correspondent. In the same vein, I will be brief. I trust the girls are behaving themselves. You must let me know what you think of Lizzy's wit—she reminds me a great deal of you at that age, and if I must do without her company I take comfort knowing that she is with you.

To answer your other question, yes, I have word on how long the girls will be staying. I could not do this had you not assured me of your willingness to keep them with you long term, and I have been staring at the page for too long trying to convince myself that this is not the best way—but it is. If you are still willing, my request is for the girls to stay with you indeterminately, at least for the next year.

I can picture that raised eyebrow, so I will elaborate. Fanny and Jane are still quite ill, but beyond that, the ordeal has taught me to consider my own mortality. I have sat here for the past week wondering when I would fall ill and regretting the lack of preparations I have made to care for my family after my death. Since I cannot turn back time, I will do my best to make wiser choices in the future, and this is one. Like it or not, Lizzy and Kitty will have opportunities to learn things and meet people in London as they never would in Hertfordshire. I would like to think that two of my daughters will have a chance at a better life than the country can provide.

I will write again when there is more news. Sincerely yours,

*

They reached Bond Street far before the fashionable hour. "I thought it best to introduce you to London without the crowds," Lady Lichfield explained as she led them past a milliner's shop. "They can be overwhelming at first."

Lizzy had thought the streets were crowded already, but she did not share her observation. Since reading her father's letter, the entire world had seemed to be tilted off its axis, and everything took more energy to complete. Besides, Kitty was proclaiming that she could not wait to see the crowds, and Lizzy did not have the heart to be cruel.

What could I tell Papa about our day? she wondered instead. They had entertained each other for as long as she could remember by pointing out the foibles and follies that surrounded them. Perhaps a letter with her observations on London would cheer her father. She had to believe it would, because the tone of his letter had nearly broken her heart. *He does not want us here any more than I do.*

"Ah, here we are," Lady Lichfield said. She led them into a store with several dresses displayed in the window, all made of finer cloth than Lizzy was accustomed to seeing.

At the chime of the door, the occupants of the shop looked up. "Lady Lichfield!" one woman—Lizzy guessed that she was the dressmaker—exclaimed, coming over to greet them. "What can I do for you today?"

"Good day, Mistress Greyson," Lady Lichfield returned. "Misses Elizabeth and Catherine Bennet have recently come to stay with me from the country, and are in need of gowns suitable for London events."

The dressmaker gave them a small curtsey, her gaze sweeping over both of them. Lizzy had the distinct impression that she could see right through their pelisses and cotton dresses. "Of course, Lady Lichfield. "Let me see—you will be Miss Bennet? And Miss Catherine, I believe? How old are you ladies? Are you out in society yet?" The last question was directed more at Lady Lichfield.

"I am sixteen, and my sister is thirteen," Lizzy answered. The mention of "Miss Bennet" pulled at her heart—that was Jane's title, not hers—but here she was the elder sister and people would make assumptions. She would meet people who might never even know of Jane. And if—but no, she would not think that.

"Miss Elizabeth is out, and Miss Catherine will attend select events," Lady Lichfield added.

Mistress Greyson was nodding. "Three dresses apiece—a day dress, an evening gown, and a ball gown for Miss Elizabeth, two day dresses and an evening gown for Miss Catherine—and I believe perhaps a new pelisse for each as well?"

"Make it two day dresses for Miss Elizabeth, but otherwise I agree," Lady Lichfield said.

"Will the young ladies need underthings?" Mistress Greyson asked.

Lady Lichfield considered. "Yes, one set each," she decided.

Mistress Greyson called one of her assistants over to take their measurements, then went back to the customers she had been helping before they entered. Lady Lichfield drifted over to the counter to look at fabric selections.

"Have you made your decisions?" Mistress Greyson asked the other ladies.

One of them shot Lizzy an annoyed look before responding, and she just had time to wonder why before Kitty stepped close and squeezed her hand. "Oh, Lizzy, it is like having a fairy godmother! Three new dresses—all truly new—and a pelisse—and Lydia cannot steal my ribbons!"

"You do not mind that you will not have a ball gown?" Lizzy could not resist teasing.

Kitty frowned. "It would be lovely. But Lady Lichfield said I should make a grand impression at my first ball and I am too young to do that. And I will still get to accompany you on other outings and go to dinner parties and, oh! Lizzy, it is so grand!"

The assistant arrived to take their measurements before Lizzy could respond. She started with Kitty, leaving Lizzy free to observe the disdainful lady and her companion. To her surprise, the second lady caught her looking and smiled.

"Is this your first time shopping in Town?" she asked.

"I have shopped for sweets and trinkets, but never dresses," Lizzy admitted.

"There is no place better than Mistress Greyson's; you are lucky your guardian brought you here. I am Miss Bingley, by the way, and this is my sister Miss Caroline. I could not help overhearing your names. You are Miss Bennet, correct?"

Lizzy smiled. "Please, call me Miss Elizabeth. I have an older sister who is not in Town with us, and when I hear Miss Bennet I look for her."

"Louisa, I need your opinion," the other lady—Miss Caroline—said impatiently, not sparing Lizzy a single glance.

Miss Bingley gave Lizzy a smile and turned to her sister. Done with Kitty's measurements, the assistant moved on to Lizzy's. Once those were taken, there were fabrics to be felt and dithered over and selected, ribbons and lace to be added, and endless questions to answer. Luckily, Lady Lichfield addressed most of those, and it soon became clear that Mistress Greyson had been making her clothes for years.

"I think the pale yellow for Miss Elizabeth's first day dress—like the one you had several years back, do you recall? —but with white ribbons instead of lace."

"Do you have anything like that lovely green you used for my evening gown last year?" "Now, I know you personally detest pink, but I think it would look lovely against Miss Catherine's skin, don't you agree?"

"You will be most fashionable," Miss Caroline remarked to Lizzy at one point during the discussion. She spoke with a smile and Lizzy wondered if she had been imagining the initial scowl. "Why, if I see you in your new clothes I will not recognize you! Mistress Greyson can make anyone look like a proper lady."

Lizzy bristled. She definitely had *not* imagined the scowl. *This is a game. You can write home to Papa about the catty ladies and how funny it was when you didn't react. Clothes do not a lady make*. "Yes, I will enjoy having new gowns. I do not need anything special at my father's estate in the country, but of course London society is different. You must have been coming here for some time, though. Did your mother bring you here for your first ball gown, as I am procuring mine?"

Miss Caroline's smile turned brittle. "I have only discovered the wonders of Mistress Greyson recently." She turned to enthusiastically greet a young lady who had just entered, leaving Lizzy bemused but glad to be rid of the lady's attention.

Several other ladies came in as the morning went on, and all of them seemed to know Lady Lichfield. Lizzy and Kitty were introduced to five young ladies and three matrons that jumbled together instantly in Lizzy's mind. Only one of them knew the Bingley sisters and left when they did. Miss Bingley said her farewells to Lizzy's group while Caroline and her friend made their way out, laughing and gossiping as they went.

Lady Lichfield and a second lady—Mrs. Samson, Lizzy remembered triumphantly—exchanged a glance as the door closed behind them. Then it was back to another round of questions on ribbons, and not until they were walking home did Lizzy have a chance to ask Lady Lichfield about the encounter.

"What did you think of the Miss Bingleys?" Lady Lichfield asked in return rather than answering immediately.

Lizzy considered. "Miss Bingley was pleasant, and I believe genuine as well, while I seemed to upset Miss Caroline simply by entering the shop. She thinks quite highly of herself. I do not think I did anything to offend her, but she took a very decided dislike to me."

Lady Lichfield gave a short laugh. "I agree you did nothing, Lizzy. Miss Caroline did not like that Mistress Greyson left them to greet us, especially since you and Kitty were the customers. If I had requested dresses, she would not have dared to show her annoyance, but you are younger and less fashionably dressed than she was, and therefore she feels justified looking down on you."

"What exactly did she mean by saying Mistress Greyson can make anyone into a proper lady?" Words were the first weapon in Lizzy's arsenal, and if she didn't fully understand the slight, she couldn't respond. Feeling as if she'd won that day's game of wits by luck rather than skill, Lizzy was determined to not leave the outcome to chance again.

Lady Lichfield laughed. "Is that what she said? I heard your response and gathered something of the sort. She meant to insult you, I am sure you gathered that, but all she did was expose her own lack of breeding. The Bingley sisters come from trade. I expect they inherited a decent amount of money and cannot wait to show it off, but only if it gives them the appearance of gentry.

"They were wearing purple and grey but ordering colored gowns, so they are coming out of mourning, and the cloth they selected was finer than what they wore. Associating with those who shop at Mistress Greyson's and showing off their wealth gives them a better chance at a good marriage." Lady Lichfield hesitated, frowning. "You will meet many marriage-hungry young ladies in London, Lizzy, but be especially careful of the newly rich, particularly those who began life in the lower classes. They have the most to prove, and some of them feel the easiest way to build themselves up is by pulling others down."

FOUR

Darcy

November 1806

Despite his intentions to live a life beyond society's expectations, Darcy was struggling to not throw himself into his new duties and ignore the rest of the world. Of course, that was likely the reason that Georgiana had broken down once again, wailing that he was going to send her away when he'd planned nothing of the sort. She had dashed out of sight, flying up the stairs to her room, where she was likely crying into her pillow like she had done the last half-dozen times.

Which left Darcy pacing his study, again, while he tried to think of anything he could do, again, and failed miserably, *again*.

The month at Matlock had been, if not enjoyable, then at least less painful than their current situation. Lady Margaret had kept Georgiana busy, distracting her with new embroidery stitches and books that she herself had loved as a girl. Lord Matlock had distracted Darcy as well, with horses and shooting and billiards on the days the weather kept them inside. Richard's older brother Henry, heir to Matlock, had spent two weeks there as well. Darcy had never gotten along with Henry as he did with Richard, but his cousin could be quite entertaining when he put his mind to it, and Darcy had appreciated his company.

It hadn't occurred to Darcy that they would struggle so much in London. Georgiana had seemed, if not happy, then at least composed by the end of their visit. She'd even laughed a few times, when Henry turned his efforts to amusing her. Somehow, within half an hour of arriving at Darcy House, that girl had disappeared, and for the life of him Darcy couldn't understand what had happened.

Finally deciding that wearing a path in the study's floor helped neither himself nor Georgiana, Darcy gave up. He had been meaning to visit the family solicitor since arriving, but originally planned to wait until Georgiana felt more secure in their new home. Obviously that wasn't going to happen as fast as expected, and he had already put matters off a month by accepting the invitation to visit Matlock. Asking Mrs. Crew, the housekeeper, to keep an eye on his sister, Darcy departed.

He chose to walk the several blocks rather than riding, hoping it would clear his head. He very much hoped to give the impression of a controlled young man worthy of his inheritance and subsequent duties; it would not do to admit that managing his own little sister was beyond his abilities.

Darcy found the correct building all too soon and enquired if the man was available. He was directed up a set of stairs to a door, where a small sign was engraved with “Mr. J Reid, Solicitor.” Darcy hesitated briefly, then knocked. It occurred to him that he should remove his gloves and he did so, shocked as always when he noticed that they were black instead of the customary white.

The door swung open as he reflexively touched his cravat—also uncharacteristically black, as befitted a man who had recently lost his father. Feeling as though he had been caught off guard, Darcy frowned at the man with more intensity than the situation required. “Are you Mr. Reid?”

Luckily, the solicitor appeared unfazed, and Darcy wondered what he usually encountered upon opening his door. He was a short man, making the small bald spot in his red hair noticeable from Darcy’s height, and his hazel eyes seemed to be disappearing into the flesh around them.

“I am,” the man responded. “Mr. Josiah Reid, at your service. You must be Mr. Darcy. I have been expecting you since I heard of your esteemed father’s passing.”

Darcy’s frown deepened. “May I inquire how you recognized me?”

Mr. Reid had retreated into the room, but at the question he turned and gave Darcy a small smile. “My secretary has a shrill voice that carries, even though our walls are thicker than usual to prevent eavesdropping. I heard her welcome you. Please, sit." He dropped into the seat behind the desk, waving for Darcy to take one of the two chairs across from it.

Two hours later, Darcy had forgotten Mr. Reid's bald spot and beady eyes. In fact, he was so impressed with the man's knowledge of law, investments, and both the Darcy estate and family history that he'd managed to forget the problem with Georgiana completely—until Mr. Reid closed his file and said, smiling, "Your sister is lucky. Not everyone has relatives that are so interested in working out the details of what was left to them—that is, other than the amount of their new inheritance."

Darcy's stomach dropped. "My sister…. has taken my father's passing harshly. I fear I am a poor substitute for him in that regard."

Mr. Reid nodded, his face turning grave. "It is a hard thing to lose a parent," he said, and Darcy got the distinct impression that the man was speaking from personal experience. "It is both a curse and a blessing that your sister is young—she feels the loss keenly, but children are remarkably resilient in the long term. For now, she may do best with distractions. Take her to Hyde Park, see the fireworks at Vauxhall. If she plays an instrument, encourage her to practice. Does she have a dog? A kitten? These things help, even if there are still trying phases. And don't blame yourself too much if you don't always know what to do. We are all only human, and thus inherently flawed. I maintain my belief that your sister is lucky to have you."

Overwhelmed by a mix of emotions, Darcy gruffly took his leave of the solicitor and walked back to Darcy House deep in thought. The easiest suggestion—an outing—he could arrange at once, for it was a pleasant day and early enough that Hyde Park would not be overrun by fashionable people who might insist on an introduction and therefore intimidate Georgiana. Likewise, the pianoforte could be tuned and new music purchased in an afternoon; perhaps they could select some after their walk.

As for an animal—well, he'd see how the other options worked first. Anne Darcy would have shrieked at the idea of a cat shredding her beautiful furniture or a puppy tracking muddy paw prints on her rugs. Still, the idea was there, should the rest of them fail. After all, Christmas was not too far away, and it was certain to be rough this year. And if anything worked, Darcy thought as he reached his own door and climbed the front steps, he would pay Mr. Reid double what he charged for the morning's session.

*

"Georgiana, I have a proposition for you."

The door to her room flew open with an alacrity that caught Darcy off guard. Equally surprising was his sister's appearance—wide eyes and flaming cheeks replaced the tears he had last seen.

"Don't send me away! I'm sorry, Fitzwilliam, so sorry. I'll behave, I promise. I promise. I didn't mean to upset you."

She thought the problem was upsetting *him*? Good Lord. "I've told you, Georgiana—"

"I'll act like a proper young lady, I'm sorry, Fitzwilliam!"

"—that I will not send you away, and I don't break my word. I mean that, Georgiana. You will stay with me unless something—and it would have to be *drastic*—happens that makes that impossible, or until you no longer wish to stay with me. *I promise*. I came to ask if you would like to go for a walk in Hyde Park."

"Is that not improper?" Georgiana asked after a long pause. She looked down at her black bombazine gown, one of three hastily made before they left Pemberley. "I did not think we were allowed to go out."

Well, maybe that was part of why she seemed so unhappy.

"We cannot attend parties or socialize with large groups, but being in mourning does not mean we are under house arrest, Georgie. It is early; the *ton* do not descend on Hyde Park until afternoon. And even if there are others there, they will understand we do not wish to make new acquaintances." Their black garb would certainly make the reasoning obvious.

"How long will we have to stay away from others?" Georgiana asked, once she had fetched her spencer and gloves—black like his own—and they were strolling down Grosvenor Street.

Darcy considered. "It's not set in stone," he said. Surely a governess would be better able to explain the intricacies than he was! "For a parent, the mourning period is around half a year, but there are distinctions. If you were out, it would not be fashionable for you to attend balls or parties in that time. Since you are *not* out, though, it affects you less. You can still see family or intimate friends. As I am taking over Father's business, it affects me even less. I am *expected* to maintain some form of contact with the outside world—whether I wish to or not."

"Father locked himself away after Mother died."

The words tore at Darcy's heart. He remembered Georgiana, only six at the time, sneaking into his room at night because her mother was gone and her father had shut himself up in his study. In her long white nightdress and pale skin, Georgiana had looked very much like a ghost herself.

"Yes, he did," he said aloud. "That was Father's choice. He missed Mother very much, and he didn't want to be with the rest of the world when she wasn't in it."

"Not even us," Georgiana observed in a small voice. Then she cocked her head. "Why would you not wish to attend parties and balls? They sound like great fun, although I'm sure the people would terrify me at first. Is it because you are sad and do not wish to be around others, like Father?"

"Well, I suppose that's part of it. But it is more than that, Georgie. You know that we have a very grand life compared to many of the people around us. Other people want that life for themselves. Since I am to inherit—since I *have* inherited—Pemberley, that means that there are many ladies who would like to marry me. Or, at least, their mothers would like them to marry me." It sounded so crass to say it aloud! Darcy knew how the world worked, knew that money and social standing often outweighed love. That didn't mean he liked admitting it to his eleven-year-old sister.

She was frowning as they entered Hyde Park, turning the thought over in her head. Realizing he had not fully explained himself, Darcy went on. "I do not always enjoy parties and balls because it is hard to know which young ladies like me for myself, and which ones like me because they have been instructed to do so. Does that make sense?"

"Oh, Fitzwilliam, that sounds horrible! I would hate to never know if someone truly liked me." Her eyes grew big. "And what if someone were to trick you, and pretend that they truly *did* love you—and then there would be nothing you could do. What if you marry someone like that, and *she* makes you send me away?"

Oh blast, not that again. "Hush, Georgie. I'm not planning on marrying *anyone* soon, and I like to think I could tell a lady's true feelings after spending time with her. Besides, there are ladies who have money and status already, and they do not need to ensnare someone to gain either. I can always marry someone like that."

But the idea had entered Georgiana's mind that an unknown evil lady would integrate her way into their lives and persuade Darcy to send his sister away, and nothing he said could convince her otherwise. Watching her, Darcy made up his mind to start inquiring about a governess immediately. Surely a female companion was better suited to help Georgiana—*he* was obviously incompetent in that regard. He knew little about women's sensibilities on a good day, and it was becoming rapidly apparent that his sister was in a great deal of distress. Perhaps a kitten *would* be a suitable distraction until a governess could be procured, shredded furniture be damned.

"Do you remember Hyde Park at all, Georgie?" he asked after they had walked in silence for several minutes. "You used to come here with Mother when we were in Town and throw bread to the geese."

Georgiana frowned. "I think so. I remember feeding geese and one of them grabbing the bread from my hand, but I always assumed that was at Pemberley." Her nose wrinkled. "I do not care for geese. They are horrible creatures."

Startled by the recollection, Darcy gave a bark of laughter. "I remember that! Yes, that happened here. You must have been five years old, and the goose was almost as tall as you. Your nurse was so flustered when the goose ran at you she nearly fell into the Serpentine. And then Mother almost pushed her in because she was of no help whatsoever."

"And then we went to the confectioners and had sweets!" Georgiana exclaimed. "I thought the geese might steal them from me even in the shop, so I held onto them so tightly Mother laughed. I thought that was in Derbyshire, too, but the store in my memory is too large to be the one in Lambton."

Encouraged by her smile, Darcy grinned as well. "Yes, that was Gunter's. We shall have to get sweets there soon, so you can update your memories of the place." Struck with an idea, he added, "Would you like to see where the goose attacked you? I remember it well, because we were at my favorite bench in the entire Park."

Georgiana nodded, and they tuned back down the lane. It had been several years since Darcy last visited the bench by the Serpentine, but it did not take him long to find the correct path. They were at the last turn in the path when a shout came from behind him. "Darcy! Is that you?"

Darcy and Georgiana turned. A young man was hurrying towards them. "Bainbridge," Darcy responded, recognizing him. He had attended Eton with Peter Bainbridge and his brother Andrew. Peter, while older than Darcy, had undoubtedly been the closer acquaintance. Still, they hadn't seen each other in several years, and Darcy couldn't help wondering how he had been recognized at a distance and from behind.

He was in luck, because Bainbridge laughed as he reached them. "I thought it was you! There aren't that many fellows with your height, even in London. Then I saw you were tapping your fingers on your leg and I knew. What brings you to Town? And who is this lovely young lady?"

Of course, Darcy thought, resisting the urge to roll his eyes. Peter—in fact, most of his friends at school—had teased him about his constant fidgeting, whether that was tapping a foot or drumming his fingers on the nearest available surface. He'd thought the habit had eased, but apparently not.

"This is my sister, Georgiana Darcy. Georgiana, this is Peter Bainbridge, a friend of mine from school."

Bainbridge bowed. "Delighted to make your acquaintance," he told Georgiana with a brilliant grin. In return, she gave a weak smile that managed to make her look even more timid than before, then began to inch behind Darcy.

He sighed silently. "I have business in Town, and I thought Georgiana would be happier with me. She has not spent much time in London."

Bainbridge lost his smile. "I heard about your father. Please accept my condolences, Darcy. He was a good man by all accounts, and will be missed by many."

Darcy raised an eyebrow. "I had not thought many of the *ton* would notice his passing. He spent little time in London these past five years."

"True, but a man like George Darcy is not so easily forgotten. My father said your parents were always favorites at the parties they attended. There are a great many who aspire to be like them." He gave Darcy a sideways look. "You'll be looking for your own lady before long, unless I'm mistaken. Or do you already have a favorite?"

Darcy stiffened. What would Georgiana think now, hearing that so soon after he'd assured her marriage was not on his mind? "I haven't given it much thought," he said coldly, turning to find his sister. She must have moved away while they'd been conversing, because he had to turn father than expected. And then—he turned in a full circle once, twice—the sinking feeling was back in his stomach.

Georgiana was nowhere to be seen.

Five

Lizzy

November 1806

Remember, Lizzy, be home in time to receive visitors!"

"Of course, Lady Lichfield," Lizzy called back over her shoulder.

"And don't lose Tom, or you won't be allowed out again."

This time, Lizzy stopped and returned to the sitting room door. "I didn't mean to lose him last time," she said, wrinkling her nose. "I thought he was right behind me—I think I was more worried than Tom was!" Sobering, she added, "I will endeavor to be more careful today."

Lady Lichfield nodded, apparently convinced of her sincerity. "Kitty, are you sure you do not wish to accompany your sister to the Park?"

Kitty giggled. "Oh, no. Lizzy walks much too fast, and she hates waiting for anyone. It didn't surprise *me* at all when Tom couldn't keep up."

At home, Lizzy would have stuck out her tongue. Here, where Lady Lichfield could decide she was too immature to go for walks and rescind the privilege at any time, she didn't dare. Instead, she turned and hurried back down the hall and stairs. Tom, Lady Lichfield's oldest footman, waited for her by the door.

"I am glad to see you have remembered your bonnet, Miss Elizabeth," he remarked, the hint of a smile showing at the corners of his eyes.

"I made sure to choose the one with the brightest ribbon, so you will have a better chance of picking me out of a crowd," Lizzy rejoined. She had always ventured out bare-headed at home, but in Town such disregard to propriety would never do—a fact that Tom had reminded of her prior to their last outing.

"I appreciate your forethought, but I do not think the bonnet makes you any taller, which was my downfall on our last excursion." He held the door open for her, then followed her out.

"I would be happy to grow taller, but short of wearing high heels and breaking both my ankles, I know no way that I can oblige." Lizzy hoped she hadn't sounded bitter. Of all her features, she liked her height the least. How she would love to be tall and willowy!

"If you broke your ankles, I should have to carry you home, and I do not believe Lady Lichfield would be happy with either of us," Tom responded.

Lizzy agreed, and she appreciated his humor even more. Tom had been a pleasant surprise. When Lady Lichfield said a servant would accompany Lizzy on all her walks, the latter had expected a stuffy, self-important manservant or a simpering, dainty maid. Instead, she had found a spry old footman with thinning grey hair, brilliantly blue eyes, and an impish smile. An old injury—the cause of which Lizzy had yet to guess and Tom seemed to delight in not telling her—had left him with a severe limp and a bent-over gait, but it had not slowed him down much. Tom didn't walk at the speed Lizzy would have liked, but his pace was far from a stroll.

They reached Hyde Park quickly. It would be hours before the *ton* descended on the Park to see and be seen, and so Lizzy had her choice of quiet lanes. Tom, remarkably adept at turning silent and invisible when he wanted to, stayed far enough away that she could almost imagine she was alone. But she wasn't, Lizzy thought in a moment of bitterness, and no artificial wilderness could replace her beloved country lanes. There were those who would thrill at catching a glimpse of London's grand buildings; Elizabeth Bennet longed for the view from Oakham Mount.

Determined not to ruin her outing with such thoughts, Lizzy turned on her heel and took a path that followed the edge of the Serpentine River. *What could I tell Papa about this place?* she mused, looking around.

But that was no good—her father would not find humor in an account of a park, and he had never cared for walks as she did. *Very well then, Jane.* How to describe the riverside path so that Jane could pretend she had seen it as well? Lizzy turned in a slow circle, drinking in her surroundings.

Had she not been looking at every detail, Lizzy would have missed the flash of movement between a pair of trees at the water's edge. Blinking, she froze, staring at the spot. The fall foliage blocked most of the area, but as she continued to watch, a shape began to take form amongst the leaves. Lizzy took two steps forward, and the shape solidified into that of a girl in a dark dress.

What is a girl doing alone by the Serpentine? And she's clearly high-born—look at that dress!

"Excuse me," Lizzy said, and the girl jumped, grabbing a tree branch to keep from falling. "Oh, forgive me!" Lizzy exclaimed, hurrying forward.

She stopped short. The girl's face was streaked with tears, and she watched Lizzy with ever-widening eyes.

"Are you hurt?" Lizzy asked hesitantly. When the girl didn't answer, she added, "Or in trouble? Can I help you?"

At that, the girl broke into fresh tears. Letting go of the branch, she wrapped her arms around herself and leaned forward so chestnut curls covered her face.

Years of soothing her younger sisters took over. Without thinking, Lizzy hurried the rest of the way to the stranger and wrapped her arms around the shaking shoulders. "Shhh," she whispered, hugging the girl tighter when she would have pulled away. "The worst thing in the world is having to cry alone, so cry as much as you want and when you feel up to it you can tell me what's wrong."

I should know, Lizzy thought, stroking the other girl's hair. *I never knew how much better Jane made everything just by being there.*

The girl pulled back after several long moments, hiccupping, and this time Lizzy didn't stop her. "I'm Elizabeth Bennet," she said instead. "I suppose I should introduce myself as *Miss* Elizabeth Bennet, but I'm not used to that." Everyone knew her at home, or someone else introduced her. "What did you say?" The other girl had whispered something.

"Miss Darcy," she repeated. "That's me—my name. Georgiana Darcy." Georgiana wiped her eyes, but her bottom lip trembled as if the tears would return at any moment.

"Pleased to meet you, Miss Darcy," Lizzy said brightly. Odd—it was easier to act positive around this sniffling stranger than with Kitty's enthusiastic approach to everything in their new life. "Are you alone?"

"No." The lip trembled more. "My brother—he will be looking for me—I oughtn't have run off, but I know he thinks I shouldn't cry, and—" she stopped abruptly, looking away.

"Why were you crying?" Lizzy asked gently, filing away the information that Georgiana's brother might appear at any moment. "If you don't mind me asking, of course."

For a moment, tears filled Georgiana's eyes, and Lizzy silently cursed her lack of tact. Then the younger girl took a shaky breath and blinked them back. "My—my father died."

"Oh, Miss Darcy." Lizzy moved to hug Georgiana again, but stopped herself. "I'm so sorry," she said instead. "You must miss him very much."

"I do." Now that Georgiana had decided to speak, the words poured out of her. "I miss him *so* much, all the time. And it makes me miss my mother, too, even though she died years ago. I know Fitzwilliam must miss them as well, but he's always so *composed*, and all I can do is cry. I hate crying, but I can't stop, and Father always made everything better but he can't make this better and I don't know what to do!"

She took a deep gasping breath and then a whole new level of dejection seemed to fall on her. "And now I've run off and I'm telling my problems to a *stranger*—no offense meant—and it's everything I'm not supposed to do. Fitzwilliam is so perfect at doing everything just as he ought, and I'm so scared he'll send me away if I don't act like him, but what if I *can't*?" Her eyes beseeched Lizzy for an answer, any answer.

Pity and sympathy filling her heart, Lizzy made a show of sighing. "Can I tell you a secret, Georgiana?"

The girl looked surprised. She blinked twice in rapid succession, clearing some of the tears from her eyes. "If you want to, of course. But, I mean, you don't know me at all."

"No, but you just opened your heart to me and it is only fair I do the same. Besides, I don't suppose it's really a secret. I just haven't said it to anyone, because it won't help my situation at all. I think I would like to tell you, though. And that way you won't have to feel bad about telling me what you did." *It might even help you,* Lizzy thought, but she'd keep that to herself.

Georgiana nodded slowly.

"My sister Kitty and I have been in London for a month," Lizzy said. "We were sent away because everyone else in our family was ill. Our father wouldn't even let us say goodbye, and I don't know if I'll ever see him or my mother or my three other sisters again. My mother and my older sister—the *best* sister in the entire universe—are still very sick." She paused, wondering how to phrase what she wanted to say. "Kitty acts like we're on holiday and it's a great lark."

"No!" Georgiana exclaimed softly.

Lizzy nodded. "It makes me so mad to watch her laugh and talk about fashions when the only thing I can think about is going home and seeing Jane. But then the other day, a letter from my Papa arrived at the same time as a new fashion magazine. Kitty turned absolutely white—she said she'd had a bad dream about home and the letter was sure to have bad news. She wouldn't even read it; I had to tell her that nothing bad had happened and one of our sisters seems to be fully recovered. Even then, though, she didn't touch the magazine until she'd read the letter half a dozen times for herself. The next morning, she acted like nothing had ever happened." Lizzy paused. "Is your brother older than you?" He had to be, but it wouldn't do to assume.

"Yes, considerably so. He's three-and-twenty."

Well, that explained why Georgiana hadn't mentioned anyone else. Her brother was old enough to be her legal guardian. "Everyone copes with problems in their own way," Lizzy said. "Your brother should understand that. I am sure he is worried about you, but you aren't disappointing anyone because you feel sad, any more than it is wrong for my sister to deal with the worry in her own way. You wouldn't want to forget your father overnight, would you?"

Oh, that had come too close to her own secret terrors. Immediately, Lizzy felt tears well up in her own eyes and she blinked rapidly to clear them.

"Georgiana!"

Both girls jumped at the shout. This time Georgiana grabbed Lizzy's arm to steady herself rather than the tree, then looked horrified with herself.

"Is that your brother?" Lizzy asked, turning her arm so she could take Georgiana's hand.

"Yes," the girl whispered.

"Come, let us get out of the trees. Everything will be fine." Still holding onto the younger girl's hand,

Lizzy made her way back up to the path. Tom, who had stayed in the shadows while she talked to Georgiana, came forward and stood at attention, his livery making it clear he was accompanying Elizabeth. She gave him a small nod, then turned to face the brother.

Her first impression of the young man standing in front of her was that of height. He was tall, with hair only a shade lighter than his black clothing and brown eyes framed by curling lashes. Despite the aristocratic face, with its strong chin and long, straight nose, the feeling Lizzy picked up from him was one of confusion. He either didn't know what to do with his sister or how to react to the presence of a strange young lady. Just as likely, both options were true. Three-and-twenty, Georgiana had said, with a sister to care for and—if their clothes were any indication—a great deal of money to manage. She didn't envy his position any more than she liked her own.

They stared at each other for several moments, then the man seemed to catch himself. "Georgiana, will you introduce your companion?" he asked, eyes lingering on their intertwined hands; Georgiana was still clinging to Lizzy.

Silence returned for a moment, and Lizzy glanced down at her new acquaintance. Seeing Georgiana's frozen face, she was about to introduce herself when Tom stepped forward.

"Sir, this is Miss Elizabeth Bennet or Longbourn in Hertfordshire. She is currently staying with my mistress, Lady Lichfield."

A relieved look crossed the man's face, and Lizzy wondered if he had been as confused as she about the proper way to proceed. Freed from the uncertainty, he bowed. "Fitzwilliam Darcy, of Derbyshire, at your service."

Lizzy curtseyed as best she could without letting go of Georgiana. "Pleased to meet you, Mr. Darcy."

He gave her an odd half-smile before looking at his sister. "Georgiana, are you well? You worried me."

She hung her head and Lizzy reached out with her free hand to touch the girl's chin. "Remember, it's okay to be upset," she murmured so only the two of them could hear. "Just keep in mind that not all people you will find in Hyde Park are as lovely as I am."

Startled, Georgiana looked up and gave a sweet smile. "But you *are* lovely, and I'm glad you found me." She half glanced at her brother.

"He's upset, too," Lizzy said in an even quieter voice, so low she could barely hear herself. "Go hold onto *his* hand. It will probably make him feel better. Surely you used to do that when you were younger?" she asked as an afterthought. The Darcy siblings clearly came from a stricter background than she did, but she couldn't imagine a younger sister never holding her brother's hand.

Georgiana nodded, then took a deep breath and spoke louder. "I am well, Fitzwilliam. I—I needed a bit of space. I've only encountered Miss Elizabeth, no one else. There weren't even any evil geese. I'm sorry for worrying you."

Lizzy frowned, wondering what geese had to do with the situation, but was glad when Georgiana released the death grip on her hand and straightened her black skirts.

A second young man came jogging down the path from the other direction. "Oh, good, you've found her!" he said, coming to a stop several paces from Darcy. "And a friend as well," he added, looking at Darcy and raising an eyebrow. Darcy scowled.

Before Lizzy could puzzle out what had happened, the other man had stepped forward to be introduced. Another round of pleasantries were exchanged, then Darcy looked at his sister. "Come, Georgiana, we should return home," he said. "It was a pleasure to meet you, Miss Elizabeth. Bainbridge, I shall see you soon, I am sure."

"Come to Jack's any day, we'll have to go a round," Bainbridge told Darcy. "I'll walk part of the way out with you—my horse is in the Row." He bowed to Lizzy. "Good day, Miss Elizabeth. I hope we shall meet again." He shot another look at Darcy, and Lizzy wondered what on earth the man was thinking.

"Good day, gentlemen, Miss Darcy," she responded, and Georgiana replied in kind. Then the party split, Lizzy and Tom walking off in one direction and the other three taking a wider lane that led back towards Rotten Row.

What an interesting group, Lizzy mused as she wandered. *I wonder what will happen to Georgiana, and if she will ever feel more comfortable with her brother. It's a shame I'll probably never see any of them again.*

Six

Darcy

December 1806

The short girl in the yellow dress was magic. How else could she have gotten Georgiana to smile when Darcy had clearly seen the telltale wobble of her lip that always foretold tears? What had she said that encouraged his sister to hold onto his hand the entire way home as if her life depended on it? Was it a skill females were simply born knowing, or did this girl have access to information he'd never before thought he'd need?

Darcy didn't know, but if someone told him that they had met an angel in Hyde Park, he would believe them. It had been three weeks since their encounter by the Serpentine, and in that time Georgiana had not run off bawling once. She still cried, of that he was certain, but her behavior was that of grief rather than hysteria. Darcy was sure it was the young lady's doing.

He looked down at the invitation in his hand and made a face. It seemed unlikely that he would meet an angel at Lord and Lady Haddington's party that evening, but he was going regardless. Darcy thought it highly probably that Bainbridge had a hand in procuring him an invitation, for the Haddingtons were no more than passing acquaintances. He'd certainly played a role in Darcy's acceptance.

"Come on, old pal," Bainbridge had wheedled during their last meeting at Jack's, as they both warmed up for a fencing match. "It's a small affair, really, the perfect way for you to ease yourself back into society. And I'll be bored without you."

"Then don't go," Darcy had responded simply.

"Not all of us have your fortune," Bainbridge said, poking Darcy in the side with his dull practice foil. "If I am to meet an heiress, I have to go to places where they will be as well."

Darcy sidestepped the jab and held his own foil out before him, keeping Bainbridge at bay. "You're in the wrong place, then," he said, making a show of looking around. "I don't see a single heiress. And you said it will be a small event—do you really think that many grand ladies will attend?"

Bainbridge stepped into position and brought his foil up to cross Darcy's. "It's been three months, Darcy. Your sister can be left alone for one evening. Just say you'll come, will you?"

And so, reluctantly, he'd promised to attend, a decision he regretted heartily as he stepped into the main room of the party and felt the crush of people all around. Darcy had never cared for parties, and several months away had not helped the matter. Bainbridge had been correct—by London standards it *was* a small party. Of course, that meant the manners of those present were more likely to fall flat and the mothers were voracious in their search for a man with money. Darcy frowned. Maybe a fancy ball would have been a better choice. It would be easier to disappear there.

He was already here, though, and people were entering behind him. Resigned, Darcy let out a sigh he hoped wasn't audible and moved father into the room.

"Darcy! There you are!" Bainbridge appeared amidst the crowd, waving his way to Darcy's location. "I didn't think you'd actually come," he said when they at last met up in the midst of the throng.

"I said I would come and I keep my word," Darcy replied, feeling put out that Bainbridge thought he would break his promise.

"Yes, you always were a stickler for that sort of thing," the other man agreed, already turning away. "Come, there are some people I want you to meet. They're from trade, mind, but the brother is a pleasant chap and the sisters have large enough dowries to risk the connection. I'll be interested to hear your opinion on the lot of them."

Darcy bit back a protest that he did not want to be introduced to every group in the room, especially the social climbers. He'd met a few of those at Eton and Oxford, young men full of ambition and more often than not determined to "show up" those from the landed gentry—but also quite keen to introduce their sisters to those same men. It was an experience he would happily forego repeating.

Bainbridge had already disappeared back into the throng, and Darcy permitted himself a single frown before he started in the direction his friend had gone. It would not do to look annoyed or—heaven forbid—roll his eyes, no matter how much he wanted to do so.

"Survive the crowd?" Bainbridge asked with a grin when Darcy at last arrived at his side. "I was worried one of the mothers had waylaid you—to give her condolences, of course." He glanced at Darcy's black-on-black attire, then turned to the group in front of him without waiting for an answer. "Darcy, this is Charles Bingley, and his sisters Miss Louisa Bingley and Miss Caroline Bingley. This is Fitzwilliam Darcy, a friend of mine from school and recent master of Pemberley, in Derbyshire."

Darcy promptly resolved to make Bainbridge pay for his last comment, although it would have to be more inventive than putting a frog in his bed, seeing how they no longer attended the same boarding school.

"Pleased to meet you," he said aloud, shaking hands with Bingley and bowing slightly to the ladies. Drat it, he'd already managed to forget their names.

"We are so pleased to meet you as well," one of them said. Catherine, perhaps? Cora? She was looking him over as well, making Darcy feel increasingly like a horse for sale. "Mr. Bainbridge has told us all about you. We lost our parents just last year, and it is a *dreadful* experience. You have our deepest sympathies—and your sister, too, poor dear! She is lucky to have a brother such as yourself."

If he never heard that statement again, it would be too soon. But he managed to murmur something polite in response and then asked Bingley if he had been in Town long.

"Oh, yes, we've been here nearly a year," Bingley replied easily. "We are from the north of England, originally. I must say that London provides a different type of life that is quite enjoyable, as I am sure you are aware. I have met more people here than I ever could have dreamed of encountering at home."

Darcy's stomach knotted and it took his mind a moment to catch up—the musicians had struck up their instruments, signaling the start of the dancing. All three Bingley siblings brightened. The first sister, who had remained silent, turned and smiled at the man who had materialized out of the crowd at her elbow. The man gave Darcy a solemn nod, then led his lady away.

The second sister—Christine? —was unfortunately smiling at *him*. Was she preening? Forgetting the question of her name, Darcy hurriedly broke eye contact. He'd let Bainbridge talk him into attending; dancing was a separate matter.

Bainbridge himself came to the rescue, though Darcy expected his reasons were self-serving rather than altruistic. Bowing over her hand, Bainbridge put on the charming smile Darcy had seen at so many previous events. "Miss Caroline, would you do me the honor of dancing with me?"

Caroline! Watching from the corner of his eye, Darcy saw that she gave *him* another look before accepting the hand that Bainbridge offered and threw yet another glance back over her shoulder as they walked away. *Damn it, Bainbridge.* The last thing he needed right now as an upstart trying to claim his attentions.

"You'll have to excuse me," Bingley said once his sisters were gone. "I met an absolute angel and she promised me the first dance. I look forward to speaking with you more later, Darcy."

He hurried off, but the phrasing stayed with Darcy. *An angel.*

As if the thought had summoned her, the crowd parted and Darcy caught sight of the girl in the yellow dress. Of course, she wasn't wearing the yellow dress tonight. Instead, she wore a gown of the palest green, trimmed with lace, and pearls were entwined in the curls of her dark hair. She was passing a fan back and forth between gloved hands, glancing repeatedly at the dance floor and looking almost as out of place as he felt.

No one had asked her to dance. With everything she had done for Georgiana, surely he could stand up for one song.

Without thinking, he moved towards the young lady. Unlike Miss Bingley, Darcy had no trouble remembering her name—Elizabeth. Unfortunately, that was the only name he remembered. He'd been told a family name, even a guardian, that day in the park. Of course, there had been a considerably amount on his mind that day, but—well, Miss Elizabeth would have to suffice for a name even if she technically should be referred to as Miss-Something-Else.

"If you do not have a partner, may I have this dance, Miss Elizabeth?"

She jumped just a little, then turned and looked up. Instant recognition lit in her eyes, and some of her previous awkwardness faded. "You may, Mr. Darcy, but only if you tell me how your sister is doing."

"I am happy to oblige." He held out a hand, she placed hers on top of it, and they took their places on the floor just as the dance began.

It occurred to Darcy as they went through the first few steps of the dance that they were still, in reality, strangers. "In case you do not remember from our rather hurried meeting," he said when the steps brought them together, "my name is Fitzwilliam Darcy."

Elizabeth smiled, a true smile that made the corners of her eyes crinkle instead of a lady's affected turn of the lips. "I remember you, Mr. Darcy. If that was a ploy for me to reintroduce myself, I am Miss Elizabeth Bennet. Tell me, did Miss Darcy inform you that I have an elder sister at home in Hertfordshire, or did you just not remember my surname?"

She was quick for a girl he would have guessed to be fifteen. "My sister has talked a great deal about you, Miss Elizabeth. I admit it is somewhat of a shock to find you are a real person, and not a friend she invented from thin air." Their hands touched as he spoke, the warmth of her fingers through her gloves underlining the sentiment.

"You promised to tell me how she fares," Elizabeth responded, either not aware he hadn't answered her question or willing to let the matter slide. Darcy wondered which one it was.

He spoke of Georgiana, saying mainly that she seemed far more composed than the day they had met, and that she spent a large portion of each day practicing the pianoforte he had had tuned just for that purpose. To say more would invite questions, and Darcy did not want to admit how little he still knew about his sister's thoughts and feelings. Instead, he turned the conversation back to Elizabeth.

"If you do not mind me asking, why does your elder sister not join you in Town?" he asked when they had exhausted several other subjects. "Is she already married, or promised to someone?"

The light in Elizabeth's eyes dimmed. "There was an illness," she said shortly. "My younger sister and I were sent away before we could catch it, too. One of my sisters recovered fully a week after we left, and another one is nearly better as well. My mother and Jane—my eldest sister—are still ill. My father seems to have been fortunate enough to avoid the sickness despite remaining at home."

"Good lord, how many sisters do you have?" He spoke without thinking and immediately winced. "Beg pardon, Miss Elizabeth, I did not mean to offend you."

Much to Darcy's relief, she laughed. "You are not the first person to say that, or something similar," she said. "There are five of us. Jane is the eldest and the dearest sister anyone could ask for—and I say that even though I know you are secretly thinking *your* sister is the best. But you have not met Jane, so I cannot fault you for being wrong, and Miss Darcy *is* a dear. I am the second, and then there are Mary, Catherine, and Lydia. Catherine—Kitty, she is usually called—is in London with me."

No wonder she had known what to say to Georgiana. Darcy was slightly awed at how different her life and family sounded from his own. Aloud, he remarked, "You must miss them."

"Very much," she replied simply. "We have been away for nearly two months and I expect we will stay in Town for much longer. As entertaining as it is here, I will express an unpopular opinion and admit that I would much prefer to return home."

Darcy opened his mouth to reply and the music faded. As much as he wanted to continue the conversation, he would not create a stir by dancing two dances with the same young lady, even if she did have a magical influence on his sister. Instead, he bowed, she curtseyed, and he watched her from the corner of his eye as she made her way across the room to a middle-aged lady who looked vaguely familiar. What name had she given as her guardian? Was the older lady a relative, perhaps?

Darcy shook himself out of his distraction and found a corner next to the room where several other men had hidden themselves away with whiskey and cigars. The smell of cigar smoke gave him violent headaches if he breathed it in for too long, but the room would provide him with a quick escape if the Bingley sisters—or any other young lady—appeared to make small talk.

"I never would have believed it," Bainbridge said, slapping him on the back as he appeared out of thin air. "Fitz Darcy danced with an unknown lady, seemingly of his own will. I think I even caught a smile. Tell me, how soon should I plan to stand up with you? Or are you still sampling the selection? If so, Miss Caroline is quite the accomplished dancer, and she seemed rather taken with you."

She'd certainly seemed taken with his credentials, Darcy thought, remembering the way her eyebrows had gone up at the mention of his estate. "You know I do not dance with people I have not met before, Bainbridge."

"You could have fooled me. Surely you hadn't met your little dark-haired partner before? You've been practically hibernating since you arrived in Town."

"I made her acquaintance previously. You did too, if you'd bother to remember. She found Georgiana the day that we met in Hyde Park. They are friends."

Perhaps not completely true, but he'd heard enough about the girl to feel better acquainted than their time together allowed.

"Oh yes, I recall now. And you? Are you, ah, *friends* with her as well? You looked quite enchanted, if I do say so myself."

He was, if not enchanted, then very much intrigued by Miss Elizabeth. She was an interesting young lady, with a quick mind, light step, and expressive eyes that had seemed to be laughing at a private joke—unless reminded of her family's illness, of course. He'd felt a kinship with her, perhaps because neither of them particularly wanted to be there. But it wouldn't do to admit any of that to Bainbridge. No, this was what he got for coming to a party—at Bainbridge's request, nonetheless—and trying to help a young lady have a more enjoyable evening. Well, he'd remember this the next time a similar situation arose.

"She is hardly more than a child, and by no means tempting enough to give up my single state. When I marry, it will be to someone who is my equal in every way, and I don't see a single lady here who comes close." *And I won't ask you to stand up with me even when I do marry.* "I've done more than you asked—I showed up *and* I danced. Now go court your heiresses and leave me in peace!"

Seven

Lizzy

December 1806

For once in her life, Lizzy actually slept late the day following the Haddingtons' ball. They had returned home at a reasonable hour, leaving before almost all of the other attendees, but Lizzy had not been able to fall asleep for over an hour. Instead, she'd relived the evening, wishing she could tell Jane everything and committing the night to memory so she could transcribe it faithfully in her next letter.

The only sour spot was Mr. Darcy's dismissal. She had been thrilled when he asked her to dance simply because it meant she didn't have to hang back like a wallflower. Then she'd noticed that he was quite likely the tallest man in the room and handsome in a classical way, with a square chin, long nose, and deep brown eyes. He'd danced superbly and made interesting conversation.

Lizzy decided she could have like Mr. Darcy very much—at least from afar—if only he hadn't brushed her off as a child! She knew very well that she was young, and her height did not help matters at all. But to think he had only danced with her because it fulfilled a duty and they had encountered each other before! And worst of all, to be 'by no means tempting enough' and clearly someone he thought below him. She was not a prop for rich men to use. No, if she were ever so unlucky as to meet Mr. Darcy again, Lizzy would know exactly what to think, and it was far from favorable!

Now, as she made her way to the breakfast room, Lizzy decided that she would not put that part of the story in Jane's letter. It would only distress her kind-hearted sister. Better to send it to her father, who would laugh at the man's haughtiness.

One of the footmen followed Elizabeth into the breakfast room and handed her a letter, then gave the rest of the mail to Lady Lichfield. Kitty reached for the newest fashion magazine, and Lizzy selected a pastry to nibble on while she read.

"Papa's sent a letter," she remarked absently to Kitty, breaking the seal. Engrossed in the magazine, her younger sister didn't reply.

My dear girls—

I hardly know how to tell you this, but you deserve to hear the news from me, before some busybody can spread the word. Your mother passed away early this morning—

Lizzy choked on her bite of pastry. Coughing to dislodge it brought tears to her eyes. That was all. Nothing else was the matter—surely she had just misread. Her father's handwriting left much to be desired, and even after years of deciphering it she sometimes made a mistake.

But there was nothing unclear about *this* letter, and Lizzy finished reading it in a state of shock and disbelief. Mother dead. Jane recovering, still weak, unable to get out of bed for long. Lydia inconsolable. And then a line jumped out at Lizzy in sharp relief. *You girls are not to come home for the funeral—that is an order.*

"Lizzy?" Kitty asked hesitantly from across the table, and Elizabeth realized that she had frozen, all the blood draining from her face. Unable to say the words, as if that would make them true, Lizzy pushed the letter towards her sister and ran out of the room. She made it halfway up the staircase before, behind her, Kitty gave a strangled cry and began to sob.

*

Of all the things she had missed while in London, Lizzy had never thought much about her mother. She thought of her now, longing for her in a way she could never remember feeling before. All children are supposed to want their mothers when something is wrong, but Lizzy had long ago stopped running to hers. Jane and her father were both more rational, sympathetic listeners, less prone to turning Lizzy's problem into one of their own. Growing up, Lizzy went to Jane with daily complaints, her father with sibling injustices, and the housekeeper, Mrs. Hill, with injuries. At some point, without even realizing it, she'd dismissed her mother as a silly creature and ceased to consider the matter.

She'd never even wondered if her mother noticed. Even now, it was Jane and Papa she wrote to, Papa and Jane she thought about lying in bed at night. How awful to realize that she had spent hours worrying about Jane without sparing more than a few minutes for another who was equally ill! While Kitty bawled, Lizzy lay on her bed and listened with an odd sense of jealousy, wishing that she could feel grief without guilt. Of course, that thought only brought on *more* guilt.

Strangely enough, Lizzy had never considered her mother's death any more than she had missed her while in Town. Her father, yes—there had always been that far off day when her beloved Papa would die and Longbourn was to be inherited by an evil, unknown other man, who would cast them out into the cold mercilessly. For the most part, Lizzy hadn't thought about that, either, for no fun was to be had by dwelling on such a matter. Now the unthinkable had happened and nothing could be done to change it.

After an indeterminate amount of time, the door opened a hand's width. "Lizzy?" Kitty asked in a choked voice.

"Come in, Kitty."

A moment later, Lizzy looked up at her sister's blotchy, tearstained face. There was a pause while they simply stared at each other and then Lizzy forced herself to act. She scooted over on the bed and patted the space next to her, opening her arms to Kitty.

The younger girl didn't hesitate, but dove into Lizzy's embrace. Burying her head in Lizzy's shoulder, Kitty immediately began to cry again, body shuddering. Moving reflexively, Lizzy curled her arm around her sister and ran the other hand over her hair. Beyond that, she remained frozen on the bed, staring up at the canopy above her and feeling nothing at all.

*

This time, Mistress Greyson came to the house. She brought her tape measure and so many fabric samples that Lizzy bit her tongue to keep from making a snide comment. How many versions of black could there be, after all, and why did it matter when they weren't to be seen in the dresses?

Lizzy moved stiffly through the fitting, drawing back from the slightest touch, but Kitty was little more than a rag doll. She sat where directed, stood on request, and allowed Mistress Greyson to move her arms without seeming to notice the woman at all. Even the question, "Do you think we should add lace or ribbons, Lady Lichfield?" failed to elicit a reaction.

Then the seamstress went away again, and the next day a black dress appeared for both of them, with another set to follow once they were completed. The garments weren't the only deliveries. Sketchbooks and pencils, new pianoforte music, and a book on French conversation all appeared as well.

"Since you can't go out, we may as well make the most of this time," Lady Lichfield told them several days after the letter had arrived. "I know that you have a great deal on your mind, but I have found that doing nothing is often the worst option in times of distress. Give your brain something to focus on and it will gladly accept the distraction, but sit idle and your grief will consume you."

Kitty looked up, and Elizabeth could read the hope on her face. Kitty would love to be distracted from the grief, would happily accept the belief that being busy could cure their problems—or at least make them tolerable. For her part, Lizzy could not see that it mattered what she did or did not do. Her mother was dead and her father did not want her anymore; she had been cast off on a stranger without explanation. Playing the pianoforte or improving her French was not going to change any of those facts.

Still, it took less effort to comply than it did to argue, so Lizzy picked up the sheet music and set her chin and pretended that she didn't feel Lady Lichfield's eyes on her. She made a mess of the song, which didn't concern her like it usually would, and restarted from the beginning. After five such iterations, the notes actually resembled the melody written on the page.

"My goodness, Lizzy, you're as bad as Mary!" Kitty exclaimed when she played the opening measures for the sixth time. "Although I will admit that you improve much faster than she does. I certainly haven't missed—"

Lizzy saw the moment that Kitty remembered. Her features froze, then drooped. "I am sorry," she whispered, eyes fixed on her sketchbook.

"Would you like to play?" Elizabeth asked, studying her hands.

Kitty shook her head. "Oh no, I—I don't think I could play at the moment. You keep playing if you want to, I didn't mean—"

She trailed off, opened her mouth to continue, and closed it again. Readjusting her grip on the pencil, Kitty turned her attention back to her sketchbook, hair swinging forward to hide her face. Lizzy watched her sister for a moment, then sighed. Rifling through the pile of music, she selected a new song and set about butchering it into submission once again. She played all afternoon, and Kitty never said another word.

That evening, Lady Lichfield surveyed the two of them as they took their seats at the dinner table. "Did you learn anything from your pursuits today, ladies?"

There was a pause. "It is a great deal easier to master the pianoforte when I spend more than twenty minutes at my practice," Lizzy said. No need to mention that at home, Mary had hogged the instrument and Lizzy had preferred walking or conversing with Jane to practicing.

"I worked on getting the shadows right to create more realistic drawings," Kitty said.

"You both looked very engaged." Lady Lichfield took a sip of her wine. "I thought perhaps this evening we could spend time on something more, ah, communal. French, perhaps?" She smiled at Kitty and asked her—in rapid French—to pass the butter.

Kitty's eyes widened and then darted to Lizzy. Taking pity on her sister, Lizzy repeated the request slowly, and Kitty complied.

"*Merci beaucoup*," Lady Lichfield said. "*Parlez-vous français*, Elizabeth?"

A pause to think about the phrasing, and Lizzy responded that they both did, but Kitty was not fluent, precisely, and she herself did not do well with complicated words or a fast pace.

Lady Lichfield nodded. "Well," she said in English, "perhaps we can improve on that, hmm?"

And so mealtimes became French lessons, and afternoons were for practice—drawing, pianoforte, curtseys, needlepoint—anything that a young lady was supposed to know but Lizzy had never put much stock in before.

"May I go on a walk this afternoon?" she asked Lady Lichfield after a week of cooped-up days, recalling that she had met Georgiana in Hyde Park while the other girl was in mourning.

But the lady frowned. "I'm not sure it that is a wise idea, Lizzy. Your father thought it best that you not wander the city at present."

Lizzy felt her face contract into a scowl and turned away rapidly until she could restore a presentable expression. So her father had written Lady Lichfield again, and clearly the letter had relayed more than the news of her mother's passing. "I wouldn't have to go far," she tried again. Hyde Park was only blocks away and could hardly be counted as "wandering the city" in any case. "Even if I could go around the block, I am sure I would feel more like myself. Of course, I would wait until Tom could go with me."

"Oh!" Lady Lichfield exclaimed. "I forgot that you do not know. Tom received word from his sister yesterday. Her husband broke his leg, and she asked that he come and help them for a couple of weeks until the man starts to recover. I didn't even think to tell you."

"Is there anyone else who could go? Nell, perhaps?" Surely, with her status as a ladies' maid in training, she could be spared for a while to accompany one of the ladies she currently served.

Lady Lichfield cocked her head. "Is there something you need, Lizzy? Please do not hesitate to tell me if there is."

I need my home! Lizzy thought instantly. *I need Jane and Papa and the normal, boring life I never thought I would miss. I need my mother.* "I am simply accustomed to walking daily, and fond of the activity," she managed. What else could she say? "And I thought perhaps it would be acceptable to visit a bookstore. I want to find a novel written in French, so I can work on my conversational fluency." Thank goodness Lady Lichfield allowed novels to be read under her roof! And a French novel would indeed be interesting, even if Lizzy had never considered the idea before opening her mouth.

"Why, I wish you would have said something about that sooner," Lady Lichfield said. "I have several books that might do." She stood up. "Come, we will go look and see. There is an entire trunk of books that I've never gotten around to adding to the library, and I'm sure that most of the volumes would interest you. They are mine, you see, rather than part of the Lichfield collection."

Stopping in the doorway, the lady looked back over her shoulder. "We can always send for more books, if there is something specific you require. For now, though, Lizzy, I really do think it best that you stay here."

And that, Lizzy thought wryly to herself as she followed Lady Lichfield out of the room, was that.

Eight

Darcy

December 1806

Something—or rather, someone—was creating a commotion at the door of Jack's when Darcy strode up the day after the Haddingtons' ball. As he got closer, Darcy recognized Mr. Bingley at the center of a group of young men. It looked like they had surrounded him, and Darcy couldn't imagine they'd done it for the sake of welcoming him.

"What is this?" he asked, picking one of them at random and leveling a glare at the man. Unbidden, a memory in his mind spoke. *Don't look away first, Fitz. You've got height, bearing, and a reputation for being unbendable. If you can't bother to be polite, then use what you have. You'll wear them down.* Darcy ground his teeth, but didn't look away. Blast Wickham. He'd happily remove any good memories he had of the man if it meant the bad ones would disappear as well.

“He’s got no right to be here,” a different man said, and Darcy shifted his gaze to the speaker. “This is a place for gentlemen, and he’s no right to that distinction.”

Unfortunately for the speaker, Darcy recognized him. “I see why you feel strongly about the matter, Rowley. Your father must have hated those in trade, since he pulled both of his wives straight out of Cheapside.”

The man flushed a brilliant red, but Darcy had moved on, targeting the only other person he knew in the group. “And you, Thompson, your name is still on your grandfather’s warehouses. It’s a pity the company hasn’t turned a profit since the old man died.” He looked at the remaining men. “Besides, he’s with me. Come along, Bingley.”

Lifting his head, Darcy shouldered his way through the middle of the group and walked inside, not bothering to look back. He heard the sound of footsteps behind him, but only after the door had closed did he turn to see who had followed.

As he had hoped, it was Bingley, and they were alone in the corridor. Bingley was grinning. “That was splendid,” he exclaimed. “It was like you pulled a wolf’s mask out of your pocket and all the sheep ran away.”

Amused but trying not to show it, Darcy raised his eyebrows. “What makes you think I’m not a wolf?” he asked.

Bingley laughed easily. "Last night you spoke to me as if I was your equal, not a servant who had borrowed his master's clothes. You didn't try to show off for my sisters, but you didn't snub them, either. And you just stood up for me, of course."

Darcy studied the other man, not sure if he was insightful or simply determined to see the best in everyone. The only thing he could tell for sure was that Bingley looked *young*.

"If you don't mind me asking, how old are you?" Not the most proper question, but Darcy didn't think that Bingley would mind.

"Eighteen," he responded promptly, not looking bothered a bit.

No wonder he looked so young. He *was* young. "I try to judge a man on his merits, not his name or amount of money he spends on clothes each season. I would imagine you have far more interesting stories than the men that do nothing beyond bragging about their wardrobe. In fact," Darcy paused, then decided he might as well finish his sentence, "I've been looking into several investments. Bainbridge mentioned you still are involved with the running of your father's business. Would you be able to advise me?"

Bingley looked at him sideways. "I can't promise I'll be any help, but I'd be happy to discuss with you." He cocked his head slightly, as if he was considering Darcy as well. "Actually—it won't be at a very fashionable address, mind—would you like to come to dinner tomorrow?"

*

Bingley had been right. The address he gave Darcy was decidedly unfashionable, but the house looked to be in good repair, with bright red brick, wide front windows set with what looked like new glass, and freshly scrubbed white-washed steps. A man wearing the dress of a high-status servant opened the door instead of a maid or housekeeper, and he was shown into a sitting room infused with all of the latest fashions.

In fact, Darcy thought wryly as he glanced around, perhaps a few too many of the latest fashions. He'd noticed before that the newly rich just *had* to show how fashionable they were, but the established families would never decorate in such a way—you didn't throw out quality chairs because they weren't exactly the right shade of brown. He stifled a smile thinking of what his aunt Fitzwilliam would say about the room. The countess was not known for softening her opinions to spare others' feelings.

"Darcy, welcome!" Bingley exclaimed, pulling Darcy from his thoughts. He crossed the room exuberantly and offered a hand to shake, beaming all the while. Bemused, Darcy found himself smiling back.

"Mr. Darcy, how lovely to see you again." *Caroline, Caroline, Caroline. Not Charlotte, not Cecelia, not Christine, not Catherine. Caroline.* She too stood and came towards him, smiling, her movements carefully calculated to be graceful rather than Bingley's youthful approach. He bowed, hoping that would be enough of a response. He would not lie and claim the same sentiments that she expressed, even if it was the socially acceptable response.

Luckily, Bingley interjected before Caroline could go on. "Darcy, I do not believe you have met Mr. Hurst." He indicated a portly young man sitting at a card table across the room.

Seeing that he was being discussed, the man pushed himself up unhurriedly and ambled over to be introduced. "John Hurst," the man said when he reached them, making his bow.

Darcy bowed in return. "Fitzwilliam Darcy," he responded. "Pleased to make your acquaintance."

"Same, same. Bingley's told us all about your support at Jack's yesterday. Not many men that would do something like that. *I* wouldn't, but then, that's because I wouldn't be at Jack's in the first place. White's is more my style. Do you play cards, Mr. Darcy?"

Darcy admitted that he did, holding back the thought that he found reading or chess far better ways to pass the time.

"Then I am indeed delighted to make your acquaintance." Having said this, he lapsed into silence, and Darcy was left with the impression that playing cards rated him higher with Mr. Hurst than coming to Bingley's defense had done.

Caroline jumped in to fill the silence as Mr. Hurst re-settled himself by Louisa Bingley. Wondering if the pair was engaged or soon to be, Darcy missed the beginning of Caroline's sentence and only caught "—must say, London society is something that simply cannot be matched elsewhere, wouldn't you agree, Mr. Darcy?"

"Let the man sit before you start inundating him with your views, Caroline," Bingley said amiably.

The comment earned him a swift glare from his sister, who put a smile back on her face with unnatural speed as she turned to Darcy. "Please, Mr. Darcy, do be seated. I hope you will forgive my lapse in manners. I find conversation with new acquaintances excessively diverting."

Darcy managed to murmur a pleasantry as he sat, although he couldn't say what it was a moment later. Lord, he hated conversations with new people on the best of days, and today could be considered average at best! But he must try. "To answer your question, Miss Caroline, London society is unique indeed. However, I believe that is due to the variety of people you find in Town. The country does not allow for such large gatherings of people, and as such the society must be diminished. That is not to say the countryside is without merits, only that it is different."

"Oh, but I am forgetting! You must be fond of the country, for I have heard that your estate is one of the best in England. What is it called again?"

In that moment, Darcy was sure that Caroline knew exactly what Pemberley was called, and likely could have told him the rumored cost of the drapes and the chimney piece if asked. But—in the next heartbeat he reconsidered. Perhaps he was becoming too jaded. Was it presumptuous to assume that all young women were only interested in his newly inherited fortune and estate?

"It is called Pemberley," he managed. "And it is certainly a beautiful place." But he didn't want to talk about Pemberley. Since coming to London, he'd found it easier to set his grief aside as long as he didn't think too much about home. It almost felt like being away at school again. "I am enjoying London at the moment, however." He looked at Bingley. "Tell me, how did you meet Mr. Bainbridge?"

Bingley laughed. "Oh, it must have been my first, maybe second week in London and I was utterly lost. I came around a corner, looking up and trying to gauge my location from the buildings I could see in the distance, and ran straight into him. So of course I start to apologize, and before I knew it he's gotten me to tell my whole tale and is leading me along to a different store than the one I was looking for, but which turned out to sell better quality for lower prices. Several weeks after that I decided to go for a ride in Hyde Park and he was there racing with his friends. That sort of thing has happened often enough that we have become friends."

Caroline shifted on her seat and Darcy glanced at her instinctively. Her lips were pressed into a thin line, eyes hard. If Caroline had her way, Darcy imagined she'd tell a very different story of how they entered London society.

"How did you meet him?" Bingley asked, and Darcy felt his lips twitch involuntarily into a smile. What would Caroline make of *his* story?

"It starts out not much different than yours, actually. I got lost on my second day at Eton, along with another boy in my class."

"Perhaps that is why Mr. Bainbridge was so willing to help you, Charles!" Caroline interjected. "He remembered being lost himself."

Darcy's smile grew. "Perhaps he felt guilty. I was lost with *Andrew* Bainbridge, Peter's younger brother. I remember how relieved we were when Peter and a group of his friends came along. Of course, he sent us in the completely opposite direction of where we needed to be, and we both got in trouble for being late."

Bingley grinned. Caroline looked put out. Before either of them could say anything, however, the door opened.

"Dinner is served."

*

The separation of the sexes had not come a minute too soon. All throughout supper, Caroline had done her best to impress him with her style and sophistication. Sadly, she did not possess the subtly required to make the desired impression, and he came away from the meal with a bad taste in his mouth that had nothing to do with the chef's abilities.

It was the same treatment he had experienced in almost all ballrooms and dining rooms since he turned eighteen, and Darcy was disappointed in Miss Caroline Bingley. It was clear she had a quick mind—the biting responses she threw out as if joking were proof of that. As such, the conversation had had the potential to be perfectly enjoyable, or as enjoyable as any conversation with near strangers. Unfortunately, Caroline had spent most of dinner either agreeing with him or praising his choices, and when she wasn't doing that she criticized others. To his annoyance, the person she criticized most was one he found no fault with at all.

"Why, Mr. Darcy, I was quite surprised to see you dancing with Miss Eliza Bennet. You're not acquainted, surely? I know for a fact she is newly arrived in Town."

Darcy had acknowledged she was a recent acquaintance of his sister's, already braced for a repeat of Bainbridge's teasing.

But Caroline did not accuse him of any *tendre* towards Miss Elizabeth. "You did her such a favor by paying her attention, I hope she was appropriately grateful! I'll admit, she looked nearly fashionable at the ball, nothing like when we first met her, don't you agree, Louisa? Her dress was three years out of date and the most ill-suited color. How she and her sister garnered the attention of someone like Lady Lichfield, I will never guess."

Lady Lichfield. He had a title for her chaperone, if not an answer about their relationship. "Her father is a gentleman, is he not? Most likely that is the source of the attention."

Caroline had laughed. "A dowager countess, chaperoning a chit like Miss Eliza? It does not follow. She's a pretentious upstart if I ever saw one, no doubt used to being the prettiest and most accomplished girl in whatever backwater town she comes from. Hopefully Lady Lichfield will marry her off to someone with a nice country estate and we'll only have to see her on rare occasions."

Forgetting that he did not want to appear overly interested in Miss Elizabeth, Darcy opened his mouth to defend her. Luckily, Louisa chose that moment to lean forward. "Miss Eliza is young and unaccustomed to Town; you very well might be looking to befriend her by the end of the season. But Mrs. Gatway is unpardonable, did you hear what she did the night before the Haddington's ball?"

The talk continued in a similar vein for the rest of the meal, with Bingley interjecting positive opinions on nearly everyone and Mr. Hurst ignoring them all in favor of his food. By the time they left the table, with Caroline hinting that there was no *need* for them to separate and bring an end to the lovely conversation, Darcy was cursing himself for accepting the invitation.

"I hope you'll forgive Caroline," Bingley said as he pressed a glass of brandy into Darcy's hand. Mr. Hurst, having already secured his glass, had made a beeline to a large leather chair and appeared oblivious to the other men in the room. "She means well. I think she believes that if we act as though we have always been here and look down on anyone perceived as an outsider, then that is how others will view us as well. I would rather win friends on my own accord, even if my sister—and perhaps men like you—find me naive because of it."

Darcy cocked his head and considered the man—boy, really—across from him. How different the siblings were! One so full of artifice, intent on dragging herself to the top even if it meant stepping on everyone else to get there, and the other as open and guileless as the Derbyshire sky on a sunny morning. How had they come from the same parents?

He had been silent too long and forced himself to speak. "I will not hold Miss Caroline against you, as long as you do not interpret my actions towards her to be anything more than what is polite."

Bingley laughed. "I think I may have the better end of that deal. And that reminds me." He leaned back in his chair, wrapping both hands around his glass of brandy. "I've given some thought about how best to advise you, and what I've come to is that I am not the best man for the job."

Darcy gave an internal moan. He was starting to like Bingley for himself, not just as a means to information, but he'd put up with Caroline's blather for this response?

Bingley went on before he could respond aloud. "I do, however, have a name for you. Not long before my father passed, we spoke of trade and the key players in London. He knew that I would not run his business as he had done, but he said he wanted me to be prepared for whatever might come to pass. There is a man who is growing his business here in Town cautiously, but steadily. He is not rich or powerful yet, but my father pegged him as the next success story, and a good man to work with. My recommendation would be to look him up, and if you like what you see, invest in his businesses."

Darcy sat forward, leaning his elbows on his knees. "And his name?"

Bingley smiled. "Edward Gardiner. I'll get his address for you as well, shall I?"

Nine

Lizzy

January 1807

"Much suspected by me; Nothing proved can be; Quoth Elizabeth, prisoner."

Lizzy made a face at her reflection in the mirror on her dressing table. It was pretentious to compare herself to Elizabeth Tudor, imprisoned at Woodstock by her own sister and fearing for her life, but she was feeling self-indulgent and thoroughly irrational.

Her seventeenth birthday and Christmas had both come and gone with little celebration. Kitty had felt poorly for several days, worrying both Lizzy and Lady Lichfield, but had recovered enough to nibble on marzipan by twelfth night. They had received a letter from Mr. Bennet, along with money to "buy themselves something nice and frivolous" but no gifts. Apparently their father feared that if Jane, Mary, or Lydia touched something and it was sent on to Lizzy and Kitty, the disease might travel with it.

Lizzy found the idea strange, especially since he undoubtedly touched the letters that were sent, but she could not generate much anger over the matter. She had hated thinking of presents, of Christmas in general, with so much changed in their life. Surely those who remained at Longbourn felt much the same. Still, the lack of effort put forth—especially in regards to her birthday—made her heart hurt. She tried so hard to be strong and happy for Kitty, and to send positive, interesting letters to her father. Was it really too much to ask that he write her a special letter for the day she turned seventeen, rather than adding it as a postscript to their Christmas letter? Had the closeness they shared in Hertfordshire been something she'd only imagined? All Lizzy knew was that, away from her father and Jane, she was *lonely*.

Struck by a sudden thought, Lizzy sat up straighter. If family wouldn't come to her, *she* could go to *them*—at least some of them. After all, she did have relatives in London. Both of the Gardiner children had felt poorly over Christmas, as small children are wont to do when the weather turns cold, meaning that Lizzy had been deprived of their company as well. Still, they should be feeling better, and surely her Aunt Gardiner wouldn't mind a short visit either way.

Having made up her mind, Lizzy found escape surprisingly easy. She went downstairs in the same manner she always did, paused in the hallway for a moment and then, hearing nothing that meant someone might be coming, snagged her pelisse and gloves and darted down the hall to the back door.

She was swallowed up by the narrow lanes and close buildings almost immediately, and paused to don her outer garments against the chill. Properly attired, with her hood pulled perhaps a bit lower than usual, Lizzy set out in the direction of the Gardiner's home.

No one bothered her as she made her way through the streets of Mayfair. In fact, Lizzy wondered if they took any note of her at all. As she made her way closer and closer to Cheapside, however, that began to change.

At first it was easy to ignore. A shopkeeper called for the little lady to come view his wares. Another one repeated the entreaty, then a third. Lizzy kept going without turning her head. A man driving a cart yelled for her to get out of the way as she crossed the road. A group of women brushed by her, talking loudly. Stepping sideways to avoid colliding with them, her foot slipped in a patch of muck, and she wind-milled her arms, hanging precipitously on the edge of falling.

"Watch it!" A rough hand grabbed her arm and yanked her back onto her feet. "You'd best be more careful than that, young miss."

Lizzy turned to face her helper, torn between thanking him and hurrying in the other direction. The man was dressed in decent clothes, but he had clearly been wearing them for some time, if the wrinkles and smell were any indication.

He raised both eyebrows, clearly assessing her from head to toe. "And what business does a young lady such as yourself have in this part of town? Bond Street's in the other direction, missy, it's there that you'll be wanting to shop."

Lizzy drew herself up to her regrettably short height and stuck her chin out. "I'm visiting family, not shopping," she said, still fighting the urge to step back. If only his breath didn't smell so bad!

"And where is this family that you're visiting, eh?"

She hesitated before answering. "Lovat Lane."

The man's eyebrows shot up farther. "Well, then. I'll not try to stop you, but mark my words: you'd best keep your chin up and your wits about you, little missy. And don't let go of your money for a second. Not everyone you'll meet on your way to Lovat Lane is as honest as I am."

"I didn't bring any money," Lizzy snapped before she could think better of it.

"Maybe that's good, maybe it's not, but you remember what I said. G'day, little missy." Touching a dirty hand to his head as if tipping an invisible hat, the man walked away.

Lizzy hurried onwards, thoroughly spooked but determined to not show it. She'd started this journey, and blast if she wouldn't finish it! Lovat Lane couldn't be that bad of a place, or else her uncle wouldn't allow his family to live there. She'd even visited once, and while it hadn't been as upscale as Mayfair or as tranquil as Longbourn, she hadn't been worried for her safety.

With that thought held firmly in the front of her mind, Lizzy marched on through ever-narrowing streets. They became considerably more crowded as well. She'd left Lady Lichfield's house at a time the *ton* considered quite early, when few were out. Apparently the same didn't hold true for London's poorer inhabitants. Still, Lizzy thought she was managing just fine up until someone else grabbed her arm—and this time, the person didn't let go.

"I don't have any money," she blurted, trying to jerk her arm free. "Let me go."

The hand tightened, fingers digging into the soft skin of her underarm. "I accept other forms of payment from pretty girls."

Lizzy shuddered at the voice and she twisted to face the person detaining her. The smell was much worse than that of the previous man, and she could see at least one rotting tooth. He stood barely taller than her own diminutive height, but Elizabeth doubted that larger men would choose to pick on him. There was something unhinged—desperate, perhaps? —in the pale blue eyes.

She raised her chin. "Let me go."

He smiled, an expression that sent a shiver down her spine. "Oh, I like you. You'll do fine indeed, just fine."

Thoroughly spooked and past caring about appearances, Lizzy opened her mouth to scream. Before she had even indrawn the breath, though, a grimy hand clamped down over her mouth and his face was only inches from hers. "Don't try it, little girl. You don't want me t' be mad at you. Now, this is what we're going to do. You—"

"Unhand the lady," a man said in a tone that brokered no argument. She knew that voice, and a surge of pure relief flooded her body, making her sag slightly into the man's hold before she recovered herself and attempted to yank her arm free again.

Her captor looked up, rage written clearly on his face—and then stepped back. It was a bare half-step, but it happened, and Lizzy felt the tables turn.

"This doesn't concern you, *sir*," the captor sneered, making the title sound like an insult. "Be on your way and leave us to our business."

"You are incorrect. It concerns me greatly. Miss Elizabeth, if you will wait by my horse?" His face and voice were carefully polite, almost void of emotion, but there was a hint of steel in his tone.

"*Miss* Elizabeth, is it?" The man leered at her. "Not so good as a lady, I suppose, but still worth somethin'." He tightened his grip and looked up at Darcy. "What's she worth t' you? Clearly someone doesn't think very much of her, not if they let her wander so far into this part of London alone. It wasn't you, was it? Don' blame me for takin' advantage o' your mistake, an' the little miss is old enough t' know better, isn't she?"

"I won't ask again. Let her go."

"An' what's a lordling like you going to do? Cry to daddy that someone didn't give you your—hey!"

Darcy's hand had shot out, but not in a fist, and it took Lizzy a moment to understand what was happening. The grip on her arm tightened, and she glanced down to see Darcy's hand wrapped around the other man's wrist, knuckles white. What in the world did he mean to do?

Then the hold loosened abruptly and she jerked herself free, stumbling back several feet so she was out of his range. Darcy, however, hadn't let go. "Miss Elizabeth, could you please take Aeolus' reins?" he asked, still sounding as if they had met in a ballroom.

She gave him a sharp look, wondering what he was doing, then turned to do as asked.

The other man yelped. Lizzy snatched up the dangling reins and turned back. Darcy's face hadn't changed, but her captor was turning red and trying to extract his wrist with as little success as she'd had. Eyes wild, he extracted a knife from his waistband with his free hand, but before she could do more than gasp, Darcy had a grip on that wrist as well.

"I could break both for you," he remarked casually. "It might teach you to keep your hands off of what does not belong to you, and that not all gentlemen are as helpless as you like to believe. What do you think?"

In response, the man let out a strangled moan and the knife fell from his grip. Lizzy thought she heard something snap—had it been the knife hitting the pavement? Then Darcy let go and the other man was running away, not even stopping to retrieve the weapon. Darcy stooped and examined it, then tucked it into the top of his boot with more ease than Lizzy expected. Who *was* this man?

Then he looked up at her, blinked once, and turned back into the person she recognized—tall, handsome, and stern, but not physically intimidating. "I'd ask how he managed to get you here, but I saw the start of the exchange, and you're lucky I did. What on earth were you thinking, coming to a place like this?"

Lizzy dropped her eyes in shame, all bravado gone. She wouldn't lie, though. "I have family nearby. I can't go home—to my real home, I mean—but I thought I could see my aunt and uncle."

He took a step closer. "Is Lady Lichfield cruel?" When she shook her head, he went on, sounding resigned. "Where are you going? We're attracting attention, and I won't let you go off on your own again. We can talk as we walk. Who is your uncle?"

She looked up. "Edward Gardiner. He lives on—"

"Lovat Lane," Darcy said, face impassive. At her look of surprise, he gave a half smile. "I was on my way to speak with an Edward Gardiner about business."

Lizzy frowned. "You aren't in trade."

He took the reins from her and clucked to the horse, who came forward like a well-trained hound rather than the great beast he was. "Come, let's walk. No, but I am still interested in investing. A gentleman who does not manage his income will find himself a slave to money rather than the master, no matter what his title is. I do not intend to rely on fate to provide for me—or for Georgiana."

Had her father ever thought of such a thing? Would she be here now if he had? Lizzy looked away again, trying to ignore the resultant stab of bitterness, and they walked half a block in silence.

"Speaking of Georgiana," Darcy said as they turned onto Lovat Lane, "if I were your guardian I would be extremely displeased with you for pulling such a stunt. What would your parents say, if they knew what you had done?"

To Lizzy's horror, tears welled up in her eyes and what felt like a fist-sized rock settled in her throat. When she didn't answer, Darcy reached out and touched her shoulder—then pulled his hand back when she flinched and jumped out of his reach. "Apologies, Miss Elizabeth. But that is my point exactly."

Anger sliced through her pain and she could speak again. "It doesn't matter what they would say, Mr. Darcy. My mother is dead"—she took ahold of her black skirts and gave them a vicious shake— "and my father has made it clear that he does not wish to see me. So think of me what you will, but do not profess to speak for my parents."

"Elizabeth Claire Bennet! What on earth are you doing here?" The door of a nearby house had flown open and Madeline Gardiner hurried down the front steps, one hand holding her hem up so she didn't trip and the other tucked under her bulging belly.

“Aunt Gardiner!” Lizzy exclaimed, moving forward to embrace her.

“Don’t tell me you walked the whole way,” her aunt said as they exchanged an awkward hug, frowning at Darcy’s horse. “Unless something happened to the other horse? I know you’re not exactly fond of riding, Lizzy.” She reached out and brushed a loose strand of hair behind Lizzy’s ear. “Still, you should know better than to come on foot!”

It wasn’t the welcome Lizzy had expected, and she hesitate before saying, “I did walk. I—I only met Mr. Darcy several blocks from here. It’s his horse. Mr. Darcy, this is my aunt, Mrs. Gardiner. Aunt—”

“Not so fast!” the woman exclaimed. “I’d like a bit an explanation before we get to the pleasantries, if you please. Do you have any idea the shock I felt when I looked out my window and saw you traipsing down the street—*this* street—looking distressed and accompanied by a strange man? I assumed you at least would have had an escort for the entire way! I worried about Kitty when we heard you were coming to Town, but never you. Even when—” she stopped abruptly, and when she spoke again it was in an entirely different tone of voice. “You could have sent a note, Lizzy. You put yourself in danger by coming here alone, do you understand that?”

The tears were back, and Lizzy struggled to contain them. She had been foolish and impulsive—idiotic, really. It was the kind of behavior she would expect from her baby sister Lydia, but never from herself. The weight of what her actions could have meant settled over

Lizzy like a wet blanket, and she felt herself sag in dejection.

"We spoke on that matter after our paths crossed," Mr. Darcy said, surprising Lizzy. "I believe Miss Elizabeth understands and will not travel here alone again."

Mrs. Gardiner gave him a long, contemplative look. "I thank you for your assistance to my niece, and I hope she has as well. Can I offer you some refreshment before you continue on to your destination? It will not be as fine as what you are accustomed to, but I have a fresh batch of scones and water heating for tea." She shifted slightly, reaching out to rest a light hand on Lizzy's back.

"Actually, I was looking for your husband on a matter of business, which is how I came to encounter your niece. Can I find him here, or could you direct me to where he is? Oh—I am Fitzwilliam Darcy. My sister is a friend of Miss Elizabeth's."

Mrs. Gardiner's eyebrows shot up, and she gave a small smile that surprised Lizzy. "I thought I recognized you, although I do not expect that you would remember me. I grew up in Lambton, but I was Madeline Fletcher then, and it has been several years since I was able to visit Derbyshire." She glanced up at the sky, then glanced back into the house and beckoned to someone with her free hand. "I expect Mr. Gardiner home for his noon meal soon, and John here can take your horse. Please come in, both of you, and we can talk more once you're settled."

TEN

Darcy

February 1807

"Georgiana, there is someone I would like you to meet."

His sister looked up from her pianoforte and for a moment she was smiling, happy to see him. Then her gaze darted over his shoulder and the smile disappeared, replaced by wide eyes, her arms leaving the keys of the instrument to wrap around her middle.

Darcy's stomach knotted. How was it possible to love someone so much and yet dread every interaction? He could never guess exactly what would set off his delicate and finely strung sister, but he knew what was coming. How lovely it would be to pass some of that responsibility off to someone else! With that thought in mind, he turned to the woman standing in the doorway behind him and stepped away so he was not blocking the ladies' view of each other.

"Miss Compton, this is my sister, Miss Georgiana Darcy. Georgiana, this is Miss Compton. I believe she will make an admirable governess for you."

"I'm so pleased to meet you, Miss Darcy," Miss Compton said with a smile, curtsying to the girl frozen on the pianoforte bench. "I'm sure we'll become great friends, don't you think? And my goodness, you play beautifully!" There was a pause, in which Georgiana should have filled the silence with her own greeting, then the proposed governess went on. "Will you tell me what you were playing? Your brother said you spend a great deal of time practicing."

Darcy silently approved of her tactic—approved, in fact, of the governess in her entirety. He had interviewed half a dozen clearly unsuitable applicants and was beginning to despair of ever finding someone he could hope to employ before Miss Compton appeared, seemingly perfect. She had the references, the demeanor, even the ideal mix of stylish-but-professional attire. In fact, he had almost forgotten to introduce her to Georgiana, so convinced was he that she was the person for the job. He'd already begun imagining how his timid sister would flourish, given such an example to follow.

At the pianoforte bench, Georgiana remained silent. "Georgie," he chided, "surely you can spare a greeting for Miss Compton." Heaven forbid the governess think his sister was simple!

But instead of responding, Georgiana stood up and rushed out of the room, brushing past him before he could collect himself and stop her. "Georgiana!" he exclaimed after her, aghast, but her footsteps continued up the stairs unchecked, followed by the all too familiar bang that meant her door had been slammed closed, a barrier between herself and the world.

"Miss Compton, I beg your forgiveness, this is most unlike my sister. Give me a moment, and I shall fetch her."

"Actually, Mr. Darcy, I wonder if I might try?" she asked. "I do not mean to intrude, of course, but Miss Darcy might feel more comfortable meeting me if she is able to do so on her own terms, do you not agree?"

There followed a quarter hour of pleasant, banal, and entirely one-sided conversation from Miss Compton, as she sat outside Georgiana's door on a stool hastily fetched up from the drawing room. When that failed, Darcy took his own turn attempting to persuade his sister to see reason, with equal success. Entreaties fell on deaf ears, persuasion failed, direct orders produced tears. Georgiana would not open the door or respond with even a single word.

In the end, there was nothing for it but to admit defeat and tell the perfect governess that she might as well go, he would send word if anything changed. He watched her walk away doubting he would ever see her again, then settled down to the business of coaxing Georgiana to open her door for him alone now that the nasty woman was gone.

Finally, Darcy reverted to the only thing that seemed to calm Georgiana after such a fuss, and a half hour later they were strolling through the gates to Hyde Park despite the chill in the air. Although she had opened the door and answered several basic questions, Georgiana remained quiet and brooding, and Darcy was beginning to wonder if they would complete the entire walk in silence when she exclaimed, "Elizabeth!" and skipped forward several steps before catching herself.

His initial reaction was one of extreme annoyance—why was Elizabeth Bennet, a troubled young lady in her own right, worthy of smiles when a perfectly respectable woman bent on making polite conversation was treated as a monster? Then Darcy remembered the escapade that had led to their last encounter and felt himself frown. Surely her guardian would have insisted she remain at home after her nearly disastrous journey to Cheapside. He knew enough of Lady Lichfield to think she would not be persuaded into allowing undeserved treats, even by someone as verbose and quick-witted as Elizabeth Bennet appeared to be.

But there was no mistaking the young lady in front of them, and Darcy had just enough time for a knot of worry to form in his stomach before he noticed that she was accompanied by both a maid and the footman who had attended her on the day they first met. She was also, he noticed, dressed all in black, and the sight of two young ladies—girls, really—greeting each other with obvious joy while swathed in winter outfits of full mourning created more than a little dissonance.

The girls had finished their greetings by the time Darcy recovered himself and attended to the conversation, but he made a half bow to Elizabeth when they paused for breath. “Miss Elizabeth, it is good to see that you are well-accompanied today. Have you been enjoying your walk?”

Her cheeks turned pink and she stiffened. “Good day, Mr. Darcy. Yes, it is good of Nell and Tom to walk with me, although I feel decidedly ridiculous with such an entourage.” She turned back to his sister, making it clear their conversation was over, and asked a question about a book he vaguely recalled Georgiana requesting from a bookstore not long ago.

Looking up from Elizabeth—he routinely forgot how short she was, given the strength of her personality—the footman caught his eye and winked. Darcy frowned, taken aback, and the man came forward, ducking his head in deference. “You must forgive my impertinence, sir. Her ladyship finally agreed to let the young miss venture out for her walks again, but only with two escorts, and she’s quite out of sorts over the arrangement. I understand we have you to thank for bringing her home safely on her previous, ah, excursion?”

So Elizabeth had been punished after all, and rules had changed. It must have been at least a month since the fateful encounter in Cheapside, a suitable amount of time to rescind any privileges. His estimation of Lady Lichfield grew, and he nodded once to the footman in acknowledgement. It was not his habit to make small talk with other people’s servants, and he did not intent to change that on a public path in the middle of Hyde Park, certainly not while he was still out of sorts from the day’s events.

Georgiana and Elizabeth had set off again, walking arm in arm, all trace of Georgiana's earlier petulance vanished. He followed them, trying not to feel so relieved that the responsibility of cheering up his sullen sister had been taken on by someone else, and his annoyance towards Elizabeth disappeared as quickly as it had arrived. Once again, she had appeared to save the day, his personal angel.

The thought gave him pause, and he reconsidered the pair ahead of him. They were very nearly the same height, but how many years separated them? Four? Five? What was it that made Elizabeth so friendly to his sister when many young ladies her age would have dismissed a twelve-year-old as a child? Was that simply who she was, or did she have an ulterior motive in mind? She certainly didn't fawn over *him*, but that didn't automatically make her blameless.

Deciding that conversing with servants was a lesser evil than allowing his sister continued interactions with a social climber, Darcy stopped and waited for the footman—Tom, was it? —to catch up. "What is Miss Elizabeth like, when she is out of sorts and no one else is present?"

Tom smiled, his bright blue eyes twinkling. "Very much like she is now, sir. I've yet to see her in a temper she can't laugh herself out of in half an hour or less. She'll stomp off at a great pace, realize I'm falling behind—I hurt my leg, you see," he patted the appendage Darcy had noticed that he favored, "and then come back and keep pace with me until she forgets herself again. She's very much used to more exercise than she's been getting of late, being cooped up in the house, and it's been hard on her. But I'm forgetting myself, sir, and going on more than you likely wanted to hear." Without another word, Tom inclined his head and moved away so that Darcy walked alone once again.

The picture Tom painted was one of an impulsive, half-grown girl, not a young lady grasping for power, and Darcy felt better for the insight. It also made him think—as he had often in the intervening month—of the impulsiveness that had lead Elizabeth into harm's way. He still shuddered to think what could have happened to her if he hadn't been there. He looked back to the chattering pair ahead of him. At that moment, they bore little resemblance to the young lady who'd run away to find comfort and the girl who cried at the drop of a hat. Was there a reason they seemed so happy with each other? There had to be. The more he considered it, the more sense it made. After all, both girls felt the pain of losing a parent and were learning to call an entirely new place home. They could trust each other to understand.

Perhaps that was why he'd thought of Elizabeth Bennet so many times in the month since they'd last crossed paths, wondering how she fared: the pain was not so different from his own, either. He'd dismissed the thoughts whenever he recognized them, but they persisted. Of course, it was not always Elizabeth herself that he thought about. In silent moments, alone in his study or over a glass of brandy in his favorite chair in the library, Darcy relived the showdown with man who'd meant to take her, and what he felt left him thoroughly uncomfortable. Catching his fingers drumming on his leg, Darcy closed his hand into a fist to still them.

He'd liked hurting the other man too much, far too much. For a moment, his responsibilities and commitments had all disappeared, and the only thing that mattered was the strength in his hands. Saving Elizabeth had been simple, clear-cut, and immensely euphoric. It was an addicting feeling, and Darcy hated himself for wishing to repeat the experience. He'd never thought to use the skills Wickham taught him. He was better than that, had to be better than that. There was Georgiana to think about, his name to uphold. A Darcy was civilized, polished, a man others could look up to and emulate. He did not relish a display of brute strength.

"History!" Georgiana exclaimed, breaking into his thoughts, and Darcy realized they had reached the path beside the serpentine while he brooded. It seemed the conversation had turned from novels to school books. "How am I supposed to remember all the brothers and cousins in the War of the Roses, or who married someone's sister or widow, and what policies they brought about that ended up killing their own family members? Every time I try to follow it, the words turn into a big confusing jumble and none of them make sense. I'll never remember all the facts correctly, and it takes up time where I could be practicing the pianoforte or drawing."

"Oh, don't think of it as facts," Lizzy said easily. "That's the fastest way to end up bored out of your mind. The secret to studying history is to think of it as a marvelous story. Imagine that you are Elizabeth of York. Your brothers have been kidnapped and no one can find them. You are in love with your uncle, and he with you, but instead you have to marry the man who killed him. What do you tell yourself so that the days are bearable? Maybe that, no matter who your husband is, you will raise your children the way that your mother raised you, and the blood of the White Rose *will* continue on the throne."

Georgiana made a face, and Lizzy stopped to hear her response. "But wasn't Richard III ugly and deformed? I would rather marry a handsome prince than my ugly old uncle."

"Perhaps Henry VII was the ugly one and he demanded that all portraits be switched, since he won the war," Elizabeth said, startling a giggle out of Georgiana. "Besides," she went on, "no one thinks practically when they fall in love. When *I* fall in love, you may think the man horrid, but there will be no one more handsome in my eyes."

Watching her, head tilted back and eyes dancing, Darcy realized he actually believed her. There would be none of Caroline Bingley's artifice, no thought of marrying an old man for money and status but continuing to flirt with the handsome young dandies. It was hardly practical, in the world where they lived, but he found her romanticism compelling all the same. It was certainly better than dwelling on the way he had felt when another man's bone began to fracture in his grip. No, he would certainly *not* think of that!

Elizabeth had continued. "But don't you see, Georgiana, it isn't just dates and lines on old family trees. These were real people, with stories just as interesting as anything Shakespeare ever wrote. Even the Bard himself has a story of his own. Did you know it's rumored that he was friends with Queen Elizabeth herself?"

Georgiana giggled. "Now I see why *you* like history. You can compare yourself to all the other Elizabeths that have done grand things. I don't know of a single interesting *Georgiana.*"

Lizzy shrugged. "So become someone interesting, and in the future all the Georgianas in the world will read about you and smile."

"Oh no, I couldn't!" his sister exclaimed, eyes widening. "It would hardly be proper." She frowned. "How do you come up with stories that make history interesting? Everything is so flat and boring on the page."

Another shrug, and Darcy wondered if anyone had ever tried to break her of such an unladylike habit. He didn't get the impression that she'd received much formal training, in either education or etiquette. "I don't know, really. I just do. Tell me what else is in that horrid history book of yours and I'll see what I can come up with as an example."

Something clicked in his mind. Elizabeth could use polish on her social skills. Georgiana needed someone she trusted, someone who made learning worth her time so she didn't just revert to practicing on her pianoforte.

And didn't Elizabeth have another sister in Town, one younger than herself? Being in the company of other young ladies might help Georgiana come out of her shell and become surer of herself. Lady Lichfield—a dowager countess, no less—was well respected and would make sure his impressionable sister was not exposed to anything improper.

Darcy sighed to himself. Clearly, it was time he called on Lady Lichfield and suggested that the girls receive lessons together. Surely there was something he could pay for, a music or language master, perhaps, that would provide incentive for her to agree. It couldn't be worse than this morning's display with Miss Compton, and—Elizabeth said something that made Georgiana giggle again—it showed promise of being much, much better.

Eleven

Lizzy

March 1807

My dearest Lizzy,

I cannot tell you how long I have dreamed of writing this letter, how many times I have thought about what I will say, and now that the time has come, I can scarcely believe it. I am better—not truly well, per se, but this morning I put on something other than a dressing gown, ate a bit of breakfast not from a tray, and I am now sitting in the drawing room with Mary and Lydia.

Lizzy, I cannot thank you enough for your letters. Even though I did not respond, you wrote as if we had just spoken. You lifted my spirits when little else could stir me, and I will forever be grateful for your help in getting through this most trying of times. I only wish you, and Kitty, of course, could be here to mourn Mama with the rest of us, but I trust that Papa knows best and I will be a much better correspondent now!

When I wrote this in my head, I confess that I had little news to relate, for what can happen of interest in a sick room? But the past week has been quite an interesting time here at Longbourn, and since both Mary and Papa say they have not yet written to tell you, I shall do so now.

A visitor arrived just over a week ago now, when I was finally able to sit up for a while and eat something other than broth and gruel. His name is Mr. Collins and he is our cousin, the man who is to inherit Longbourn from Papa due to the entail. I understand that our father and his had a falling out many years ago and all contact ceased at that time. However, his father recently passed away, and when he heard of Mama's passing, he decided it was time to extend an olive branch and mend the rift.

Oh, Lizzy, he is the most peculiar man! I saw him but little, and I do not hesitate to say you would have laughed at him if you were here—I know that Papa did. He came to my room after he had been here several days, with Papa of course, and made the most impressive speech about how pleasant it was to meet me and see me on the mend. And then, right in front of me, told Papa that it was his utmost desire to secure a wife from among his cousins and had set his sights on me—quite prematurely, since this was our first meeting—but did not think it wise seeing the precarious state of my health and the length of my illness.

He then inquired after you and was rather put out when Papa said he did not expect you home for some time, nor was he willing to give Mr. Collins the necessary direction to London to claim you. I believe Mr. Collins might have pushed the matter farther, but Papa reminded him that we are in mourning—and indeed, Mr. Collins himself is still in mourning for his father—and that by the time a six-month had passed Mary would be of a suitable age to marry. I believe he also hinted that you were learning expensive tastes in Town and Mary would be a better choice for a parson's wife, for he means to go into the Church and spoke of the need for economy. I lost track of the conversation there, not being accustomed to such excitement.

Whatever was said next, he is now engaged to Mary. She will be sixteen when they marry, if not older, for he still has three months at Cambridge and then will need to find a living so he has a home for his bride. I wonder that none of this occurred to him when he decided to sweep me off my feet, but the logistics seem to work for all involved, and Mary appears satisfied with the arrangement. I believe she is more pleased about being the first sister engaged than about her husband, but I still have every belief that they will find happiness together.

I must end here, for my hand is unaccustomed to holding a pen and I fear if I continue my writing will become illegible. In any case, I have little else to tell. Please write soon and tell me more of your new friend Miss Darcy, she sounds delightful and I am so pleased to hear you are making acquaintances in Town. Give my regards to Kitty as well. Let her know I will write to her directly when I can next summon the energy to put pen to paper.

Your devoted sister,

Jane

P.S. Best wishes for your birthday, belated as they are! I so wanted to be able to write to you in December, but it was not to be. I have now had seventeen years of the best sister anyone could desire.

Lizzy looked up from her letter just as Georgiana entered and went to sit on the pianoforte bench next to Kitty. The younger girl had been calling at Lady Lichfield's house for nearly a month now to share in Lizzy and Kitty's lessons, while they went to Darcy House to meet with music and dancing masters.

While Georgiana's presence—and Mr. Darcy's interest in the matter—had increased the amount of time and effort their lessons required, Lizzy couldn't hold it against her. Georgiana was still quiet, nervous, and likely to run if confronted, but she'd begun to laugh freely and occasionally offer an unsolicited opinion or advice on their lessons. Lizzy thought that change was more than worth the frustration. Besides, what else was there to do in London in March, when one was still in mourning and visits to relatives across town were strictly regulated?

Georgiana pointed something out on the sheet music, then stood as Kitty began to pick her way through the piece. Kitty had changed as well. Without Lydia's exuberant schemes to distract her, she poured her attention into improving her drawing skills. It was clear that the pianoforte and French lessons would never hold the same place in her heart as her sketchbook and pencils, but she still made noticeable progress. Kitty had also taken to watching Georgiana and asking her to repeat the tiniest motions so she might be seen as a highly-bred lady rather than a country miss. Watching them, Lizzy thought that her younger sister would soon outshine her as the more graceful young lady. She also knew the attention helped Georgiana come out of her shell even more—and she gave good advice. Lizzy had picked up several tips that she had been practicing ever since.

Lost in thought, Lizzy didn't notice that Georgiana had approached her until the other girl sat down on the adjacent chair. "Good morning, Miss Elizabeth," she said with a smile.

"Miss Darcy, a pleasure to see you," Lizzy returned serenely. Following a lecture on proper addresses, they had fallen into the habit of greeting each other properly when they first spoke each day, then promptly reverting to nicknames. "How are you today?"

Georgiana made a face. "Well, I suppose. Fitzwilliam found a companion for me."

Lizzy felt her eyebrows shoot up. "I am surprised you don't sound more upset. Have you met her yet?"

"Yes, briefly. She is not so horrible. You will notice I said companion rather than governess. Fitzwilliam said he would not stop our lessons together, especially since she doesn't join us for another two weeks. She is to keep me company at home when Fitzwilliam has to be away on business and to teach me the things we do not learn here. Her name is Mrs. Younge, which I find funny because she is not *young* at all, but quite middle-aged. She seems to be kind, though, and did not try to make me talk any more than I wished."

"Where did Mr. Darcy find such a creature?" Lizzy asked.

Georgiana shrugged, a habit she had picked up from Lizzy and would now need to unlearn. "I'm not sure, exactly, but she was highly recommended by an acquaintance of his. It seems her past charge was recently married and is no longer in need of a companion."

"So that is the secret of escaping unwanted companions," Lizzy exclaimed, laughing. "If you do not like her, Georgie, you need only to find a husband and she will be gone."

Georgiana blushed. "But I don't *want* a husband! I'm far too young. *You* are the right age for thinking of husbands. All the men will be falling over themselves to dance with you, and you will have to tell me how it feels." Her eyes fell on the letter still in Lizzy's hands. "Oh! Have you had news from home?"

Kitty stopped playing abruptly. "Yes, Lizzy, I meant to ask you earlier—is that Jane's writing? Is she truly well? She must be, if she can write a multiple-page letter."

"Come and see," Lizzy said, waving her sister over to share her couch and handing the letter over. "It is from Jane, and it sounds like they have had quite the exciting month at home. Read it aloud, Kitty, Lady

Lichfield said you should practice and I am sure Georgiana would enjoy the contents despite not knowing the participants." She gave her sister an impish grin. "Besides, that leaves me free to respond."

Dear Jane,

Your letter brought me more joy than I can do justice to in words on a page. Now that it has arrived, I do not know how I survived without word from you in so long, and I am replying at the earliest opportunity so I can look forward to hearing from you once again. Of course, I do not want you to tax yourself overmuch, but then I know you will be sensible about your limits, even if that means you write only two pages instead of the twelve that I desire.

So Mary is to be married! I am glad she is satisfied, and gladder still that you were not forced into an understanding with such a fool. Yes, dearest, I will call him that even though I can hear your voice scolding me. You may apply to Papa for his opinion if you will not take mine, for I am sure he will support me. You are meant for someone who will cherish you and treat you like a queen, not barge into your sick room and discuss you like a mare for sale! I am quite put out just imagining the scene. Is it horrid that I feel a great deal of relief that I was not present to be an option? It may be the only good thing that has come of my exile to date.

I will contradict that statement, actually. You are correct that Miss Darcy is delightful. She is closer to Kitty's age than to mine, but is well-taught and intelligent. Her greatest failing is a nearly overwhelming shyness, but she is accustomed enough to Kitty and myself to show a hint of a playful nature beneath. I occasionally have the strangest feeling that I am teaching her to play for the first time in her life. Both of her parents have died—her father not long before Mama passed, and her mother when she was quite young—and she is now in the care of a much older brother. Mr. Darcy is not *the type to encourage silliness, of that I am certain, and so I am glad that Georgiana is at ease with Kitty and myself.*

I must end here, for I have only snatched a few moments of time and I am sure Lady Lichfield will soon arrive and scold me for neglecting my studies. We are focusing on drawing today, and you likely remember that it has never been my strong suit. Give me French or music or dancing and I could bluff my way through, but creating depth on a flat page still alludes me! It does not help that both Kitty and Georgiana (who spends mornings with us most days) are truly gifted artists. That reminds me, Kitty is very excited about the prospect of a letter from you, and I believe you will be pleasantly surprised by the handwriting on her reply—it has become not only legible but pretty in the past months, but borders on pretty as well. I will even suffer a longer wait for a letter, knowing how much Kitty looks forward to one of her own.

Your loving sister,

Elizabeth

Twelve

Darcy

March 1807

"But surely, Mr. Darcy, Georgiana will be happier in the long term if she were to go to a school. I know it must be hard giving her what she needs rather than what she wants in the moment, but you must see my point. If *I* had a girl of her age in my charge…"

Darcy quit listening. Miss Caroline had not stopped talking since she found out that Georgiana would be taking various lessons with Elizabeth and Catherine Bennet rather than learning from a governess or going away to school. She had let the idea of a governess go almost immediately, but was still pushing strongly for a boarding school—namely, the school that she herself had attended. Why she thought that Darcy wanted her advice or would listen to her, he had yet to determine, and he had been considering the matter for nearly a month.

The drawing room door opened and Georgiana herself entered, followed by the Bennet sisters, who had come to share Georgiana's lesson with a dancing master. Georgiana stopped short upon seeing their visitors, and Elizabeth frowned.

A look of annoyance crossed Miss Caroline's face, quickly hidden behind a smile. "Why, Miss Darcy, how lovely to see you again! And Miss Eliza and Miss Catherine, I did not expect to see you here. I have not encountered you lately, but then I suppose it is quite possible that you move in different circles." Her condescending smile made it clear that by *different*, she meant *lesser*.

Startled, Darcy was barely able to keep his face impassive. Georgiana looked horrified, and Catherine blushed scarlet. Elizabeth, however, raised her chin and smiled beautifully. "Miss Caroline, I did not realize you were on such terms with the Darcy family. Had you called on Lady Lichfield she would not have admitted you—both households *are* in mourning, after all. You must have known the family for quite some time."

Elizabeth dropped a brief curtsey that encompassed both Darcy and Bingley, then crossed the room and settled on the sofa across from Caroline. Georgiana and Kitty followed. "As for not seeing us, the circles we travel in matter little—we have been all but cloistered away. I *am* looking forward to encountering more of society again, once our six-month has passed. Kitty is not out, of course, but I was ever so pleased when an invitation came for Lady Granby's ball later this spring and Lady Lichfield said we might go. Will you be attending?"

Darcy was torn. On one hand, he did not approve of the cattiness ladies so often used with each other, especially when his impressionable sister was present. However, it was a beautifully delivered put-down, given to a lady he had wanted to put in her place for the entirely of her visit. And where he would have stayed silent or forced out something overtly rude, Elizabeth had managed to make her points entirely within the conventions of polite conversation, saccharin smile never wavering. To top it off, the look on Miss Caroline's face said plainly that she had *not* received an invitation to Lady Granby's ball. He was left with the bemused feeling that Miss Elizabeth's presence often inspired.

"Oh, I can hardly recall where I was last night, let alone something weeks away," Caroline managed after a moment's pause. She turned away from Elizabeth deliberately. "Miss Darcy, we were discussing schooling when you came in, and I fancy that I may understand how you feel a little better than your brother does—not, of course, to say anything less of him. Tell me, would you not find it most exciting to attend a school filled with girls just like you?" Clearly, Miss Bingley did not consider the two other young ladies in the room as Georgiana's equals.

Darcy bit back a snarl and braced himself for the flight and tears. Caroline Bingley had no idea what she had just done, and for a moment he wanted nothing more than to bodily remove her from the house. To make the presumption worse, she did not really know his sister at all—they had been introduced once weeks before, and had not met since. What on earth was she thinking?

Bingley clearly picked up on his tension, for he shot Darcy an alarmed look and said, "Now, Caroline, you have to admit your situation was different, since Louisa was there as well, and Miss Darcy is not lacking company here."

Caroline frowned at her brother. "But Louisa went on her own at first, and I hardly noticed she was there after a week or two. I became *such* good friends with the other girls, they were absolute dears."

"It would be interesting to hear Miss Bingley's take, then. Will she be joining us today?" Elizabeth asked, though Darcy scarcely heard. Why had his sister not made a dash for her room yet?

He crossed the room, presumably to look out the window, but still could not discern what kept her in her seat. She certainly looked on the verge of flight, white-faced and tense.

"Oh, no, Louisa will not be joining us," Caroline said with a tinkling laugh. She shot a look at Bingley. "I daresay she will not have much time for visiting in the foreseeable future, since it will take time to assemble her trousseau. And of course her fiancé will want to see her as well."

"Miss Bingley is engaged?" Kitty asked, perking up and looking interested in the conversation for the first time. "Is she shopping for her trousseau today?"

"I can't imagine she would be, not without her dear sister's input," Elizabeth said before Caroline could reply. She gave the other lady an even sweeter smile. "It was clear to me when we first met, Miss Caroline, that your sister greatly values your opinions. It must be quite the hardship for her to give you up today."

Darcy moved closer and finally discovered why Georgiana had not run. Tucked in the folds of their skirts, at an angle where Caroline could not see, she and Elizabeth had joined hands. It was strange, he thought, that she could breathe easily even as she hung on with white-knuckled fingers. He stifled a sigh once again at the thought of Miss Compton. His sister *would* take to a headstrong imp who still needed guidance of her own rather than a sweet, accomplished lady.

But as he continued to observe the joined hands, Darcy realized it was past the point of mattering. Georgiana had chosen to trust Elizabeth Bennet, and that meant his duty was plain. Rather than judging the headstrong imp, he needed to remove Caroline Bingley from his sitting room before Georgiana gave up and ran—or squeezed so hard Elizabeth lost the feeling in her fingers altogether.

*

It was raining that evening when the butler knocked on the door to Darcy's study. "Captain Fitzwilliam to see you, sir."

Darcy looked up, surprised—his cousin was not usually announced when he chose to visit Darcy House, but simply showed himself in. Sure enough, before Darcy could respond the Mr. Crew's stern visage disappeared from the doorway to be replaced by Richard's grin.

"That's Major Fitzwilliam, Crew," Richard Fitzwilliam said, turning to direct the grin at Crew now out of Darcy's sight.

"Of course, my apologies, Major Fitzwilliam. I was not aware of your promotion."

Darcy joined his cousin at the door. "Do not be concerned, Crew. I would not put it past *Major* Fitzwilliam to have planned this entire scene." He arched an eyebrow at the other gentleman. "A tactic I would expect from a child, not a major in His Majesty's army, I might add."

Richard clapped him on the shoulder. "I knew you would appreciate the joke, Darce," he said with a grin, unconcerned by the reprimand.

Darcy shook his head and stepped aside so his cousin could enter the study. Richard was one of the few people who dealt with his reserve by ignoring it altogether. He'd never admit it, but Darcy thoroughly enjoyed the banter.

"Congratulations," Darcy said, retrieving a second glass from the sideboard and pouring Richard a measure of whiskey from the decanter already sitting on his desk.

His cousin accepted the glass with a questioning look. “I’m acquainted with your surly nature, but that response lacks enthusiasm even for you. And you never have more than a single drink.” He indicated the decanter that Darcy had placed back on the desk. “Has something happened?”

Darcy dropped into his chair and indicated that Richard should sit as well. “I’ve just received a letter about our old friend George Wickham.”

The smile disappeared from Richard’s face and suddenly he became the respected army captain—now major—rather than the daredevil boy that Darcy had grown up with. The change eased the knot in Darcy’s stomach; whatever they decided to do, he wouldn’t have to deal with the situation alone. “And what has our dear friend done now?” Richard asked, settling back into his chair and taking a sip of whiskey.

Darcy sighed. At one time, George Wickham really *had* been their friend, Darcy’s closest friend in the world. He’d been the son of Pemberley’s steward, and when Richard came to visit in the summer the three were inseparable. They’d learned to ride horses and climb trees together, had spent hours fencing and boxing, and stolen countless sweets from Pemberley’s kitchen. Wickham had always been particularly adept at wheedling treats from Cook.

“Darce?” Richard asked, pulling Darcy back to the present.

"Here," Darcy said, picking up the letter he'd been staring at when Richard was announced. "It's a bit hard to make out in places, but legible."

He sat in silence while Richard read, thinking about the note. The woman who signed her name as Betsy Hall had clearly seen more of Wickham than he had recently, if she was to be believed. He had promised her marriage, but disappeared in the night with anything of value in the house. She was left alone, with no recourse and nowhere to turn, for she now had a newborn daughter—Wickham's child—that her remaining family refused to acknowledge. Betsy had heard Wickham speak of him several times, and after several inquiries managed to find the addresses for both Pemberley and Darcy House. Although paper was expensive and her writing poor, she had written to both locations, hoping for much-needed assistance.

On the other side of the desk, Richard swore. "What could have given her the idea that this is *your* problem?" he asked, looking up with a frown.

Darcy have a half-hearted shake of his head. "I imagine she was with Wickham when I paid off yet another of his debts, or at least heard about it. There have been several in the past year or so that I settled."

"Good God, Darcy, perhaps you should stop paying and see if that keeps him out of your life!"

Darcy fixed his cousin with a scowl. "He used *my* name on the account, and not a single person was willing to admit the man who had run up the debts was clearly someone else. They likely knew they'd never get a penny out of *him*."

Richard sat back, somewhat mollified, and studied the letter again. "What are you going to do?" he asked after a long pause.

It was the same question Darcy had been asking himself all night. "I'm not sure," he admitted, letting his fingers drum on the whiskey glass. "I can hardly blame the woman for being taken in—you know as well as I do that Wickham could charm leaves off a tree in July. I had thought to send her two hundred pounds. It is enough to see her and the child more comfortably settled somewhere, and is far less than some of the other bills Wickham has sent or attempted to send my way. There *have* been some I refused to pay, before father died."

Richard shook his head and threw back what remained of his whiskey. "It's a good thing these walls can't talk, and you know I don't gossip. Your reputation would be in shambles, elsewise. The great stern Mr. Darcy is in truth a bleeding heart. No, don't argue with me, you know it's true."

Darcy scowled. "A position such as mine comes with a great deal of responsibility, and I take that very seriously, Richard. It is not so different from your responsibility to your men, which I am sure has increased now that you are a major. I do not like seeing people in pain when I have the power to help them—and like it or not, Wickham falls under my responsibility. You know how my father was about him, know that he made me promise to look out for the man."

It was Richard's turn to grimace. "I wish your father could have seen him for what is really is. Wickham milked Uncle George for all he was worth, and only the pair of us were ever the wiser. No offense meant to your father, of course."

Darcy waved off the comment, unfazed. "He was happier believing that Wickham was who he pretended to be. I couldn't begrudge him that, not after Mother died. So little made him happy for a while."

Richard cocked his head slightly and Darcy got the distinct impression that he was being closely studied even though his cousin's expression didn't change. "And how are you doing, now that your father has passed? Are there any imps that make you happy even though they shouldn't?"

Elizabeth Bennet's face sprang to mind unbidden, followed quickly by her set-down of Miss Caroline that morning. Startled, Darcy gave a short laugh. "Yes, actually, there is one," he said, feeling a genuine grin tug at the corners of his mouth for the first time since he'd received the letter from Betsy. "Oh, don't look at me like that, I haven't lost my senses. It isn't like Wickham and my father, I promise you that. No, it's—"

He stopped to consider. How to explain Miss Elizabeth, or, as he heard from Georgiana countless times a day, *Lizzy*? He certainly couldn't tell Richard that he'd sometimes thought of her as an angel in disguise, and anecdotes would fall flat without her playful manner and sparkling eyes. He didn't even know what *he* thought of Elizabeth Bennet. She puzzled him exceedingly.

"Georgiana has a friend that by all rights should not be any good for her," he said finally, considering each word before it left his mouth. "Miss Elizabeth is older than her—sixteen or so, I believe—and comes from a lower station in life for all that she is a gentleman's daughter. She loves to argue, and I can't imagine what it must be like making her sit still and attend to her work. And yet since she has been in Miss Elizabeth's company, Georgiana is much calmer. She laughs some days when all she used to do is cry. And," he finished, thinking yet again of Elizabeth's perfect handling of Caroline Bennet, "I have had cause to find her amusing when I ought to have told her to mind her tongue."

Richard was watching him in astonishment. "Well," he said after a considerable pause, "forgive my caution, Darcy, but I would feel better if I can meet this young lady. I have never met *anyone* who has made you so verbose, and I would like to form my own opinion that we do not have a female Wickham on our hands. She could mean to ingrate herself with the family using Georgiana's timidity and your tendency to give in to your sister, have you considered that?"

Of course he had. "You'll like her," Darcy said without a shade of doubt. And she would like him as well; everyone loved his dashing cousin, most especially spirited young men and lively ladies. "You know I've considered that she is using Georgiana, and if that is her intent then she's a far better actress that Wickham ever was. If you want to meet her, however, come round for tea on Thursday. She and her sister will both be here then."

"Well," Richard said again, "I believe I will do that." He smiled suddenly. "I might bring a surprise for Georgie. It will be good to see her again, too."

THIRTEEN

Lizzy

March – May 1807

To Elizabeth, it seemed like spring had never come at a more fitting time than it did that year. She and Kitty had settled into their routine on Hill Street over the winter, taking lessons in the morning and amusing themselves in the afternoons. Georgiana joined them at least once a week, although she came less frequently now that she had a companion at home. Mrs. Younge had arrived and seemed sufficient to keep Georgiana company and listen to her conjugate French verbs, a task Lizzy was happy to give up. She still called often enough that Elizabeth didn't feel a need to bemoan the change, and in turn the Bennet sisters continued to visit Darcy House at least once a week, more often if a dancing or music master was due to visit.

With the groundwork of their new life laid, spring slowly gave way to the joys. Numerous changes occurred over the season, but few made Lizzy happier than the first. Convinced that her oldest charge had learned her lesson, Lady Lichfield agreed that she could once again take walks with only Tom as company and chaperone. Freed from the plodding pace and frequent complaints of the maid that had joined them before—and helped by the fact that Tom's sore leg fared better in the warmer weather—Lizzy set off into the city parks feeling closer to her old self than she had since they'd arrived in the city.

The next change began over dinner one evening in late March. Lizzy guessed the moment she sat down that Lady Lichfield had something to discuss, but their guardian waited until the servants were out of the room before she said anything beyond pleasantries.

"I have no doubt, being that you are intelligent young ladies, that you are aware your mourning period will be officially over on the 29th. Since that is Easter Sunday, I think it would be best to continue wearing mourning until Monday. Do you agree?"

To Lizzy's surprise, Kitty turned to look at her rather than replying immediately. After a moment of silence from all ladies, Kitty asked slowly, "Would it not be appropriate to come out of mourning when we celebrate Jesus' rebirth? Or would it honor Mama if we keep our mourning?"

Lady Lichfield smiled, and Elizabeth knew Kitty had asked the correct question. Giving her own opinion, she said, "I think we should keep our mourning. We cannot visit Mama's grave, but we can remember her in our dress—and I don't believe anyone would fault us for doing so, whereas they might if we come out of mourning on a day that should not be focused on ourselves. Was that your conclusion as well?" she asked Lady Lichfield.

The lady smiled. "It was, but I thought you should have a chance to give your input. That was well reasoned, both of you. I will tell Nell to remove your previous clothing from storage. I have a suspicion that you both have grown, so we will need to confirm which of your dresses still fit." She smiled at them both, eyes lingering on Lizzy. "Besides, I have heard that there is a ball coming up, and it would not do to show up in a dress six months out of style."

*

Her new ball gown was lovely, Lizzy thought once again as she dressed for Lady Granby's ball. Kitty had insisted on watching all the preparations, and Lizzy, who had been braced for endless whining and jealousy from her younger sister, was surprised to find Kitty cheerful instead. "I'm still so clumsy," she admitted. "Lady Lichfield has promised that we will go to the opera soon, and I can wear your old ball gown then and practice being a grand young lady. Besides," she added, plucking at the front of her dress, "I don't want to just *go* to a ball. I want to be the *belle* of my first ball. If I go now, that will never happen. I still look like a boy with curls!"

Lizzy laughed. "You've been reading too many novels," she accused, "but I know what you mean. I enjoyed the few dances I went to in Hertfordshire, but I stood next to Jane for most of the evening, and that means I was all but invisible."

Kitty laughed as well. "Jane's the most beautiful girl in the world; it would take something impressive to divert attention from her."

"Well," Lizzy said, turning around so she was facing Kitty rather than looking at her in the mirror, "there was the time I tripped and spilled punch all over my new gown. If you're anything like me, you're wise to avoid such potential embarrassments until you feel equal to the task. What's wrong?" she added, because Kitty's face had turned reflective.

"You don't have Jane to hide behind tonight," Kitty said after a moment. "I think you *will* be the belle of the ball. You're beautiful, Lizzy."

Touched but determined not to show how much, Elizabeth raised an eyebrow. "I think you're biased, but thank you, Kitty. I might be lucky enough to have several dance partners, although the ball last fall made it clear there is no guarantee of that." Thinking about the other event, Lizzy grinned. "If nothing else, I'm sure Mr. Darcy will dance with me so he doesn't have to make any new acquaintances. Georgiana says he absolutely loathes dancing with strangers, but he is back from his trip to Kent and doesn't have an excuse to not attend. It will be better than sitting out, even if he does act standoffish all the time." She had not forgotten his comment from the Harrington's ball. *She is hardly more than a child, and by no means tempting enough to give up my single state.*

Lizzy looked down at her new dress, creamy white and accented with lace. She had grown, as Lady Lichfield had feared, and even if Mr. Darcy thought of her as a child, Elizabeth noted with smug satisfaction that she at least did not look like a boy with curls.

*

In the end, Lizzy found a variety of dance partners and a reason to believe that Darcy did not think well of *anyone* in a ballroom. She had procured herself a glass of punch and was standing against the wall to drink it when the group to her left moved, revealing Mr. Darcy and Mr. Bingley. She was briefly surprised, for Lady Lichfield had told her Lady Granby took pride in keeping those from trade out of her parties. Then again, Bingley was the most agreeable gentleman of Lizzy's acquaintance, and ballrooms were always in need of handsome young men who actually liked to dance.

"Darcy, come, you must admit that she is an angel," Bingley exclaimed, his eyes on a young lady across the room. "I have never met anyone like her in my entire life."

Darcy's eyes flickered to Elizabeth rather than the lady across the room and quickly away again before he replied. "You said as much about Miss—oh, what was her name? Last fall, when we were introduced." Unlike Bingley, Darcy kept his voice low, and Lizzy had to strain to hear it. "If all women are angels, then it stands to reason that none of them are."

"They may all be angels, but I see only Miss Heart. Even her name is perfection, is it not? I must have you agree with me."

Darcy's stern expression didn't waiver. "I should think your preference would be for me to *not* agree, for then the lady in question would be faced with a choice between gentlemen."

Bingley looked taken aback for a moment, then his face cleared. "Oh, you jest," he said easily. "Look, here comes Bainbridge, I am sure he will agree with me."

"No doubt he will," Darcy replied, "and if he is here you will not be in need of my company. Excuse me; I have had my fill of silliness for the evening." And so saying he disappeared into the card room, where Lizzy had no doubt he would stay for the rest of the night.

And that is the sort of man that society seeks to emulate, she thought, exasperated, as she watched him go. *What an impressive gentleman. I didn't see any behavior that I found gentleman-like at all.*

She was somewhat mollified when Bainbridge, having greeted Bingley and agreed that Miss Heart was indeed lovely, looked around and caught sight of her just as the music started up again. They had encountered each other again at Darcy House, and if Lizzy had not cared for his interest in her at those times, she was glad to know him now.

"Miss Elizabeth, it is delightful to see you again. Are you engaged for this dance?" She admitted that she was not, and he bowed at once, holding out a hand.

"Then will you do me the favor of dancing with me? For the entire ballroom will suffer if your loveliness is hidden here by the wall."

She laughed, not believing a single word, but took his hand readily enough. "Tell me," he went on as they joined the other dancers, "did I see Darcy just now?"

Lizzy cast a look around them and turned back with an arch smile. "You could hardly mistake him. I see no other men of his bearing present, but the truly distinguishing feature is his scowl. It is not common in a ballroom, and therefore must be recognizable even through the crush."

Bainbridge laughed. "You have described him well! Darcy has never been one to seek out pleasure, even when it is staring him in the face, and so he detests these events. I would go after him, but he will most likely be arguing politics or crop yields with a rheumy old man, and neither would welcome my interruption. But enough of that, or soon we will be just as boorish. Did your sister accompany you tonight?"

As she spun in the dance, Lizzy thought she caught sight of Darcy, not arguing politics but watching the revelers from a balcony above the dance floor, his face set in its usual mask. Then she turned again and he was gone, leaving her to wonder if she had seen him at all. Refocusing her attention back to Bainbridge, she said, "No, Kitty is not yet out. She has extracted a promise that I recount all the details of tonight, however, so she can image that she was here."

He smiled, spinning her around again. "Well then, we must make sure you have a wonderful evening. It wouldn't do to come home without a wonderful story to tell."

*

Kitty was appropriately delighted with Lizzy's account of the ball, although she seemed to take more offence than her sister that the grand Mr. Darcy had ignored her and was determined to think ill of him for the slight. While Lizzy reassured Kitty she had not been injured by the gentleman's lack of attention, she secretly delighted in her sister's solidarity.

Mr. Darcy's manners mattered little for the rest of the spring, for they saw each other only in passing. Lizzy's morning routine continued on as it had through the winters, but afternoons and evenings became considerably more varied. She was not particularly interested in any of the young men she encountered at various events, but they did entertain her—and stoke her confidence. Kitty professed that seventeen was a perfect age to marry; Elizabeth was more than happy to spend the year simply enjoying herself whether young men were involved or not.

As promised, Lady Lichfield took both young ladies to the opera, where they sat in a box with another countess and Kitty preened every time someone glanced their way. Lizzy was far more excited by the note that came from her Aunt Gardiner, informing them that they had a new cousin, and would they like to come meet her soon?

Lady Lichfield was happy for them to spend time with family as long as they continued to make progress on their studies, so soon Kitty and Elizabeth took to visiting at least once a week. Lady Lichfield always offered her carriage, even if she was not coming along, and Lizzy said nothing although she happily would have walked. She loved seeing her aunt and uncle and found baby Frances adorable; she would not risk losing the privilege of visiting now that it had finally been offered.

Having spent most of the winter indoors, often beset by boredom and uncharacteristically in low spirits, Lizzy was surprised to discover that she did not hate London. The noise and filth that permeated most of the city often made her think of Hertfordshire's clean air and quiet walks, but she was not one to remain dejected for long. Now that the girls were out of mourning, Lady Lichfield attended many more events, often with them in tow, and even when they were home it became a common occurrence to have at least one afternoon caller.

It was during one of their outings to Bond Street for shopping that Elizabeth and Kitty encountered the Bingley sisters, where the latter pair was making the final purchases for Louisa's trousseau. They had just finished exchanging pleasantries—rather coolly from Caroline, and mostly genuine where Louisa was concerned—when Mr. Bingley came bounding up to them, accompanied by a young lady and a woman who appeared to be her mother.

"Well met!" he exclaimed. "Is it not a lovely day? I am so glad the weather has turned, there is nothing more pleasant to me than a spring day and good company. I was lucky enough to encounter Miss Lucy; have you met?" he asked Lizzy. When she replied that they had not, Bingley performed the necessary introductions, calling them all dear friends and happily ignoring Caroline's subsequent eye-roll.

Miss Lucy soon fell into conversation with Louisa, and Elizabeth took the chance to step slightly away as she prepared to extricate herself and Kitty.

"Pathetic, isn't it?" Caroline asked quietly, flicking her eyes towards her brother. "He fancies himself head over heels in love. She's an angel, the most delightful thing in the world. I doubt he knows two sincere things about her. Have you ever met someone genuinely perfect?"

"My older sister, Jane," Elizabeth responded promptly, smiling at the thought. "I've never seen her equal for sweetness or beauty, and I'm convinced I never will. Tell me, is that Miss Heart?" Mr. Bingley had said the lady's last name, but in the loud street Elizabeth had struggled to hear.

Caroline laughed. "Oh goodness, no. Miss Heart's engagement was announced last week, but Charles had already met Miss Lucy by then. Her family name is Carter. Horribly common, isn't it?"

Elizabeth, who saw nothing wrong with the name, smiled and made a noncommittal noise. "Drat, you must excuse us," she said a moment later, finding her excuse as Lady Lichfield emerged from a nearby store. "Lady Lichfield has finished at the jeweler's and will be wanting to be home in time for tea. Kitty, we must go," she said. "Good day, everyone."

She spent the ride home wondering if it was better to be friendly to everyone with no consistency, like Mr. Bingley, or reliably unsociable but considerate of a very few people, like Darcy.

Fourteen

Darcy

June 1807

Summer had descended and most of the *ton* had taken themselves and their families away to country estates, forsaking London's heat and stench now that the Season had ended. For the first time he could remember, Darcy did not envy them. Pemberley held no appeal for him now, not without his father there to welcome him home. Strange that George Darcy's gruff greeting had never raised any particular emotions before, when it was now all he wanted.

Georgiana said nothing about the fact that they remained, and for that he was grateful. In the past few months, his little sister seemed more and more lively, whereas for him nothing had changed. She was happy, Darcy reflected—at least as long as no strangers were introduced suddenly and no one asked her opinion on a subject other than music. Now that the notion of going away to school had been settled, Georgiana seemed to have found her place in their world. Darcy refused to think about the topic much, because when he did the feeling in his gut came precariously close to jealousy.

All around him, people's lives seemed to be falling into order. Georgiana spent her time with the Bennet sisters and went to Mrs. Younge when she encountered a problem, Richard had settled into his role as a Major and was left with less time than ever for his cousin, and Pemberley's steward wrote that everything was well handled despite Darcy's continued absence.

Even Miss Elizabeth seemed to have changed from a fiery girl to a young lady, which Darcy found nearly as disconcerting as his sister's newfound contentedness. He could still picture her dancing with Bainbridge at Lady Granby's ball, clad in white lace and altogether unrecognizable from the rascal in black he had rescued in Cheapside. Darcy still wasn't entirely sure he liked Elizabeth, but she had often been his ally over the past eight months, and he was accustomed to her ways. If Bainbridge had singled her out, it meant that the young men of the *ton* had taken notice of Miss Elizabeth Bennet. After all the time she had spent with Georgiana, Darcy reasoned that it was natural he would view her as another sister. Yes, that definitely explained why he had not liked Bainbridge paying her attention, had not liked it at all. Unfortunately, he could no longer discourage Bainbridge's advances with a frown as he'd done when they first met Miss Elizabeth.

At least one event that summer brought joy as well as dissatisfaction. Louisa Bingley married John Hurst in early June and the couple departed London for a wedding tour immediately after. Darcy cared nothing about the match, but the new Mrs. Hurst took her sister with her for company, and the lack of Caroline Bingley's assertions and over-familiarities was appreciated by everyone at Darcy House. The threesome was scheduled to return from Bath in September, and Darcy looked forward to the long respite.

Unfortunately, the absence of his sisters meant that Bingley, untiringly social, looked more and more to Darcy for company and advice. And while London's elite had dwindled, enough of the *ton* remained to form parties that Darcy found just as tedious as any Season ball.

That evening found them at the Earl of Shrewsbury's London residence, although Darcy doubted the Earl had anything to do with the party. He would likely retreat to his library before the night was half over while the countess entertained, and Darcy would envy him greatly. If Bingley had anything to say about it, Darcy himself would have to make small talk until the early morning—and despite the younger man's inconvenient social tendencies, Darcy had come to value his company. Bingley was one of the few people who accepted him for who he was, and part of that friendship meant Darcy now spent time at garden parties.

He'd made it three steps into the garden before Lady Shrewsbury descended upon him. "Darcy, what a pleasant surprise!" she exclaimed. "How lovely to see you. I was beginning to think you had left London." She leaned a bit closer. "I am quite amazed I managed to not call you Fitz, do forgive me if I slip up over the course of the evening. Oh, dear boy, I still can't quite believe your father is gone."

Darcy bowed to his mother's closest friend. "Lady Shrewsbury, it is good to see you as well. I imagine you didn't see my father much these past few years, so his passing would not change all that much in your social sphere."

She gave him a sad smile. "No, I hadn't seen George for nearly five years. It's been far longer than it feels since we spent our summers together at Pemberley or Wanfield. And I suppose I will have to accept 'Lady Shrewsbury' as well. You're too proper to call me 'Auntie Maude anymore. But enough of that. Come, introduce me to your friend," she said, nodding to where Bingley stood just behind him. Then, immediately, "Oh, and there's Lady Lichfield and the girls. I don't suppose you know them? That's a lady that's done well for herself, companion to countess, can you imagine? She handled it well, though, and I know your mother respected her."

Darcy turned to see Lady Lichfield, closely flanked by Elizabeth and Catherine Bennet. Responding to Lady Shrewsbury's smile, they came forward and made their curtseys. Always loquacious, Lady Shrewsbury greeted them and began introductions before Darcy could correct her misconception. "I must introduce you to my godson, Fitzwilliam Darcy of Pemberley. His mother and I were the dearest of friends. Darcy, this is Lady Amelia Lee, dowager Countess of Lichfield, and her wards, Elizabeth and Catherine Bennet of Hertfordshire."

Elizabeth's eyes had lit with amusement while Lady Shrewsbury spoke, but it was Lady Lichfield who answered. "Thank you for the introduction, but the need has long since passed. Miss Darcy is friends with Elizabeth and Catherine, and we have seen much of each other this past six-month. I am actually quite surprised that you never encountered Georgiana when you called in Hill Street."

Lady Shrewsbury smiled brilliantly, recovering from her mistake without batting an eye. "We shall have to coordinate a visit. Darcy, you must assist me in making it happen, for I would love to see your sister again. Now," she said briskly, turning to him expectantly, "it seems that I am the only one who does not know your friend, here. Will you do the honors?"

*

It soon became clear that Bingley was not in need of any other introductions. He flitted from one group to the next, trailing laughter and smiles in his wake. Luckily for Darcy, that meant he was soon able to step back and fade into the shadows, taking up his preferred role as observer rather than participator. There was a perfect bench, set beneath a tree where the open garden turned to divided sections, that gave him a clear view of the revelers while he remained mostly hidden. Still, he doubted he would stay unbothered for long, and indeed it had been barely a quarter hour before Elizabeth Bennet appeared, her blue gown blending in with the shadows cast by the setting sun, a glass in her hand.

"I'm supposed to give you this," she said without preamble, holding it out to him. "From Lady Shrewsbury. She said you would appreciate it."

He took the glass and peered inside, catching a whiff of the contents in the process. As he had expected, it contained some of Lord Shrewsbury's best whiskey, the kind that he kept locked away. Darcy knew it well—Shrewsbury had brought his father a bottle every summer, and George Darcy would savor it all year.

"Thank you, Miss Elizabeth," Darcy said, taking a sip. He looked sideways at Elizabeth. Lady Shrewsbury could have sent the glass with a maid, and he hoped Elizabeth had not minded the request.

To his surprise, she did not leave but instead looked around them with interest. "I've never seen so many trees at a private residence in London," she remarked at last. "I didn't know it was possible."

"The earl hates London. Lady Shrewsbury loves it; you must have noticed how social she is. This was part of their compromise."

Elizabeth frowned. "I wonder if he feels like it is enough. It is a beautiful cage, but that does not mean one is less trapped. You cannot walk in a garden, not really. You cannot ride, not that I do, but I assume a man like the earl does. There is nothing new to discover. Silence will never be the loudest sound."

They both stopped talking, and even with the noise from the party, a kind of peace settled over their small part of the garden. The light cast by the candles and lanterns did not reach their alcove, and for a moment Darcy felt as though they stood in a separate world, held apart from the revelers that had no love for silence. He felt the same sort of kinship he had with Elizabeth at Lady Haddington's ball, that of two people who did not care to perform for strangers. It felt so *right*, he did not consider that they should not be alone together until someone spoke on the other side of the hedge to his right.

"Do you really think he means to propose?" a female voice asked.

A giggle, then "Of course he does, silly. He follows me everywhere like a puppy. It's annoying, really; I nearly had to sneak off just to get away and talk to you. He'll make the most *agreeable* husband, though, don't you think? A smile, or perhaps something more, and I'll have anything I want. He certainly has the money for it."

"Lucy!" the first lady exclaimed. "You wouldn't—wouldn't *seduce* him, would you? Besides, you'll have to put up with Miss Caroline. That one thinks she knows what is best for everyone around her, and she's not afraid to tell you so."

"Oh, phooey," Lucy said. "Caroline Bingley is nothing. I'll manage her brother easily enough, and she'll just have to live with it. He is the head of the family, after all."

They moved away, giggling, and for a long moment neither Darcy or Elizabeth moved. A previous comment came back to him, ringing through his mind: *No one thinks practically when they fall in love.* Clearly, love was not the main thing on Miss Lucy's mind.

"Do you know who that was?" Darcy asked in an undertone when he could no longer hear the rustling of skirts.

"Miss Lucy Carter," Elizabeth responded promptly, surprising him. He hadn't expected her to know someone clearly so disingenuous. "Caroline does *not* like her. I can't imagine Mr. Bingley would find any domestic bliss with those two in his household." She turned her face upwards, catching some of the first moonlight on her skin. "I should make sure Kitty is still behaving." After two steps, though, she turned back. "Are you going to do anything about it? He's your friend."

Darcy nodded slowly, taking another sip of the whiskey while he considered. "I don't think I have much of a choice," he said.

"Good," she responded. "Oh—pink gown, blonde curls." Without another word, she turned and walked off, disappearing into the throng.

*

He found Bingley standing near the punch table, a giggling lady dressed in pink clutching his arm. Bingley was paying no attention to anyone else, and the unease in Darcy's stomach increased at the sight. His friend was creating expectations, and if the behavior was not stopped soon, he might be honor bound to follow through on them. They would have to speak tonight, not later as Darcy had originally planned. He only hoped it wasn't already too late to save his friend from the dainty fortune hunter.

Swallowing a sigh, Darcy made his way towards the group, refusing to look in either direction for fear of being waylaid. Having decided on his course of action, he wanted to complete it as soon as possible.

"Bingley," he said when at least he stood beside the other man, "I need to speak with you."

He had interrupted Miss Lucy, and the quick glare she sent at him contrasted drastically from Bingley's smile. Her face smoothed into a perfect smile, but Darcy knew what he had seen. The pretty girl who looked the very picture of womanly innocence could ruin the right man.

"Darcy! There you are, I wondered where you had gotten off to. I must introduce you, this is Miss Lucy Carter, one of Caroline's dear friends."

Darcy set his teeth and waded through the pleasantries, then turned so he faced Bingley directly and Miss Lucy was cut out of the circle. "If we might speak? I believe it is urgent." When Bingley waited, eyebrows raised in anticipation, Darcy added, "Privately."

"Oh, of course! What do you need? Is everything alright?"

Darcy didn't say a word until they were inside the house, in the corner of the library opposite the door and away from anywhere that someone could hide. "Bingley, what are your intentions towards Miss Lucy?"

His friend turned a light pink. "I meant to speak to you about that, actually. I mean to propose to her, but am I moving too quickly?"

"Bingley," Darcy paused. No, he would not sugar-coat this. Bingley needed to hear this, he needed to grow up if he was going to survive as a tradesmen's son in a gentleman's world. "I overheard your Miss Lucy speaking to a friend earlier. She did not know I was present; I was on the other side of a hedge. She is expecting you to propose—no, listen to the rest," he added hurriedly when Bingley's face lit up. "She is expecting you to propose, and she means to accept, but not because she harbors any fondness for you. I am not saying she dislikes you, but it was very clear that she means to take advantage of your money and your happy nature."

"You must have misheard," Bingley exclaimed. "Or it was another lady, speaking of a different gentleman.

"She spoke of you by name, and said that a smile 'or something else' would get her anything she wanted. She means to have you send Caroline away, once you are wed. And Bingley, she began all of this by saying she'd nearly had to sneak away, because your attention was like that of a puppy. Do you want a wife that thinks of you in such a way?"

"I want a wife who loves me," Bingley said, whose face had turned grim. "And I am still not convinced that you are correct." But his shoulders were rounded, and

Darcy could see the question on his face even in the low light of the room.

"I will say no more," Darcy said. "You are your own man and make your own decisions, but please, think on what I have said. I do not want to watch someone take advantage of you." When Bingley made no reply, Darcy turned and left him to his thoughts. He had done the right thing, he reflected as he made his way back out into the garden. It must hurt at the moment, but Bingley would thank him for it someday.

"I declare, you have spent all evening in hiding!" Lady Shrewsbury exclaimed, appearing at his elbow as he exited the house. "In some ways you are your father all over again. I've no idea how you disappear so well when you tower over half of the people here. Come. I have someone I would like you to meet, and this time I am positive she is not already in your acquaintance." She turned to a young lady standing behind her. "Darcy, may I present Miss Isabella St. Clair? Miss St. Clair, my godson, Fitzwilliam Darcy."

Miss St. Clair smiled and curtseyed; he bowed. "Mr. Darcy, it is delightful to meet you. Lady Shrewsbury is clearly fond of you, and I have never yet had cause to disagree with her. I am sure you and I will be great friends before long."

Darcy returned her smile feeling rather nonplussed. He had heard similar statements from numerous young women, but somehow Miss St. Clair made the words seem genuine, personal. She was tall, he noted, the top of her reddish-gold head on level with his eyes.

“Miss St. Clair,” he responded. “I have known Lady Shrewsbury all my life, and while I cannot pretend to understand her fondness for me, I value her opinion greatly as well.” He paused, smiled again, and held out his arm. “Would you care for some punch?”

FIFTEEN

Lizzy

July 1807

Lizzy had long ago realized that Georgiana and Kitty would never be ideal walking partners, as both preferred a pace far slower than her own. However, it rarely took much effort to convince them that a trip to one of London's parks was in order, because therein was an ever-changing supply of things to sketch. Lizzy could then wander, and while the situation was less than ideal, it was better than spending her afternoons stuck in a drawing room.

She and Kitty had traveled to Darcy House that day, and so they set out from there, the three girls accompanied by Mrs. Younge and a maid. Elizabeth, watching the maid from the corner of her eye as they exited the house, knew the girl was there to chaperone her when the group inevitably separated. Mrs. Younge would of course remain with Georgiana and Kitty, and Lizzy could not walk alone. She was wishing very strongly that Tom would be accompanying her instead when footsteps sounded on the stairs behind them and Mr. Darcy joined the group.

Sure he meant only to greet them in passing, Lizzy paid little attention to the addition and resumed her contemplation of the coming afternoon. They would find a nice bench and both the younger girls would settle down to sketch. Elizabeth would join them briefly, then set off again, alone with her thoughts and a maid who refused to talk. Some days she found this the perfect respite, but Lizzy loved dearly to laugh, and that activity usually required at least two people if one did not wish to look mad. Stifling a sigh, Elizabeth glanced around and forced herself to admit that she was thoroughly unimpressed with her prospects for the day.

And then, of course, was the fact that Georgiana and Kitty could never replace Jane's company. As much as she loved them both and had spent many pleasant days in their company, Lizzy often felt as much like a mother as she did a friend. The things that had been on her mind recently seemed far removed from the worries of twelve- and fourteen-year-old girls. Unfortunately, she also couldn't image writing a letter to Jane with the line, *I'm beginning to think all the people around me are either eaten up with self-importance or too stupid to know what's good for them.* Jane believed the best of everyone, no matter the evidence, and she hadn't spent the better part of a year giving fake smiles all over London.

"Miss Elizabeth, you look lost in your thoughts."

Lizzy jumped and looked up. "Mr. Darcy, you've caught me at a disadvantage," she managed. "I was indeed thinking."

"It must have been something serious, to put such a frown on your face."

Oh yes, Lizzy thought to herself, *he truly is a flatterer*. Then something clicked in her mind, and she realized that Mr. Darcy might be a good sounding board for her recent thoughts. If nothing else, he would not take serious offense. He might have better principles than Miss Lucy Carter, but Lizzy had seen plenty of evidence that the man fell squarely into the 'full of self-importance' category.

"I believe it is serious," she replied. "I have been thinking that many of the people I've met in London can be divided into two groups. The first believes that they are correct in thought, action, and manner of dress to the extent that they ignore evidence to the contrary. Their pride blinds them to any cruelties they cause or improvements they might make.

"The second group," she went on, "is somewhat of the opposite. These people seek to please those around them at the cost of their own judgement. They are amiable without distinction, mirrors of the strongest personality near them. My current struggle is that I cannot make up my mind about which fault is more severe. What say you?"

Darcy frowned, a deep V forming between his eyes, but he answered quickly. "A man who lives his life with an excess of conviction will, to me, always be preferable to someone who exhibits no conviction at all. You say that pride blinds, but it also guides. If a man is proud of his estate, for example, he will work harder to maintain it, and all who live there will benefit. Put a weak-willed person in charge and all predictability and consistency is lost. Those who depend on such a man do not know when or if they can expect the assistance that is their due."

"And what of a man who is proud of his image and his fortune, but not of the workers who toiled so he can wear his expensive clothes?" Or a woman, Elizabeth though dryly, thinking of Caroline Bennet. She had often heard the woman scoff at those in trade when everyone knew that is where her father had earned his money.

"In such a case you speak not of pride, but of vanity," Mr. Darcy returned, "and vanity is a weakness indeed. But pride—where there is a real superiority of mind, pride will be always under good regulation."

"If that is the case then the answer is clear: one who remains true to their original beliefs and actions is to be exalted, no matter how circumstances are altered, which clearly puts the amiable in the wrong."

Darcy turned towards her sharply. "Do you always argue by willfully misunderstanding those around you?" he asked.

Pleased to have elicited a response, Lizzy smiled. "If we all must have a defect, then mine is to argue when I ought to acquiesce. How I do so varies with the circumstances. What is your defect, Mr. Darcy? Here, I will save you the trouble: it is pride, and therefore you would say you have no defect at all."

Darcy gave her a reproachful look. "I have made no such assertion, as you well know. I have faults enough. My temper I dare not vouch for. It is, I believe, too little yielding—certainly too little for the convenience of the world. I cannot forget the follies and vices of others so soon as I ought, nor their offenses against myself. My feelings are not puffed about with every attempt to move them. My temper would perhaps be called resentful. My good opinion once lost, is lost forever."

The words echoed Lizzy's previously formed opinion of Mr. Darcy, and she wondered that he could state such a list calmly, without shame. Surely it indicated that he found himself justified in some way; his superiority allowed for the faults to remain unchecked. Aloud, though, she said, "It sounds as though you are well acquainted with your own mind."

He opened his mouth to reply, but they had reached the entrance to Hyde Park and Georgiana was watching her brother expectantly. "Will you be spending the afternoon with us?" she asked, clearly hoping for a yes.

Darcy was already shaking his head. "No, I have an appointment with Reid on several important matters. I will see you this evening, Georgie. Enjoy your afternoon, ladies." He bowed, sending one more look in Lizzy's direction that she couldn't read, and walked off briskly.

They continued on, Lizzy falling back into her thoughts. When Georgiana stopped in front of her,

Elizabeth caught herself at the last moment before she collided with the younger girl. Georgiana didn't notice. Instead, she stood staring at a young man on a bench just up the path. "George?"

He looked up, and Lizzy was struck by dark wavy hair and white teeth that stood out against tanned skin. His dress marked him clearly as a gentleman, and as he came to his feet Lizzy noted that he also had a fine, lithe build.

"Well, if it isn't Miss Georgette," the man said with a smile. "And looking very grown up indeed! You're a proper young lady now, Georgie. I wouldn't have recognized you if you hadn't said something."

Having moved out from behind Georgiana, Lizzy noticed her flush and wondered if she took that as a compliment or a set-down. Then again, a sheltered twelve-year-old girl might not wonder why a young man would fail to notice her.

Whatever her thoughts, the words had brought Georgiana's shyness out in force, and she ducked her head as if trying to hide. The man noticed and grinned, apparently well aware of the predicament. He looked at the group in general and then gave a full bow. "Greetings, ladies," he said. "My name is George Wickham, and I knew Miss Darcy before she grew up and met such fashionable friends. My father was the steward at Pemberley when I was young."

Lizzy, shooting another look at Georgiana from the corner of her eye, reconsidered her previous thought. Did Georgiana harbor a childhood crush on her prior playmate? She could certainly understand the appeal, Elizabeth admitted to herself as she turned back towards Mr. Wickham.

There was another hesitation where an introduction would usually fall, and Lizzy stepped forward to fill it when no one else did so. “It is a pleasure to meet you, Mr. Wickham. I am Elizabeth Bennet, and this is my younger sister Catherine, although everyone calls her Kitty. And Mrs. Younge is Miss Darcy’s companion.”

Wickham turned the full force of his smile onto her. “Charmed, I’m sure, Miss Elizabeth. Or is it Miss Bennet? I do not want to offend.”

She could not help but smile back. “No, it is Miss Elizabeth. We have an older sister—three other sisters, actually—at home in Hertfordshire.”

“Five sisters!” Wickham exclaimed. “How delightful; you must all be the best of friends.” He winked at her. “And how is it that you two were lucky enough to come to London? Oh, I am stopping your walk. Shall we go on together?”

They walked on, Wickham transferring his attention between all three young ladies in turn. When they reached the desired bench, Kitty and Georgiana produced sketchbooks and Wickham was delighted in their work, calling out details that made Lizzy wonder if he could draw well himself. Then he turned to Elizabeth.

“And where is your sketchbook, Miss Elizabeth?”

Lizzy tilted her head to the side and pretended to consider. "On the table by my favorite chair in the drawing room, I believe," she mused. "It did not feel up to the outing today, and so I left it to rest."

Behind Wickham, Kitty gave an unladylike snort and Georgiana smothered a giggle. The gentleman raised an eyebrow.

"I have no great love for drawing, Mr. Wickham, and this is time that I may spend as I choose. Why would I attempt to capture an image of the outdoors when I can revel in it instead? I have no sketchbook with me because I intend to walk."

He grinned, clearly amused. "Would you care for company, Miss Elizabeth? I am afraid I will only be a distraction if I remain here. Assuming that Mrs. Younge will permit it, of course."

Mrs. Younge smiled at him, as much under his spell as the young ladies. "Millie will accompany you," she said, "but I see no great harm. You are an old family friend, after all. Do be back in an hour, Elizabeth, and try to not get covered in muck." With another look at Mr. Wickham, she settled herself on the bench by Georgiana and apparently gave them no more thought.

Mr. Wickham turned to Lizzy and held out his arm. "Shall we, milady?"

It was her turn to smile. "I would be delighted, sir."

*

If only all new acquaintances could be as pleasant as Mr. Wickham, Lizzy reflected several days later, the world would be a very enjoyable place indeed. She had traveled to Darcy House alone that day, since Kitty was feeling poorly, and was at the pianoforte discussing music with Georgiana when the drawing room door opened to admit Mr. Darcy.

"Brother, you must tell Lizzy to stop teasing so!" Georgiana exclaimed, noticing who it was.

Lizzy readied her own argument—she had not been teasing much, really—but Darcy paid no attention to the words. "Georgiana, we have a guest I would like you to meet." Elizabeth heard what he did not say: *So I will need you to act like a lady.*

Georgiana apparently understood as well, because she jumped to her feet and smoothed her skirt. "Of course."

Darcy looked around and frowned. "Where is Mrs. Younge?"

"Resting. She has a headache, and the light in the room hurt her eyes." Georgiana settled herself on one of the couches in the room and, once she had straightened the sheet music and closed the instrument, Elizabeth joined her. They had gone through this routine often enough, and while Georgiana no longer needed a hand to hold, Lizzy knew she felt better with a friend beside her.

The door opened again before anything else could be said, revealing two ladies. "Mrs. Northcott and Miss St.

Clair," Crew said, standing out of their way so they could enter.

Darcy almost smiled and made his bow. "Miss St. Clair, welcome. Will you introduce me to your friend?"

The lady in front, with strawberry blonde curls and a tall, willowy figure, smiled back and curtseyed. "It is my pleasure, Mr. Darcy. This is my elder sister, Mrs. Edward Northcott." The second lady curtseyed as well, and with her head lowered Lizzy could see that her hair was truly red.

Georgiana and Lizzy had stood when the ladies entered and were ready when Darcy turned towards them. "May I present my sister, Miss Georgiana Darcy, and her friend, Miss Elizabeth Bennet." There were more curtseys and with a bit of shuffling, everyone was seated.

They had been speaking for some minutes, the conversation dominated by Mrs. Northcott and Miss St. Clair, when the latter turned to Lizzy. "You must tell me the secret to your appearance, Miss Bennet, for you look far too young to be a companion."

Blood rushed to Lizzy's face at the woman's tone. Darcy, in the middle of a conversation with Mrs. Northcott, jerked his head around to face the pair. Eyes drawn to his movement, Lizzy glanced up at him and read alarm in his eyes. No doubt he was recalling his introduction, wondering if he had indicated she was Georgiana's companion. That, or perhaps his concern was for her reply—clearly he wished to impress Miss St. Clair and her sister, and he was well acquainted with

Lizzy's preference for wit over tact. She hesitated, but he did not step in to correct the mistake, and that told her everything: he did not wish her to offend Miss St. Clair. Very well then, she would prove to the dratted man that she could be polite, even if the other woman couldn't.

But Georgiana responded before she could say a word, surprising the entire room. "As my brother said, Miss Elizabeth is my *friend.* My companion did not feel well enough to join us this afternoon." Confidence expended, Georgiana sat back on the couch and Lizzy had the distinct impression that she would prefer to simply disappear. Darcy looked astounded.

"My goodness, please forgive me!" Miss St. Clair exclaimed. "I did not mean any offence, Miss Elizabeth. You do look familiar, now that I think on the matter. Would I have seen you at any events this summer? Your surname is Bennet?"

A multitude of quips filled Lizzy's mind, especially now that she had reason to bring up Lady Lichfield. More than one person had whispered about her rise from companion to countess in Lizzy's hearing, although the lady herself had never once mentioned her origins. Georgiana shifted beside her, however, and Elizabeth knew a glib remark would only cause her friend more stress.

What would Jane do?

Lizzy smiled, hoping she managed to look sweet rather than mocking. "Do not concern yourself overmuch, there is nothing to forgive. Yes, I am a Bennet, of Longbourn in Hertfordshire, but my sister and I have been staying with Lady Lichfield for the past ten months. We were at the Countess of Shrewsbury's garden party—were you perhaps there as well?" *See, Mr. Darcy, I am capable of holding my tongue.*

"Oh, yes, of course," Miss St. Clair said, and Lizzy noticed that she was being subtly reassessed now that she was the ward of a countess instead of a presumed companion. *How wonderful, you find me worth your notice now.* "Tell me, what did you think of her garden? Is it not delightful?"

I rather thought it was her husband's garden, Lizzy thought, determinedly not looking in Darcy's direction as she remembered their conversation. But she did not say that. She was suddenly reminded of Lady Haddington's ball, when Mr. Darcy had dismissed her so clearly as beneath his notice. This lady was exactly the same, and Elizabeth could only hope they made each other miserable.

You think I'm not as good as you. You think I'm a child. Fine. You can think whatever you want, but I don't need your approval. One of these days, she would manage to leave this blasted town and all its petty people behind.

Elizabeth tilted her head prettily and smiled. "Tell me, Miss St. Clair, do you play the pianoforte?"

SIXTEEN

Darcy

July – August 1807

"Well, it certainly took you long enough to return," Darcy said, leaning back in his chair and lifting an eyebrow at Richard. "You were so set on interrogating Georgiana's new friend and exposing her as a fraud I'd begun to fear for poor Miss Elizabeth."

His cousin grinned, knowing that Darcy was teasing. "You should be glad I was called away," he said. "I'd planned on bringing Georgie a kitten as a surprise this spring, but I got my orders before arrangements could be made."

Darcy laughed. "And that would have been truly horrible indeed! Did you know I actually thought about getting her a kitten when we first arrived in Town? Perhaps it was a puppy, I've forgotten which. Something to keep her company and cheer her up."

"Why didn't you?" Richard reached out and topped off his glass of brandy, then settled back.

"It wasn't necessary," Darcy said, fingers drumming on his thigh. "I considered it when she was horribly sad, almost hysterical, but almost immediately she met Miss Elizabeth and—I swear, Richard, it was the strangest thing. They had a conversation in Hyde Park and Georgiana has been steadily improving ever since."

"Yes, Miss Elizabeth seems like she could have that effect," Richard said slowly. "Especially since she has continued to be present. I am glad to see my interrogation skills were not necessary." He frowned and took a sip of brandy.

Feeling like he was being bated, Darcy took a sip of his own drink before he said, "There's no need for theatrics, you may as well spit it out." He was, in truth, interested to hear what Richard thought of Elizabeth Bennet, who he had finally met that afternoon. Despite his best intentions, Major Fitzwilliam had been summoned away in the spring before he was able to meet his cousin's new friend.

"I liked her," Richard replied easily, frown disappearing. "You're right, she isn't a female Wickham. She's clever, but it's clear she's kind as well. She kept an eye on Georgiana even while we were talking—and I'm sure you've noticed that Georgie looks to her for reassurance before you or Mrs. Younge?" Seeing Darcy's nod, he went on. "If I met them without knowing better, I'd think they were sisters."

"You might until they stood next to each other," Darcy rejoined.

Richard grinned. "Yes, as young as Georgie is she'll be taller before long. Miss Elizabeth is a bit short by comparison. Actually, Darce, that comment reminds me of something else I noticed. I was surprised how comfortable you seemed around Miss Elizabeth. And did she ask you something about a *baby*?"

"Miss Elizabeth is a bit short compared to anyone," Darcy said, because that was the statement he actually knew how to answer. He thought of Miss St. Clair, tall and willowy. Georgiana might look a good deal like her eventually. Catching himself, he went on. "Richard, you seem to think I hate anyone outside the family, and you should know better. I certainly do not have the talent which some people possess conversing easily with those I do not know, but acquaintance grows over time. Elizabeth has spent hours—days—with Georgiana. Of course I am easier around her than I am with strangers in a ballroom."

"Elizabeth?" Richard queried.

Darcy gave his cousin an admonishing look. "Be grateful I have not taken to calling her 'Lizzy,' for that is what I hear ceaselessly from Georgiana." He certainly would not admit that in some small portion of his mind, she remained the angel in yellow who had magically altered Georgiana that day in Hyde Park.

"And the baby? I *did* hear that, didn't I?"

"Oh, you mean Frances. Yes, we spoke of a baby. *Miss* Elizabeth's uncle is in trade—actually, he's quite an impressive businessman—and I've met with him several times to discuss my investments in his company.

He has an infant daughter of whom Miss Elizabeth is very fond. We were speaking of her."

Richard settled back in his chair and fixed Darcy with a searching look. "I thought for a moment you might be speaking of Wickham's child. By God, I cannot imagine that man as a father! I really wish you'd have put him away, Darce. It's not right, what he did." He quirked an eyebrow. "But a baby cousin, well, that is quite a different matter. How familial."

"Oh, stop it," Darcy said testily. He did not want to think of Wickham and the many questions he posed, especially since months had gone by without any word from the blasted man. Elizabeth was a more pleasant topic, true, but she was not the lady on his mind. And perhaps his cousin could provide some insights, if only Darcy could bring himself to ask.

He took a deep breath and curled the hand Richard couldn't see into a fist, attempting to relieve the tension that had settled over him. "Tell me, Richard, do you know of Miss Isabella St. Clair?"

*

Darcy approached Miss St. Clair's home with considerable trepidation. He'd fussed far more than usual over his attire that morning, wondering all the while what his valet was thinking behind his professionally detached expression. Georgiana had even commented how well he looked when she appeared in the breakfast room, and so Darcy had felt comfortable with his appearance until Richard arrived wearing his regimentals and an easy smile.

Now, as they climbed the steps to the St. Clair residence together, Darcy couldn't help but shoot a sideways look at his cousin and wonder again if inviting him had been a mistake. In the three weeks since he'd mentioned Miss St. Clair to Richard, Darcy had vacillated frequently between relief that he could express his feelings to someone and certainty that he'd made an unfixable mistake. At the moment, he was a firm believer that it had been a mistake.

Lord, please don't let her take one look at him and forget me. It had happened before, because *everyone* found Major Richard Fitzwilliam charming and agreeable. Next to him, Fitzwilliam Darcy often paled by comparison, and not just because his attire wasn't bright red. Darcy usually found it preferable to fade into the background while Richard took center stage. Today, however, the thought was almost unbearable.

They were met at the door and shown in with a swiftness that told Darcy they'd been anticipated—or at least he had been. On his first visit to Miss St. Clair, the wait had lasted far longer while the butler ascertained if the ladies of the house 'were home.' Did he dare read into the change? Before he could decide, the butler was opening the parlor door and they were shown in with the announcement of, "The Honorable Major Richard Fitzwilliam and Mr. Fitzwilliam Darcy."

"Mr. Darcy, have you brought us more company?" Miss St. Clair asked, standing to greet them. She was wearing a pale green dress today, and Darcy had time to take note of how lovely it looked next to her pale skin before he made his bow to her, Mrs. Northcott, and a Miss Bertram he'd met during his previous visit.

"Miss St. Clair, this is my cousin, home from his duties for a fortnight. He said he is in need of pleasant company after too long a time surrounded by men, and I could think of no better persons to remedy that problem than the ladies present."

Had that sentence actually come out of his mouth? True, Richard likely could have done better, but Darcy was—for once—pleasantly surprised with himself.

Miss St. Clair laughed, a delightful tinkling sound. "You are too kind, Mr. Darcy, but we shall endeavor to perform to our best. It will not do for our officers to lack anything that is in our power to provide." She turned her dazzling smile on Richard, and the knot reappeared in Darcy's stomach.

Luckily for his peace of mind, Richard turned his attention to Miss Bertram once introductions had been properly made and Darcy was free to talk to Miss St. Clair. Of course, that meant his newfound verbosity disappeared as quickly as it had appeared.

"How is your sister, Mr. Darcy?" Miss St. Clair asked once they had been seated.

"Georgiana is well," Darcy responded, relieved she had picked one of the few topics he could approach with relative ease.

"I found her delightful, everything that a young lady should be," Miss St. Clair went on. "Pray tell, how old is she?"

"She is twelve years old presently. I wonder, Miss St. Clair, if you would give me your honest opinion on something?"

Both of her eyebrows went up, and Darcy noticed that they were darker than her reddish blonde hair. There were flecks of green in her hazel eyes as well. How had he not noticed previously? Had they never sat in such a well-lit place?

"Most certainly, Mr. Darcy, if it is something on which I can claim authority. What will you ask of me?"

"You have an infinitely better claim to authority than I, so do not worry on that account. I have simply been wondering if Georgiana is outgoing enough. She has improved much over the last six months, but she is of a shy nature and our father's death did not help. I suppose I am asking if you truly mean she is what a young lady ought to be, or if you say that only to be kind."

Miss St. Clair tilted her head in a most becoming fashion and considered for a moment. "I believe she is well on her way to becoming an ideal young lady by the time she is presented. If she has been improving, there is no reason she will not continue to do so. I wonder, though," she paused. "If you are worried about her sociability, would it not be better to send her to school rather than employing a companion?"

"No." The word came our harsher than he had intended and Darcy involuntarily held out a hand. "Apologies, Miss. St. Clair. I did consider a school for Georgiana, but she was terrified that I would send her away after our father died. Perhaps in another year or so I will reconsider, but for now, she will remain at home."

"You are a kind brother," Miss St. Clair said. "Do not worry about Miss Darcy for the moment, she will blossom in time, and there are ways to give her a woman's guidance without sending her away." She smiled at him and Darcy's heart soared. Before he could think of an answer, she went on. "Your mention of home reminds me of our last conversation. We were interrupted, but I am still curious: do you mean to make London your home, or will you return to Pemberley? It sounds like such a delightful place I cannot imagine ever wanting to leave, should I ever be lucky enough to visit!"

Did she mean anything by that? Rather than being glad for Richard's distance, Darcy now wished he was close enough to serve as interpreter. "Pemberley is indeed delightful, but I will not be returning for some time." Oh, damn it! Richard would say something about London being even more delightful in her presence; Darcy thought the words, pictured her answering smile. But they would not move from his brain to his lips. He was left frowning instead, wondering what on earth made conversation so hard for him when his cousin navigated every social situation with ease, or at very least the appearance of it.

"Isabella, have you heard from Miss Caroline?" Mrs. Northcott asked, and Miss St. Clair turned away to answer her sister.

"Only once, and do not forget that she is Miss Bingley now, Alice. She says Bath is charming, but they will still be returning at the end of August."

Richard caught Darcy's eye. "We were speaking of acquaintances," he said. "It seems that Bingely's sisters attended the same school as Mrs. Northcott and Miss St. Clair."

"Yes, Louisa was a year younger than me, but Caroline and Isabella were in the same year and quite close," Mrs. Northcott said.

A look passed between the sisters that Darcy did not even try to interpret. "Oh yes, she is a dear," Miss St. Clair said. She turned back to Darcy. "I meant to ask you, Mr. Darcy, what do you miss the most about Pemberley in the summer?"

Now he was truly confused. Did this have something to do with Caroline Bingley? "I miss the peace of the countryside, Miss St. Clair." Better not to think about how much his father had enjoyed it as well.

"That does sound wonderful. London is more of a place for drawing rooms, in my experience."

"Perhaps we could have an outing," Richard suggested, glancing towards Darcy with raised brows before looking back at the ladies. "Darcy here has a most magnificent curricle that has not seen nearly enough use as of late, and I am sure my brother would not miss his for an afternoon if I were to borrow it. What say you?"

Why couldn't he have thought of that! Miss St. Clair beamed at Richard, clearly delighted, and Darcy felt his stomach sink for what seemed like the tenth time that hour. But then her eyes found his and the smile softened into something sweeter, filling his chest with a flood of warmth that took him completely by surprise.

"I'd like that," she said, still looking directly at him. "I'd like that very much."

*

The warm feeling lasted until that evening, when Darcy settled in to attend to the pile of letters on his desk. He'd gotten through a letter from Parker with an update on Pemberley and another from an old acquaintance of his father's when the handwriting on the third letter made him pause before ripping it open.

Fitz,

I suppose I should call you 'Mr. Darcy' now, shouldn't I? You look the part, certainly—I caught sight of you in London the other day. But I only picture your father when I hear that name, so Fitz you will remain. I know you won't mind.

I am writing to request something quite within your power, which I believe, in fact, to be more of a formality than anything else. Your father often spoke to me of the parsonage near Pemberley and

I know it was his wish to see me settled in the living. I may have had my doubts when I was younger, as you well know, but it has recently become dear to me as well. Having heard that the previous incumbent has unfortunately passed, I hope you can find it in your heart to grant me the desire of mine.

G. Wickham

No. Darcy dropped into the nearest chair, the word reverberating in his mind. *No*. After what Wickham had done, after all the pain he'd caused, he had the audacity to ask for *this*? Darcy had hoped, given time to reflect, Wickham would come to repent what he'd done. Apparently that day had yet to come. He didn't even have the training for the position!

Darcy picked the letter up from the floor where it had landed half under a side table and forced himself to reread it, searching for some insight into what Wickham had been thinking. In the end, though, there was really just one thing he could say with certainty: George Wickham was absolutely not a man of God.

Seventeen

Lizzy

September 1807

They arrived at Vauxhall by boat, with Kitty bouncing on the seat much like she had done when they pulled up outside Lady Lichfield's house for the first time. *Goodness, had that really been almost a year ago?* Lizzy wondered, watching Kitty settle down reluctantly under Lady Lichfield's stern gaze, smoothing the fine fabric of her gown across her legs. Even sitting still and despite the elaborate mask covering the top half of her face, Kitty's excitement was more than apparent.

Then again, Lizzy admitted to herself as they exited the boat with the help of two smartly dressed workers, she was far from ambivalent. They had arrived in the most fashionable way to a masquerade ball that was sure to be attended by the majority of the *ton*. If only Jane was here too! A letter from her had arrived as they were preparing for the ball, bringing with it news that the Bennets may come to Town for Christmas. Perhaps that was why Lizzy felt so strangely disconnected as they made their way up the bank towards the growing crowd.

"Miss Elizabeth! Miss Kitty! Is it not a grand evening?"

Even in his mask, Mr. Bingley was unmistakable, his enthusiasm on par with Kitty's. Lizzy looked around for Miss Lucy Carter but saw no sign of her. Mr. and Mrs. Hurst were present, looking bored, and Miss Bingley was talking to Miss St. Clair, both of whom were watching Mr. Darcy walk up from a boat with Mr. Bainbridge and two ladies that Lizzy did not know.

Kitty and Lady Lichfield had turned to speak with Bingley, but after making her curtsey Lizzy stepped back, taking in the scene. Given the attention of the other ladies, she was surprised when Mr. Darcy stopped beside her.

"Georgiana bid me to pass on her wishes for a pleasant evening," he said. "May I say, for myself, that your mask is—well, having often been tickled by feathers under my nose, I am most appreciative of a mask with more restraint. It is quite elegant."

Lizzy smiled, pleased despite his stiff manners. "You are not fond of peacock feathers, then, Mr. Darcy?"

A shadow of a smile crossed his face, and she caught the glance he sent at Miss Bingley. *That* lady had no fewer than eight peacock feathers either on her mask or in her hair. "As I have no great love of sneezing, I cannot say that I am, Miss Elizabeth."

“What can you be speaking of?” Miss Bingley asked, coming to stand beside them as they both laughed. Miss St. Clair was only a step behind her.

“We were speaking of masks, Miss Bingley,” Lizzy answered, knowing Mr. Darcy would say nothing.

“Oh yes, I am very pleased with how mine turned out. I had the feathers added specifically, you know; there is no other mask like it in London.”

“Do you often encounter masks outside Town?” Miss St. Clair asked.

“Not as often as I should. I feel for those people who are not able to join in the culture of our city. It must be quite boring.” Miss Bingley sniffed.

“I was just thinking how pleasant it would be to return to Hertfordshire,” Lizzy stated blandly. “But then, I think it would be different if I was not separated from family I love and a place I think of as home.”

Miss Bingley laughed. “I would gladly take the separation rather than be confined to some backwater country town.” She pursed her lips. “I suppose it is fine for some people, though. One must not reach too far from their beginnings.”

Lizzy noticed Mr. Darcy’s frown deepen, but she smiled. “Yes, my father’s estate has been in our family for over two centuries now. My ancestors had much to do with building the nearby town as well, and so it seems quite natural to feel connected with both Longbourn and Meryton. I do not recall if we have spoken of your home, Miss Bingley. Has it been in your family long?"

Over Caroline's shoulder, Miss St. Clair's lips curved into a smile and she raised one gloved hand to her mouth. Clearly discomposed, Caroline herself tossed her hair back over her shoulder. "Oh look, people are sitting down for supper. We had best join them if we want good seats."

A retort rose to Lizzy's lips—Lady Lichfield had reserved a box with several of her friends, and Lizzy was sure the others had done the same—but she bit it back. *What would Jane do?* "Enjoy your supper, Miss Bingley."

As the other woman hurried off, whether for show or otherwise, Darcy caught her eye. The masks and fading light must have been playing tricks on her, because Lizzy swore he winked. His voice was as solemn as ever, though, when he said, "I hope you enjoy your supper as well, Miss Elizabeth." Then he offered his arm to Miss St. Clair and they too walked away into the dusk.

*

Never before had Lizzy attended a supper where the food was so clearly the second priority. She still found it delicious, especially the paper-thin Vauxhall ham and the cheese custard, but even those paled in comparison to the gardens themselves. Having never eaten a Vauxhall Supper before, Lizzy and Kitty both jumped when a whistle was blown at night fall. Shock turned almost instantly to delight as lamps flared to life all around the gardens, illuminating the entire scene.

"How do they do that?" Kitty demanded, tearing her eyes away from the scene to look at Lady Lichfield. "It's incredible."

Lady Lichfield laughed. "There are servants all around the gardens, waiting for the whistle." She looked back at the scene. "I've seen it nearly a dozen times over the years, and it never gets old."

They ate in silence for a time, all examining the gardens under their new light, until a strain of music cut through the night. Kitty set her silverware down with a clatter, and Lizzy followed suit, although she managed the feat quietly. "Is the ball beginning now?"

"Wait ten minutes," Lady Lichfield told them both. "It wouldn't do to get sick by dancing right after you eat."

"I won't, I never do," Kitty protested, but Lady Lichfield would not be swayed. At last, though, their masks were re-secured and their guardian willing to let them go.

Or almost ready. She fixed them both with a stern look and said, "If I hear so much of a whisper about either of you disappearing down one of the dark paths, you will both be confined to the house until Christmas. They are not suitable for a young lady, under *any* circumstances. Am I clear?"

"You are," Lizzy said. Kitty stopped bouncing on the balls of her feet and managed to look serious for several seconds, adding her own reassurance.

"Then go enjoy yourselves," Lady Lichfield said. "I will be here if you need me."

Lizzy lost sight of her sister almost immediately, but she was not alone for long. The orchestra was beginning its second song of the night as Lizzy approached the crowd of dancers, and Mr. Bingley appeared by her side. "Might I have this dance, Miss Elizabeth?" he asked with a bow and a smile.

As long as you don't start calling me *an angel,* Lizzy thought, wondering how long it would take for Mr. Bingley to find a new lady on which to focus his attentions. Surely it wouldn't be her, though! "Of course, Mr. Bingley," she replied, taking the offered hand and letting him lead her towards the dance. "That would be delightful."

Three dances later, she had just decided that punch was in order when a man grabbed her hand and pulled her into the dance without saying a word. She was opening her mouth to tell him off when he leaned forward and lifted his mask.

"Mr. Wickham!" Lizzy exclaimed, scowl turning into a smile. "I should have recognized you!"

"Perhaps, but there are many men here tonight, and you did not know I would be in attendance," he replied, grin now clearly familiar from across the line. "You, on the other hand, cannot be mistaken for anyone else. I declare you stunning, Miss Elizabeth."

Lizzy blushed, for once not sure what to say, and was glad when the dance separated them for several steps. By the time they came back together, she had collected herself and said with ease, "I have not seen you for several days and had to walk alone in your absence. Is anything the matter?"

"My sincerest apologies; my intent was certainly not to deny you pleasure. I was kept busy with several matters of business which sadly left little time for the things that give me joy. But do not worry, everything should be concluded within a few days and I will be free to accompany you again."

They continued to banter until the dance ended and Lizzy expressed her need for something to drink, amazed at the dryness of her throat. They had made it halfway to the punch bowl when a shout of, "Wickham!" cut through the crowd.

"You go on," Lizzy said, noticing the crowd of young men waving Wickham over. "Thank you for the dance."

He bowed over her hand. "It was my delight, Miss Elizabeth. I will find you again tonight, do not fear."

She continued on alone, filling up a cup and drinking it with relish as she watched the rest of the revelers. Claiming a second cup when the first one was empty, Lizzy wandered away from the crowd around the punch table and found a bench where she could watch. The lamps placed around the gardens continued to burn brightly, their light flickering slightly and giving the landscape a surreal, magical feeling. For a moment, she wasn't a girl in a gilded cage, surrounded by people who wanted only to mock her. Her worries were weightless, ephemeral. Anything was possible, and being Elizabeth Bennet in London did not seem like an impossible act to maintain. Perhaps she should gulp glasses of punch at more of the dances she attended.

Then she heard the voices.

"Oh, but you must dance the next with me! I have heard you are the best dancer here, and I have no reason to doubt such a statement. We must stand up for the next dance!"

"I assure you, I was serious when I said it is not possible." That was Mr. Darcy, and he was using his most haughty voice.

The lady was not to be deterred. "La, you are too serious! Tell me, Mr. Darcy, what is it you do for enjoyment? I must know."

A pause, where Lizzy could only image the lady was waiting for a response. *La indeed!* she thought, rolling her eyes. Mr. Darcy was one of the few people she knew that did not feel a need to fill silences with useless chatter. Lizzy stifled the urge to giggle. She didn't like the man personally, but she was accustomed to him, and it *was* entertaining to watch him deal with females in pursuit of his fortune.

"If you will not tell me, then I shall guess," the lady continued. "I guess, Mr. Darcy, that you enjoy fencing, and horseback riding, and above all else that you enjoy the hunt."

"Those are common gentlemanly pursuits," Darcy said, voice betraying no emotion of any sort.

"Then you have answered my question, for you are the epitome of a gentleman!"

So you think him common? Lizzy countered silently, turning so she could see the pair at last. Darcy was tapping his fingers on the back of his leg, the motion hidden from the young lady. Even with their faces concealed by masks, Lizzy was certain she had not met the lady before. It would be only too easy to remember those rounded cheeks, the overly styled gold curls. Was she dressed as an angel? *Oh, that's original.* She snorted and covered her mouth automatically, although it seemed unlikely that anyone had heard her.

Darcy's eyes jerked to hers. Had his attention been drawn by the sudden motion? Lizzy couldn't be sure, but his relief at seeing her was clear. "Miss Elizabeth, there you are!" he exclaimed with more enthusiasm than she had ever heard him muster. "I was beginning to wonder if you had forgotten our dance."

Lizzy hesitated, and she saw desperation flare in his eyes. "Of course not, Mr. Darcy. I *was* wondering the same thing about you, though." She placed her mostly empty punch glass on the bench and stood, shaking out her skirts and pointedly ignoring the still unknown young lady.

"Miss Powell, please excuse me, but as you can see, I am previously engaged for this dance." He gave the lady the most perfunctory bow Lizzy had ever seen, then turned away. "Shall we, Miss Elizabeth?"

She placed a hand on the offered arm and followed him onto the dance floor just as the musicians struck up a new song. "You have fortunate timing, Mr. Darcy. It would have been quite awkward if you attempted to escape in the middle of a dance."

"I believe the good timing is mostly on your part, Miss Elizabeth, and I thank you for, ah, playing along. Not that I would be less than happy to dance with you in other circumstances, but I did not ask as I ought to have done."

"Think nothing of it, Mr. Darcy." His high-handedness was nothing surprising, and it would make an amusing anecdote for Georgiana. "So tell me," Lizzy went on after several beats of silence, "what *do* you do for enjoyment? Or is it something you seek to avoid at all costs?"

He grimaced, and they then were separated for a moment, switching partners for the movements of the dance. When they came back together, Lizzy's right toes were sore, and she had a new appreciation for her partner; Mr. Darcy truly *was* a good dancer.

"I would hear your guess, Miss Elizabeth, since it is far more likely to be correct. What do *you* think I do for enjoyment?"

She cocked her head as if considering, but she already knew how she would answer. "I believe you *do* like fencing and riding, Mr. Darcy. The hunt, no, although I daresay you tolerate it for the sake of friends on occasion. You read, definitely, and listen to music, particularly when Georgiana plays—some of us butcher the instrument too much for it to be truly enjoyable to you. I might even say you enjoy dancing, for you do excel at it, but only when all the parties are previously known and someone has barred the door against all grasping females."

Darcy laughed and Lizzy was on the receiving end of a rare, genuine smile. "You have outdone yourself with that answer, Miss Elizabeth. I would trade a dozen beautifully refined females for your company. I've yet to meet anyone else with your way for words, although Richard may come close."

They were separated again, and Lizzy used the reprieve to clamp down on her emotions. Nothing could stop the thought that ran through her head, though: *so you find me coarse and over-opinionated, Mr. Darcy? It's a wonder you tolerate my friendship with your sister!* She did not bother to restart the conversation, and aside from a few banal remarks they finished the dance in silence.

As she walked off the dance floor, however, Lizzy caught sight of something that put Mr. Darcy completely from her mind. A man that looked very much like Mr. Wickham was slipping into one of the dark paths directly in front of her, head bowed to whisper to the giggling lady on his arm. She frowned, then pushed the thought away. It couldn't be him; she knew it couldn't. He had been correct earlier when he said there were many men present and dressed similarly. He would come find her before long, and maybe she would tell him the story for a laugh.

But despite the fact that she stayed for many more dances and spent a good deal of time searching the crowd, Mr. Wickham never reappeared.

Eighteen

Darcy

October 1807

Darcy returned home from what had become his weekly meeting with Mr. Gardiner to the sound of the pianoforte. In and of itself, that was nothing noteworthy—given half an hour of leisure time, Georgiana ultimately found her way to the instrument. What stopped Darcy in his tracks, hat in one hand and gloves in the other, was *what* she was playing. He hadn't heard *that* song for over a year, when it had been Georgie's favorite to play after supper at Pemberley. It carried with it remembered laughter and comfort and the sense of calm his father had brought to everything he touched.

Coming back to his senses, he handed off hat, coat, and gloves, then went directly up the stairs to the music room rather than stopping in his office as he had planned to do. He hesitated in the doorway, wondering if the Miss Bennets were with her, but she was alone and clearly lost in the music.

“Beautiful,” he said when she finally reached the end of the piece.

Georgiana jumped. “Fitzwilliam!” she exclaimed. “You surprised me!”

He came farther into the room. “I didn’t want to disturb you. I have missed hearing that piece.” Settling himself in the chair nearest the pianoforte, Darcy searched his sister’s face. “Are you happy, Georgiana?”

She turned on the bench to face him fully. “I am, or at least I am most of the time. I do feel guilty sometimes—I still miss Father, of course, but I don’t think about him like I used to. Is that bad?”

Darcy smiled at how earnest her face had become. “No, that is perfectly natural. I felt similarly when Mother passed away. The first time I laughed it seemed like a betrayal. Luckily Richard was there, and he asked if Mother would want me to mourn forever. He knew the answer. Do you remember how much she used to laugh?”

Georgiana pursed her lips, considering. “I think so. I remember she had a beautiful smile and I loved to sit on her lap and play with her necklaces. My memories of her feel like someone who would laugh a lot. Like Lizzy does.”

Darcy felt himself frown. Knowing Georgiana would have picked up on it already, he didn’t change the expression. “I suppose you are correct,” he said. “I had not considered that before.”

"Brother," Georgiana stopped, looking down at the hands folded in her lap.

"What is it?"

Georgiana plucked at her skirt; Darcy locked his hands to keep from batting hers away from the garment. He fidgeted enough that he had no right to stop her. Finally, she looked up. "I hope you are happy as well, Fitzwilliam. You seem so serious most of the time, but that has always been your way. It makes sense that your happiness would look different from mine."

Despite his proclivity to find conversations taxing, Darcy only struggled with speaking to his sister when she was in the middle of a breakdown. Her statement, given with such sincerity, caught him off-guard and left him momentarily speechless. Wasn't he supposed to be the one taking care of her? For heaven's sake, she was only twelve.

"I appreciate your concern, Georgie. Don't worry about me; I am well. And it makes me very happy to hear you play that song again."

She beamed at him, and Darcy managed a convincing smile in return. "You'll have to excuse me," he said, standing. "I have correspondence that needs my attention, but the music caught my attention and I wanted to see you first."

Georgiana turned back to the instrument and Darcy made his way to his office, but he could no longer think about the letters he'd mentally composed on his ride home. Happy. When was the last time he had thought about being *happy*?

He thought back to Elizabeth listing the things he did for pleasure—when had he ridden last? He'd didn't even fence as often as he'd like. Frowning, Darcy thought about the outings and dances with Miss St. Clair on his arm. Had that made him happy? Yes, undoubtedly—but always clouded by a sheen of uncertainty, of hesitation. He held back for fear of making yet another social blunder. If that fear was gone, though, how would he feel?

Continuing down that thought path, how did Miss St. Clair feel? Was she similarly afflicted with doubt? After the months of steady attention, she must be wishing for or at least expecting him to declare himself. Once they were engaged, he could approach society with more ease, knowing how Miss St. Clair felt and without the need to worry about engaging the expectations of any other young lady. Yes, proposing to Miss St. Clair would clear up many of the obstacles to his happiness in social situations.

And what about at home? Georgiana seemed to welcome Miss St. Clair. True, she remained reserved in her presence, and let Miss Elizabeth carry the conversation whenever possible, but that could be overcome. In fact, having another female presence in the house could only help Georgiana more. She could not always rely on Elizabeth, after all. Darcy envisioned sitting by the fire with Miss St. Clair after supper while Georgiana played the pianoforte. What better picture of domestic felicity could he ask for?

It was decided. He would offer for Miss St. Clair—*Isabella, he must think of her as Isabella*—at the earliest opportunity. Feeling considerably better, Darcy stood. He would return to his letters soon, but first a trip to Bond Street seemed appropriate. His betrothed must have a token of his affection, and Phillip's was sure to have just the thing.

*

A possible opportunity provided itself swiftly. An invitation arrived for a supper gathering the following week; a few discreet inquiries confirmed that Miss St. Clair would be present. The rest of the week oscillated between dragging on endlessly and passing far too fast. He longed to speak with Miss St. Clair—*Isabella*—and have everything settled. Unfortunately, that meant he needed to decide on what to say! Darcy considered asking Richard for advice, but he was gone again with military duties. Bingley would be of little use, and Bainbridge would tease him ceaselessly. No, he'd simply have to come up with the right speech on his own. *Blast.*

The party arrived at last and Darcy tucked the bracelet he'd bought in his pocket, looking forward to settling the matter at last. Unfortunately, there were few places to speak privately and no terrace or garden he might reasonably suggest to Miss St. Clair that they visit alone. Frustrated and growing ever more anxious, Darcy slipped into what looked like a small library to reassess his plan. He had placed the bracelet for Miss St. Clair in an easily accessible pocket, which meant it was also less secure. If he couldn't present it to the lady tonight, there was no reason to risk losing it.

Task completed, Darcy took a deep breath and forced himself to relax. He would do his best to enjoy the rest of the evening; there would be other opportunities to talk. At least now he did not need to be hyper-aware of Miss St. Clair's location, he told himself reasonably. Unfortunately, logic could only calm him so much, and so Darcy wandered over to peruse the rows of books. It couldn't hurt to take several minutes for himself and let the quiet room and smell of books rebuild his equanimity.

He'd made his way through the titles on the middle shelf and stood in the far corner of the room when a rustle of fabric sounded at the door, followed by footsteps and a giggle. Reacting automatically, Darcy stepped back so he stood in a nook created by the end of the bookshelf and the wall. Unless the intruder—intruders? —came halfway across the room, he would be fully hidden from view.

"Tell me!" a female voice whispered, clearly excited but keeping her volume down.

"No, you must guess," a second lady replied. She sounded smug. "And if you can't determine what I thought worth pulling you aside to say, then I will think you a fool indeed."

A gasp. "Not Mr. Townsend? Has he proposed?" Darcy frowned. Was the speaker Miss St. Clair?

"Better. He's proposed *and* kissed me. He has gone to speak to my father now, but I know Papa won't turn him away. I'll be Mrs. Townsend by Christmas."

Both ladies collapsed into giggles for a moment, and Darcy was beginning to wonder how long he would be trapped in the room when the second lady spoke again.

"What of you, Isabella? Do you expect an offer from your Mr. Darcy in the near future? We could have a double wedding!"

It *was* her!

Another laugh. "Oh yes, I suppose so. He's too much of a gentleman to pay me attention like he has and not make an offer."

"And you mean to accept? He doesn't seem the sort to sweep you off your feet with kisses, and you once swore you'd accept nothing less in a suiter."

"Well," Miss St. Clair said, and Darcy forced himself to not lean forward, "he'll never be as dashing as Mr. Townsend, I envy you that! But he is handsome, and he's been nothing but a gentleman towards me. It will be a good match. Have *you* stayed true to all the promises you made at fifteen?"

Her friend snorted. "You sound as if you're convincing yourself, not me. He's horribly awkward in social situations, is he not? Don't you think that would mean he's reserved at home as well? And perhaps in other places?"

"Absolutely awkward, rather boring, and unnaturally devoted to his sister," Miss St. Clair said matter-of-factly. "But Celia, I refuse to be unmarried by two-and-twenty. The rest of it can be managed. I'll convince him to send Miss Darcy away to school and make sure we spend plenty of time in company with lively people. It will make Caroline Bingley furious, she's quite determined to marry him, so I'll make sure to invite her often. And you are horrid to suggest what you did, but—" she giggled again— "if it's really so horrible, you know there are always other amusements that can be found, once a couple of children are born. The men do it all the time."

The second lady replied, but Darcy could not hear her through the buzzing filling his mind. *There are other amusements to be found. Boring. Send Georgiana away.* This was the lady he had wanted to marry? *Georgiana.* She'd been worried about this exact thing, and he'd assured her it could never happen. How had he been so blind? Darcy stood frozen, hands shaking, the bracelet in his pocket suddenly five times heavier than it had been at the beginning of the evening.

He needed to leave. Making up his mind, Darcy caught himself as he started to stride out into the room where the ladies still stood. *Oh, God, how much longer would they stay?* Fisting his hands to keep from drumming on the wall behind him and making noise, Darcy forced himself to focus on his breathing. *In. Out. In. Out.* The ladies slipped back out of the room, their parting laughter feeling like a slap in the face. *In. Out.* How to leave without being noticed?

Darcy counted to one hundred before making his way out of the room. In the hallway he paused, looking back towards the dinner party with its mass of silks and jewels and immoral ladies. There had to be another exit, a way to escape without encountering anyone who might question his departure. Glancing around, Darcy caught sight of a servant's stair at the end of the passage and moved decisively towards it.

The stairs were steep and narrow and became considerably darker the further he descended. By the time he reached the passage at the bottom, Darcy had to keep his hand on the wall to find his way. Surely this would lead to an exit eventually? Was that a glow of light up—

"Oof!" Darcy exclaimed, running into someone he hadn't noticed in the dark.

His accidental assailant recovered herself first. "And just what do you think you're doing, sir? I'll not have anyone sneaking down to accost my girls, I will not stand for it. This is a respectable house!"

"I beg your pardon," Darcy replied, rubbing a hand over his face. "I had no intentions of finding anyone. If you would show me the exit I would be most obliged. I am not feeling well and wish only to leave."

There was a pregnant pause, and Darcy could only imagine the woman, most likely the housekeeper or cook, was glaring at him in suspicion. "It's this way," she said finally, turning on a heel and walking away. "Come with me and I'll show you out."

"My horse is in the stables," Darcy said, hurrying to keep up with her but also nervous to get too close for fear of another collision.

"Aye, the door opens up to the back. And here you go, stables are just through there. If you change your mind, come back in the front, understand?"

"Of course," Darcy replied, stepping out into the night air with relief. How lovely it would be to sink down on the stone steps and simply sit in the dusk! But no, he needed to return home first. *In. Out.*

He reached the stables without further mishap and Aeolus' reins were handed over within minutes. Only as he rode away did he realize he'd been taken to task by a servant for coming to seduce one of the maids. The thought was preposterous—a Darcy would never do such a thing! It was an outright insult to his honor!

But Darcy could not bring himself to be properly angry. Everything about his world had been turned on its ear by Miss St. Clair's unguarded comments, and he didn't know how to feel or what to think anymore. What had Elizabeth said that summer? *People are either eaten up with self-importance or entirely lacking in conviction.* He'd dismissed it at the time as the ponderings of a young lady caught at the transition from girl to woman. Now, though, he wasn't so sure. Yes, Miss St. Clair had been expecting his offer, just as he'd thought. But she cared nothing for the joining of their families, the security and stability and happiness that he'd considered so carefully. Happiness! What a fool he was. *In. Out.*

He'd never thought such a thing would happen to him. Bingley, yes, was easily directed and therefore had invited the chance for deception. But for it to befall him as well—for him to overhear essentially the same conversation but with regards to himself! He, who so carefully studied his mind and the situations around him so as always to do the correct thing, had fallen prey to the exact same malady as his friend. Only hours ago he would have thought it preposterous, impossible. *In. Out.*

Was all his pride, his belief in the propriety of his actions and correctness of his understanding, based on false assumptions? Good God, what else had he been so blindly mistaken about? He had assumed Elizabeth asked his opinion on pride and amiability because she valued his insight, but Darcy was no longer sure. *What is your defect, Mr. Darcy? Here, I will save you the trouble: it is pride, and therefore you would say you have no defect at all.* Had she been teasing, or making a statement about his behavior? *In. Out.*

Aeolus turned into the stable yard behind Darcy House without prompting and Darcy handed over the reins. "Thank you," he told the hostler without registering which one it was, concerned only on reaching the silence and sanctity of his study. *In. Out.*

Up the stairs, take a left, take a right, more stairs, close the door. Should he lock the door? No, Georgiana didn't know he was home and the staff knew better than to enter if the door was closed. *In. Out.* Where had he put the brandy? There it was; thank goodness he'd requested the new bottle from the cellar.

Collapsing into his favorite chair by the fire, glass in hand and the bottle of brandy within reach, Darcy allowed himself at long last to slump down and lose himself in a world of confusion, alcohol, and regret.

Nineteen

Lizzy

November – December 1807

"I say, Miss Elizabeth, I find your pink cheeks most becoming. I should have known you would blossom even more in the cold weather."

"Good day, Mr. Wickham," Lizzy said, smiling at the gentleman before her. "I find the cold refreshing, although I know I will be ready to curl up in front of the fire after our walk."

"Go on now, Miss Elizabeth, but don't wander too far today," Mrs. Younge said from her spot on the bench between Georgiana and Kitty. "It's too cold to do much drawing today."

Lizzy doubted her sister would be willing to leave until her fingers could no longer grip the pencil, but she didn't argue. "I will return shortly."

"Good," Mrs. Younge said. "Millie, go with them." She turned back to look at what Georgiana was drawing, clearly considering her duties done. Well, she wasn't paid to be a companion to Elizabeth, even if the ongoing lack of concern struck Lizzy as strange. But no matter—Lizzy was free for her walk, and she couldn't complain about that!

"Do you return to Darcy House after your outing?" Wickham asked as they strolled down the lane.

"We do. I am surprised, Mr. Wickham, that I have not seen you there. Your past disagreements with Mr. Darcy cannot be so great as to bar you from visiting, surely."

Mr. Wickham looked pained, and Lizzy half regretted bringing up the topic. "I am afraid he dislikes me most thoroughly," he told her, "and I can offer you proof of my belief, should you wish to hear it."

"I would not cause you pain, but must admit to considerable curiosity."

"Do not fear, perhaps speaking of my losses will help bring me to a state of equanimity. It is quite a tale, so I shall beg your patience." At her nod, he set his shoulders and began. "The church ought to have been my profession—I was brought up for the church, and I should at this time have been in possession of a most valuable living, had it pleased the gentleman we were speaking of just now. The late Mr. Darcy bequeathed me the next presentation of the best living in his gift. He was my godfather, and excessively attached to me. I cannot do justice to his kindness. He meant to provide for me amply, and thought he had done it; but when the living fell, I applied to Darcy and was refused in no uncertain terms."

"Good heavens!" Lizzy exclaimed, but there was a problem with that scenario and she went on, "But how could that be? How could his will be disregarded? Why did you not seek legal redress?"

"There was just such an informality in the terms of the bequest as to give me no hope from law. A man of honor could not have doubted the intention, but Mr. Darcy chose to doubt it—or to treat it as a merely conditional recommendation, and to assert that I had forfeited all claim to it by extravagance, imprudence—in short anything or nothing. I cannot accuse myself of having really done anything to deserve to lose it. I have a warm, unguarded temper, and I may have spoken my opinion of him, and to him, too freely. I can recall nothing worse. But the fact is, that we are very different sort of men, and that he hates me."

"This is quite shocking! He deserves to be publicly disgraced." It was shocking indeed; Lizzy had not imagined Mr. Darcy capable of any such malice. Then again, had he not placed himself readily in the group that let their pride blind them to the faults of others, when they had discussed the matter that summer? Had he not called his temper resentful and implied he was unwilling to change his opinion, once his mind had been made up? But Wickham had gone one speaking, and Lizzy forced herself to focus, to show that *she* cared for his plight.

“Some time or other he will be—but it shall not be by me. Till I can forget his father, I can never defy or expose him.”

Elizabeth honored him for such feelings, and thought him handsomer than ever as he expressed them. “But what,” said she, after a pause, for the matter still sat poorly with her, “can have been his motive? What can have induced him to behave so cruelly?”

He answered without hesitating. “A thorough, determined dislike of me—a dislike which I cannot but attribute in some measure to jealousy. Had the late Mr. Darcy liked me less, his son might have borne with me better; but his father's uncommon attachment to me irritated him, I believe, very early in life. He had not a temper to bear the sort of competition in which we stood—the sort of preference which was often given me.”

Lizzy could certainly feel for the young Mr. Darcy—had she not known herself to be the least favorite of her mother? Between the two, however, she felt far worse for Mr. Wickham. “I had not thought Mr. Darcy so bad as this—though I have never liked him, I had not thought so very ill of him. I had supposed him to be despising his fellow-creatures in general, but did not suspect him of descending to such malicious revenge, such injustice, such inhumanity as this.”

Mr. Wickham gave her a sad smile. “There are injustices in all of life, Miss Elizabeth. This is mine to bear, just as yours is staying in a place like this when you so clearly wish to be elsewhere. *That* is an injustice, however, which I may be able to help remedy."

"Oh, I did not tell you!" Lizzy exclaimed, his words reminding her of the news. "Jane's last letter brought with it news that my family will be coming to London in December and will stay through the Christmas holidays!"

"I am happy for you, but disappointed I could not be of the assistance I hoped. I am traveling to Derbyshire to visit my aunt, who is ill and wishes to see me in case the unthinkable happens. It is not much of a detour into Hertfordshire, and I would happily have delivered you home on my way. Of course, I would engage a maid to ensure all propriety is met, and if I have offended you then I beg your forgiveness. Perhaps I ought to have said nothing, now that the case is moot."

"You would do that?" Lizzy asked, heart swelling with the idea. Someone had noticed how unsatisfied she was here and sought to correct it, asking nothing in return! Would that everyone had the kind heart of the man in front of her.

"Of course. I have come to value your friendship greatly, and it pains me to see you suffer. But come, we should return. The others will be waiting for us."

*

Lizzy spent the next two weeks feeling lighter than she had since her arrival. Further conversations with Mr. Wickham buoyed her spirits and she spent long hours imagining what it would be like to see Jane again.

What would they whisper to each other as they lay in bed, the way they had done for as long as she could remember? And to see her father! How she had missed him.

It was the first week in December when Lady Lichfield met Lizzy and Kitty in the entryway as they returned from a visit to Georgiana, and the look on her face gave Lizzy pause even as Kitty continued to chatter about their day.

"What is it?" Lizzy asked sharply, cutting across her sister.

Lady Lichfield's eyes met hers and in them Lizzy read pity. She didn't want pity. "A letter came from your father," the lady said, voice steady. "There has been a change of plans." She held out a letter. "I thought you should see for yourselves."

Forcing herself to take the letter gently rather than snatch it from Lady Lichfield's hand, Lizzy swallowed back the lump in her throat and looked down at the familiar handwriting.

Lady Lichfield—

I will be brief. There has been a change of plans, and we will not travel to London for the holiday season this year. I do not find myself equal to the excursion, and can only apologize for any inconvenience I have caused you. I hope you did not have any grand plans, but then you are well acquainted with my feelings on the sort of events that may be deemed 'grand.'

Thank you very much for the book you sent with your last letter. You were correct; the second half more than made up for the drudgery of the beginning.

Yours, etc.

Thomas Bennet

P.S. Mary has married Mr. Collins and returns with him to the living he recently secured in Kent. I am sure you will hear more details when Jane writes to Elizabeth. TB

Something inside Lizzy snapped. This was *it*? Over a year of longing to leave London and return home, the all-consuming excitement of finally seeing her family again, both brushed aside without a mention. Her father did not wish to inconvenience Lady Lichfield, an acquaintance she'd never once heard him mention before being shipped off to her doorstep. Kitty might as well not exist, and she herself was a postscript mention, a way of transferring information. He might as well have written of a servant, and he'd only ever called her *Elizabeth* when she misbehaved. What had she done now? Nothing!

She handed the letter carefully to Kitty and made her way up the stairs to her room without a word, refusing to look anywhere but directly in front of her. Was this how Mr. Wickham had felt when he wrote to request the living, sure that his godfather's love and support would see him through? Had he been equally as confused and heartbroken and furious to be brushed aside with no explanation?

Mr. Wickham. Mr. Wickham said he would take me home.

Lizzy closed the door behind her and sank down onto the edge of her bed. Was she too late? Had he gone already, leaving her behind? Goodness, did she actually mean to accept the offer? Even with Mr. Wickham's promise to bring a maid, leaving unchaperoned and without permission was horribly improper.

It's not like Papa will care. He's made that abundantly clear, and it's equally apparent I can't rely on him for anything. I'll get myself home. It can't be worse than staying here forever.

*

To Lizzy's surprise, planning to leave London was almost as easy as walking to Cheapside had been. She refused to think of it as running away, just as she ignored the memory of how nearly disastrous her last desperate excursion had been. Mr. Wickham would be with her this time, and they would have a proper carriage. Everything would be well.

She was relieved he did not ask what had changed her mind. Despite their previously shared confidences,

Lizzy had no desire to discuss the letter and the burning motivation it had provoked. Her father's betrayal ate away at her, but he was still her father and she was not ready to share the tale. It reminded her again of Mr. Wickham's story, how he could not denounce the son for love of the father, and she took relief in the fact that someone could understand. Perhaps she would tell him on the way to Longbourn. Oh, thank heavens for Mr. Wickham!

Getting away went so smoothly Lizzy took it as a sign that she had made the correct choice. Kitty felt poorly, so Lizzy called on Georgiana alone, sure her sister was not truly ill and therefore thrilled with the convenience. "Don't worry about coming back for me," she told Lady Lichfield's carriage driver upon their arrival at Darcy House. "Mr. Darcy has offered the use of his carriage for my return, since the timing is unfixed." The man agreed, unconcerned, and the second of her obstacles was removed.

She spent the next two hours forcing herself to be calm, turning the pages for Georgiana at the pianoforte or playing duets. Georgiana laughed at how poor her playing was; Lizzy blamed it on her excitement for a ball two day's hence.

"Just you wait," Mrs. Younge declared, wagging a finger at Elizabeth and winking at Georgiana. "She says the ball is distracting her, but I believe the true reason is a gentleman," Mrs. Younge declared, winking at Lizzy. At the latter's denial, she shook her head. "Say what you like, but I remember being your age. I thought of nothing but gentlemen! It is a shame Mr. Wickham does not have a steady income, he would make some young lady a very lucky wife, don't you agree?"

Lizzy could only pray her face did not look as flushed as it felt. She certainly didn't want to be Mrs. Wickham, but thinking of the man made her tremble with anticipation for her scheme.

Just then, the bells chimed one o'clock, and she jumped up. *Finally*! "Oh! Excuse me, Georgiana, but I must go. I promised Lady Lichfield I would be home in time to receive other visitors today."

"Do you need the carriage?" Georgiana asked.

"No, no, I knew I would need to leave now so Lady Lichfield's carriage will be waiting." She smiled at Georgiana, resisted the urge to pull her into a hug, and said her farewells. Surely she would see Georgiana again, given how close they had become. It was not truly goodbye. And letters could be sent back and forth no matter where she was. She was doing the right thing, really she was.

Crew opened the door for her to exit and she paused, remembering the rest of her plan at the last moment. She pulled the letter from her pocket. "Would you give this to Miss Darcy, Crew? I brought it for her but forgot to pass it on. It does not contain anything urgent."

"Of course, Miss Elizabeth," he replied, taking the missive and placing in on the tray used to convey calling cards.

She gave him one last smile, then hurried down the steps and made her way to the carriage that stood just far enough away it could not be easily identified. Suddenly overtaken by a fit of nerves, Lizzy bit down hard on the inside of one cheek. She could not back out now, for there might not be another chance to go home. There was no reason to wonder desolately if she would ever see Crew again, ever climb the steps to Darcy House knowing she was a welcome friend.

Home. You are going home, and none of this will matter there.

But she glanced back once more, taking in Darcy House just in case. As she turned away, something in an upstairs window caught her eye, but she refused to double-check. Instead, Lizzy stepped around the carriage and smiled to find Mr. Wickham on the side hidden from the house. What did it matter if Mrs. Younge was watching from the window? At long last, she was going *home.*

*

Georgiana,

I am leaving this for you because I know if I give it to Kitty I will never get away in time. I do not wish to cause anyone pain or worry, but I simply cannot stay in Town any longer. There is no reason for me not to go home. Please pass word to Kitty and Lady Lichfield that I have left for Longbourn, and I intend to stay at least through the Christmas season. They need not worry about my safety or reputation. Mr. Wickham has very gallantly offered to see me home on his way to visit his aunt and has secured a maid to travel with us for propriety.

I do not leave because of anyone here, and in fact will miss all of you—but I feel so out of place here, and I am so, so worried about my father. He never once turned me away, Georgiana, and now he barely acknowledges my existence. I need to see him and Jane and be home. *I pray you will all forgive my sudden departure. I will write upon my arrival.*

Yours most sincerely,

Elizabeth Bennet

Twenty

Darcy

December 1807

Brother?"

Georgiana's panicky voice jerked Darcy's attention from the book he was reading. He forced a calm voice. "What is it, Georgie?"

"Lizzy has left London," she said, eyes huge in her white face.

Damn! How was he going to handle Georgiana feeling abandoned when the person who usually cheered her up was the one that had left? "Did Lady Lichfield take them to Longbourn?" Darcy asked, hoping they would be back soon.

"No—Lady Lichfield didn't take them anywhere, and Kitty is still in Town. Lizzy left with George Wickham, to go home. She didn't even tell Lady Lichfield or Kitty." Looking even more frightened, she held out a half sheet of paper.

Darcy stood and snatched it in one smooth motion, book tumbling off his lap to the floor. He felt as if someone had thrown icy water on him as he read, numbing him from head to toe. *Damn, damn, damn George Wickham!* And then—*God, let me not be too late to save her.* She would need saving, of that he was certain. All other matters aside, George Wickham didn't have a living aunt.

"When did you get this?" Darcy snapped, wincing at his tone but not willing to take the time to apologize.

"Crew gave it to me just now," Georgiana said, hunching her shoulders. "Lizzy left it when she was here early this afternoon. Mrs. Younge said I shouldn't bother you with it, but—I thought you should know."

Two hours, then, give or take. And they would be traveling in a carriage, not expecting to be pursued. At least, Elizabeth would not expect it. Would Wickham? Even if he did, he would have to play the part so as not to alert his quarry. There might still be time. There had to be time.

"You did right to show me this, Georgie," Darcy said, mind full of plans for how to proceed. "I will bring her back, do not worry."

"But she wanted to go home so badly!" Georgiana exclaimed, catching at his sleeve as he made to pass. "Is it so horrible, truly?"

He bent down so their faces were on the same level, forcing himself to sound calm and certain. "George Wickham isn't taking her home, Georgiana. He is an evil man who has no compassion for young ladies that miss their families. There will be a way that he means to profit from this, likely at Elizabeth's expense. I will explain everything when I return, but I need to go *now*. Promise me that you will not say *anything*, not even to Mrs. Younge." He would need to mitigate the damage to Elizabeth's reputation as well as save the lady herself, and that meant no one could know what she'd done. He would speak with Mrs. Younge when he returned. *Headstrong imp!*

"I promise," she whispered. Darcy dashed out the door and hurried down the hallway, calling for his horse. A brief stop in his study saw a note written to Lady Lichfield, professing that Elizabeth was feeling poorly and had been given a bed to rest in; he would ensure she returned safely home in the morning. Then he was gone, running down the steps just as his horse Aeolus was led out of the stables.

"Take this and deliver it to Lady Lichfield," Darcy snapped at the groom, grabbing the reins and vaulting into the saddle without any of his usual finesse. "I will be out late."

Without waiting for a response, he kicked Aeolus forward and barely missed a group of walking ladies as he turned onto Grosvenor Street. "Think," Darcy admonished himself once he was out of the ladies' hearing. He would never reach Elizabeth in time if he tried to gallop the whole way there. Aeolus was an incredible horse, but he had mortal limits despite being named for the wind god of Greek mythology. He would tire, or injure himself, and Darcy would be stranded on foot. Reluctantly, Darcy pulled back on the reins and settled Aeolus into a fast trot, letting his fingers drum out a rhythm on his thigh. They would canter once they'd reached the edge of the city, and he would simply have to pray that it would be fast enough.

*

The sight of the slightly ragged black carriage filled Darcy's stomach with a mixture of dread and elation. *Please, please, please let it be them.* The sun was on the horizon; if this equipage did not hold the people he sought, he would have to stop for the night in defeat, and it would be an uncomfortable night indeed. His hat had blown off several miles ago, and his gloves were still somewhere back at Darcy House, useless against the chilly wind. *Please.*

Sending up a final prayer, Darcy maneuvered around the carriage so he rode abreast with the driver. "Halt!" he yelled, doing his best to imitate the voice he'd heard Richard use with the men he commanded. "I need to speak with the people in this carriage!"

"An' what's in it for me?" the man yelled back.

Thank goodness he'd remembered to bring money. "I'll pay you," Darcy responded. "If you were hired by the man I think, I'll pay you more than he did."

For a heart-rending moment, Darcy thought he'd be told to sod off, but the driver gave a jerky nod and pulled back on the reins. Darcy followed suit, watching the carriage with mounting trepidation.

Then, as it slowed almost to a stop, the door flew open and a mass of fabric and flying hair tumbled out, followed by a shout. Darcy knew that green dress, those curls. *Elizabeth.* George Wickham appeared in the carriage door above her crumpled form, a long scratch down one side of his face.

Before Darcy knew he'd decided to dismount, he stood between them.

"You bitch!" Wickham was yelling, face turning redder by the moment. "You—oof!"

All sound left the world and everything ceased to exist other than the sensation of his knuckles sinking into Wickham's stomach. As if through a haze, Darcy felt himself grab the other man's cravat and jerk him out of the carriage. He stumbled on the landing and Darcy helped him fall the rest of the way to the ground, hooking a foot behind Wickham's legs and shoving his shoulders back. Wickham landed with a thud.

Come on, Fitz. You can do better than that. Don't start a fight unless you mean to finish it.

The words taunted him across half a decade. Wickham had been goading him then, hoping to see Darcy lose his head. Now, though, the thought settled into Darcy's mind and his head cleared. Wickham was rising, scrambling towards Elizabeth—or perhaps towards Aeolus, looking for escape—but Darcy was ready. His left hand found Wickham's shirt front, and he saw realization of what was coming flash through the other man's eyes a second before his fist connected squarely with Wickham's jaw and he dropped like a stone.

From years of sparring with Wickham, Darcy knew he would be nasty when he came to, and the last thing Darcy wanted was a drawn-out fight. Gritting his teeth, he bent over the prone form on the ground until Wickham began to moan. Then very deliberately Darcy placed the barrel of his pistol between Wickham's eyes. A bullet wasn't chambered, but Wickham didn't know that; his eyes flew open and he went white.

"If you try to run," Darcy said with equal deliberation, "I will shoot you in the leg and leave you here. You know I can. And don't even think about taking my horse. You taught Aeolus to hate you years ago. Am I clear?"

Elizabeth made a strange, strangled sound somewhere between a sob and a laugh and his attention jerked back to her. She sat in a huddle on the ground, knees pulled up to her chest and her hands clasped over her mouth, knuckles white. The fading light concealed much of her condition, but Darcy could tell her hair was a mess and one shoulder of her gown had been ripped away. Had it happened when she jumped from the carriage, or before?

Let her be well, let her be unharmed. If his angel from Hyde Park was injured or ruined because he had failed to deal with Wickham earlier—*No.* It wasn't possible. *Not Elizabeth.*

Darcy turned his back on Wickham and knelt beside her. She was shaking, but with fear or cold he couldn't tell. "Are you hurt?" he asked in low tones, linking his hands together to stop from reaching out. She had been scared, been assaulted if not actually harmed; it wouldn't do to startle her.

Elizabeth tipped her head back, eyes closed, and Darcy's stomach clenched. But then she let out a long breath of air and opened her eyes. Something wild lurked at the back of her gaze, but he could almost see the composure forming around her. The shaking lost its intensity. "No," she whispered at last. "No, I am not hurt."

"Scared you'd have to pay me to marry her?" Wickham rasped from behind them, and the relief flooding through Darcy snapped back to anger.

"Was that your plan, George?" he asked coldly, looking over his shoulder without moving away from Elizabeth. "She has a bit more to recommend her than a kitchen maid in Kent, after all, and no bothersome brothers to deal with."

"And yet in essentials, how different is any woman from another? Perhaps you'd better pay me after all. You never know what might happen, several months from now."

"No!" Elizabeth shouted, voice ragged. She was breathing hard now, fury and anguish mixed on her face, shaking harder than ever. "I will not—I am not—*No*! I *will not* marry you."

Caution be damned. Darcy reached out and drew her to him, then raised both of them to a standing position. He'd expected Elizabeth to pull away, but she simply brought both her arms in and tucked her head down, huddling under the arm he locked around her. "You heard the lady, George." *By God, I'll marry her myself if I have to.*

The thought made him catch his breath, forgetting for a moment he stood on a dusty road three hours from home, forgetting Wickham and the driver, forgetting everything except the girl tucked against him and the realization that made him feel as if *he'd* been the one to take a hit in the jaw. She was not just his sister's friend or a young lady he had grown accustomed to over the past year. She was *his* Elizabeth, his angel in the yellow dress that had fallen into his life when he needed her most. And to think he'd wanted to marry Miss St. Clair when all the while *she* had been right in front of him!

She was also still trembling, and that brought Darcy back to the present. "Have you a coat?" he asked, bending so his lips were only inches from her ear and barely managing to not kiss the top of her head in the process.

"My pelisse is in the carriage," she whispered.

He could not let her go, not with the newfound knowledge coursing through him. Instead he led her to the carriage, extracted the garment, and released her only so she could slip her arms into the sleeves. She leaned back from the equipage, turning her face rather than look inside. He had planned to use the carriage for her return journey, but he could not make her ride back in something that clearly frightened her. Frowning at the carriage, an idea for how else it might be used unfurled itself in Darcy's mind. Yes, that would do.

Tucking Elizabeth back under his arm once her pelisse was secured, he turned at last to the driver, who had hovered in the background throughout the entire scene. "Where were you taking them?"

"Well, that's a wee bit of a problem," the man said, shooting Wickham a sideways scowl. "The man, there, hired me to take them to Hertfordshire and paid me as much, but once we was leaving he changed the destination to Scotland. That's a fair bit longer drive, and I've not seen a penny more."

Darcy nodded, unsurprised. "Are you willing to travel to Scotland, assuming you are paid for the drive?"

"Oh, willing enough. I've made the drive before, it's not difficult."

Darcy reached into his coat pocket with the hand not holding Elizabeth's shoulder. "Name your price for the journey and I will pay you. You will take that man," he nodded towards Wickham, "to the first town across the border. You are under no obligation to him after that time, which includes bringing him back to London with you when you return. In fact, you will specifically *not* bring him back into England. What say you?"

Rubbing his chin, the man named a price that Darcy assumed was twice his normal rate. It would be worth it to be rid of Wickham, if only for a while—it would give him time to make sure Elizabeth was safe, decide what was to be done with the man. Once the coachman had been paid, Darcy walked Elizabeth over to stand by his horse. "Stay here," he told her, then gritted his teeth and approached Wickham.

"Get up, George," Darcy commanded, then watched the man struggle to his feet without offering a hand to help. "You are going to get in that carriage and go to Scotland, just as you had planned," he said once Wickham was standing. "I've paid for your journey, and I'll even throw something in for rooms and food along the way. Don't be stupid with it, because it's the last money you will ever see from me or my family. Take this as your opportunity to make a new life; if I ever see or hear from you again I'll have you tried for murder. You know I have enough to put you away."

Wickham glared at the bag of money Darcy held out. "You wouldn't dirty your hands to find me," he sneered, "and you wouldn't succeed even if you tried."

"Maybe not," Darcy replied with a grim smile, "but Richard has the means to ferret you out of just about anywhere, and he hates you even more viscerally than I do. Keep that in mind before you do anything rash. He's not as even-tempered as I am, and he's spent the last year casually planning how you might be detained."

Wickham touched his swelling jaw gingerly, scowl deepening as he appeared to consider the truth to Darcy's statement. "Right." Making up his mind, he snatched the bag of money from Darcy and marched to the carriage. Turning back at the door, he glanced to where Elizabeth stood by Aeolus, head bowed. "She hates you too, Fitz. You think you know better than everyone around you, but all you do is drive people away. Do you even have any friends left?" He slammed the door and rapped on the top of the carriage, signaling the driver to drive away.

Darcy didn't bother to watch his old friend disappear into the ever-darkening night. The past was done and nothing he did now would change it. Instead, he walked over to the lady he hoped would be his future, still standing motionless next to Aeolus.

"We have a long ride ahead of us," he said, avoiding all thoughts of what it would be like to ride double with Elizabeth pressed against him. Her safety and comfort must come first. "If we get back before morning, no one ever has to know you were gone—I sent a note to Lady Lichfield that you felt ill and were staying at Darcy House. I am sorry, I should have consulted you, but you looked quite opposed to reentering the carriage. Can you manage the ride, or do you need to rest?"

She took a shuddering deep breath and Darcy wondered if her bowed head hid tears. "Do not apologize, you judged correctly. I do not need rest, but I am no horsewoman," she said, voice tight but steady. A surge of pride shot through Darcy. Elizabeth would come through this trial admirably.

"Do not worry, you will ride in front of me and I will not let you fall," he replied. "If you are uncomfortable, you only need to let me know and we will stop for as long as you require." A single nod of her head indicated her acquiescence. "I'm going to lift you onto the saddle," Darcy continued, not wanting his touch to come as a surprise. Another nod and his hands found her waist, lifting her up with ease. She was so light! Then he was mounted behind her, his chest pressed against her back, one arm wrapped around her waist while the other managed the reins.

He would think about this later, once she was safe—how he was aware of every movement she made, how her hair smelled of lavender, the way his heart swelled when she turned her head so it fitted snuggly under his chin. The ride with *his* Elizabeth would be imprinted on his brain for the rest of his life. He could savor it later.

But right now, he would focus on taking her home.

TWENTY-ONE

Lizzy

December 1807

They arrived at Darcy House as the bells rang two in the morning, the noise echoing around the deserted Grosvenor Square. Even late-night socializers were home for the night, which suited Lizzy just fine. She didn't want any witnesses to her shame.

The long ride back had lulled Lizzy into a false sense of ease. Darcy had unbuttoned his great coat and wrapped the front around her, sharing the warmth of both the garment and his body. For several hours, reality ceased to exist and Lizzy let herself doze against Darcy's chest. She was safe and warm, headed south with a gentleman rather than north with a rake. Even the uncomfortable saddle, not meant for two riders, was unquestionably preferable to sharing the carriage with Wickham.

The sight of Darcy House brought all of her worries back in a flood that nearly made her ill. She sat up as straight as the saddle would allow and concentrated on not throwing up. She focused on breathing as Darcy dismounted and lifted her down from the horse, who he handed off to an anxiously waiting hostler, then led her into the house. Lizzy followed blindly, paying no attention to where she was until, blinking, she looked around and realized that she sat in a leather armchair in Darcy's office while the man himself crouched before her. *God, what he must think of me.*

Her eyes found his, and he swallowed, looking uncomfortable but resolute. "Elizabeth, I have to ask you, and I need to know the truth: did he violate you?"

How could she look him in the face and think about what he suggested? Dropping her eyes to the ground, Lizzy shook her head. "Not how you mean. He kissed me, multiple times, and tried to—to touch me, but no more. He was…" *Enough.* "Yet again, Mr. Darcy, you arrived with perfect timing." She couldn't keep the bitterness from her voice on the last sentence.

"Perfect timing would have meant keeping you out of this situation all together. I should have dealt with Wickham months ago, so he would have not been able to hurt you or any other woman. I naively hoped the problem he presented would simply disappear. I am sorry, Elizabeth."

She gave a strangled laugh, burying her head in her hands. "I fail to see how this is your fault, sir. You do not control my actions; responsibility for that lays with me alone. I was so thrilled to have someone who shared in my abuse of you and complimented me all the while that I let myself be led into a situation that would have ruined me for life, had you not arrived when you did. *You*, who I have treated astonishingly ill, in word if not in deed. I let a man of only several months' acquaintance, who was not known to my family, talk me into leaving behind all propriety, and all because he paid me compliments and made me feel justified in my prejudices!" She raised her head to find Darcy a handbreadth's away and caught her breath for a moment before she could continue. "I was wrong. Tell me, Mr. Darcy, how is any of that *your* fault?"

He sighed and stood, pulling a matching armchair over so it faced Lizzy's and settling into it. "I will tell you why it is my fault—will tell you anything you want to know—but I need to understand something first. No matter what you think of yourself at the moment, I do not take Elizabeth Bennet to be a blind fool. Something convinced you that Wickham was a gentleman worthy of your trust, and you mention months' acquaintance. How is it you came to know him, when I was not even aware he was in London?"

At that, Lizzy looked incredulous. "You did not know—but I was sure Georgiana would have told you. We met him on one of our walks this summer, and he has often joined us in Hyde Park since then. He would walk with me while Kitty and Georgiana drew, and Mrs. Younge—" She stopped abruptly, a cold feeling settling over her. "Mrs. Younge encouraged them to let us walk alone, although she always sent a maid along for propriety. She convinced me there was nothing wrong with the acquaintance, since he was a longtime friend of your family and so clearly a gentleman. It would not surprise me if she also convinced Georgiana to say nothing to you. There were times when I wondered if they knew each other, but I always dismissed it as impossible."

Darcy nodded, his face a mask, but the way his fingers drummed on his leg belied his agitation. They stilled under her gaze, clenched into a fist, then returned to drumming. "What did he tell you of me? I would hear all of it, no matter what it is."

Lizzy took a deep breath, thinking back on their conversations. How best to condense the weeks of shared grievances that filled her with such shame as she considered them now? "He said you were raised together, but you cast him off at school and turned your father against him. His main complaint, though, was that you denied him a living that had been left to him in your father's will. It seems like so little, saying it now. I assume there is more to the story, in any case?" It was her turn to lock her hands together.

"There is much more. Did Wickham happen to mention how my father died?"

Good God, what had he done? "He did not. He said only that it was sudden."

Darcy closed his eyes, and for a moment Lizzy wondered if he would refuse to say more. Could she blame him if he didn't? It was a private matter, after all, and undoubtedly one that caused him pain. She had not exactly earned his confidences.

But he continued. "A letter came from my cousin, Major Fitzwilliam—you have met him. He meant it to go to me, but it was addressed hurriedly and the outside direction smudged almost beyond reading. A servant assumed it was for my father. Richard had written to say that Wickham had," Darcy hesitated. "He had gotten a girl with child, and when her brother tried to, ah, persuade Wickham to marry her, he shot the brother and killed him. None of this was confirmed, but there was enough evidence to create reasonably certainty.

"My father doted on Wickham. Since I had done my best to conceal from him the poor manner in which Wickham behaved when we were at school, the news came as a complete shock. My father's health had not been the best for several months, but the letter sent him over the edge. He collapsed and was in and out of consciousness for several days before he passed away. I cannot blame Richard; he did only what he thought was right. But Wickham—I can and do blame him for my father's death.

"I still do not know why he thought himself entitled to the living after committing such a crime, especially since it was never officially left to him. It was simply one of those things spoke of as a possibility. I have an aunt who is convinced I am engaged to marry her daughter because she and my mother discussed the match when we were in short clothes. Wickham's appointment to the living was much the same—it required him to take additional steps on his own, such as becoming a clergyman. Since he has not done so, and has at least the death of one man on his hands, I felt perfectly justified in denying the request."

Darcy sighed and rubbed his hands through his hair, causing it to stand on end, and Lizzy was seized by a sudden desire to fix it. She tucked her hands together instead as Darcy continued. "In fact, I sent him a thousand pounds with the promise of two thousand more if he expressed interest in additional schooling or training for a career. When I did not hear back from him, I assumed the matter was closed. I know Wickham; I ought to have known better. In ignoring the problems he presented, I was lazy and naïve, and you paid the price for my inaction."

He stopped talking and they sat in silence for several minutes, the only sound the crackle of the fire. Was it exhaustion or something else that scrambled her thoughts, Lizzy wondered. Her head swirled with images and phrases: Wickham's face too close to her own, Darcy's pistol, the way the carriage driver had frowned at her before she climbed in and discovered Wickham hadn't brought a maid after all, a thousand pounds—a *thousand* pounds—an imaginary baby that looked like Wickham, and finally, Wickham's words just before he climbed into the carriage and disappeared: *She hates you too.*

Had she been nothing more than a prop in a plot to settle a score? Lizzy looked up, the words falling from her lips before she knew what she meant to say. "He picked me because it would injure you, didn't he?" Even if society didn't blame Darcy for her ruin, he would blame himself, and she was willing to bet Wickham knew it.

Darcy sighed. "I'm not sure his main purpose was to hurt me. I think his motivation was more financially driven than that. Wickham knew if he married you I would make sure you were cared for, and that meant he would have access to money. I had time to think on the ride back, and I considered the idea that he meant to charm Georgiana. She is little more than a child, though, and he would have to wait years before marrying her, even if they eloped to Scotland." His eyes raked over her so fast she might have imagined it. "You are not a child."

She felt like one, a naughty child who had disobeyed her mother and gotten into a scrape entirely of her own making. "But I am nothing to you," Lizzy said viciously. "Of course you would ensure Georgiana's safety and comfort, and she has a substantial dowry besides. I have only a thousand pounds, and my father's estate is entailed away from the female line to a cousin. Mr. Wickham knew all of that, and he knew you are not fond of me. Why would he take such a gamble?"

Darcy sat forward, elbows on his knees and eyes intent on her face. "Desperate men do desperate things, Elizabeth. I wonder, though, why you think I am not fond of you. Or, I should say, why Wickham would think that. I may be able to shed light on the situation if you give me more details."

Why was he watching her like that? Lizzy licked dry lips to wet them, then blinked in surprise when

Darcy stood. Several moments later he held out a glass of wine, which she accepted gratefully. After pouring himself a glass of an amber liquid, he settled back into the chair opposite her and resumed his intense observation of her face.

Frustrated, confused, and exhausted, Lizzy stared back desolately. "It has been clear since I began my friendship with Georgiana that you do not like me. You have spent hours in a room with me and very rarely acknowledged me, you have insinuated that I am coarse, argumentative, and un-ladylike, and whatever you may have just said, I will never forget when you told your friend that 'She is hardly more than a child, and by no means tempting enough to give up my single state.' What was I to think, Mr. Darcy? You may have danced with me and made conversation when no one else was available, but I felt that you looked at me only to find fault, never that I was your equal, let alone a friend."

He gaped at her, glass frozen halfway to his mouth. "By God, Elizabeth, is that what you truly think?"

When had he dropped the 'miss' before her name? For that matter, when had he ever been so loquacious? Lizzy brushed the thoughts away to deal with later. "Of course that is what I think. Regardless of my other faults, I am not in the habit of professing opinions that are not my own!"

Another pause and then Darcy said slowly, with what sounded like forced calm, "In that case, I can only apologize. I esteem you more than any other young lady of my acquaintance, and I thought I had made that clear.

It seems I was mistaken. However, I do know why Wickham was so sure I would see to your wellbeing." At her questioning look, he smiled and said simply, "You told him I danced with you on multiple occasions."

"Why on earth would that mean anything to him?" But she knew, even as the words left her mouth: Darcy did not dance with the same ease and frequency that Bingley and Wickham and Bainbridge did. He danced with her because she was familiar and uninterested in pursuing his fortune, she had known that. He couldn't truly esteem her. Had Wickham read too far into the matter?

"I have not the talent which some people possess of conversing easily with those I have never seen before. I cannot catch their tone of conversation, or appear interested in their concerns, as I often see done. Dancing is even worse. Wickham knows very well how I feel. He knows that I only dance routinely with those ladies whom I find worth the effort, meaning that they are also people I would feel obligated to protect."

Lovely. Now she was an *obligation*. Would she ever be anything pleasant to the man? Opening her mouth to snap at him, Lizzy caught herself. Wasn't today proof enough that she could misjudge him? No matter what he thought of her, she owed him her reputation and quite possibly her life. "I am tired, Mr. Darcy, and overwrought. I should go to bed before I say something that would reflect poorly on both of us."

He stood immediately, placing his glass on a side table and offering her a hand. "Let me show you to your room."

Drained and confused, Lizzy accepted the hand rather than arguing, noting how warm his palm was as he helped her to her feet. For the first time, it occurred to her that she had spent more than enough time alone with Mr. Darcy to be ruined yet again. "Your servants won't talk, will they?" she asked as she followed him out of the study and up the stairs.

Darcy stopped and turned back, causing her to nearly collide with him in her tiredness. He caught her arm, steadying her, and Lizzy could only imagine the picture they made. "They wouldn't dare, Miss Elizabeth. You are safe here, and with luck this will soon be nothing but an unpleasant memory."

He left her at the door to a spare room just as the clocks chimed three in the morning. "Mr. Darcy?" She had to say it.

He turned back. "Yes?"

"I don't hate you. Mr. Wickham said—well, you should know that."

She thought she saw the ghost of a smile. "Thank you for telling me. Sleep well, Miss Elizabeth." He disappeared down the dark hallway and Lizzy let herself into her room.

Someone—one of the many Darcy House servants, she could only imagine—had built a fire in the grate and left more wood stacked to the side. *Good*, she thought with satisfaction, building the fire up from the glowing coals. Double-checking that the door was locked, Lizzy divested herself of pelisse and dress and promptly shoved the latter garment into the flames. When the gown was well on its way to being ash, she removed her torn petticoat and fed it to the fire as well, ignoring the chill of the room. Finally, clad only in her chemise, Lizzy climbed onto the bed and buried herself in the bed clothes.

Unbidden, the day replayed itself in her mind as soon as her eyes closed. She felt Wickham's hands on her again, his breath in her face, her terror and the horrible understanding that everything she'd believed about him was a lie. When the carriage had slowed, she'd thrown herself out of it, not realizing how tangled her skirts had become in her struggles to avoid Wickham's advances.

And then Mr. Darcy had been there, just like before, appearing out of nowhere when everything seemed hopeless. She had never felt such an overwhelming desire to throw herself into someone else's arms and turn over all responsibility, because clearly he had the situation in hand better than she ever could have managed. The desire had embarrassed her, bewildered her, and his subsequent gentle handling only exacerbated both feelings.

I was so wrong, Lizzy thought as she stared at the ceiling. *I wonder how many others have made the same mistake about Mr. Darcy and Mr. Wickham. One has got all the goodness, and the other all the appearance of it.*

She considered the differences in their behavior today, when appearances were finally set aside and true character revealed. Wickham had thought only of his own gain, Darcy only of hers. There was no doubt who the superior gentleman was. The way she had felt when he held her—*No*.

Lizzy rolled over and buried her face in the pillow, although the only person in the room to hide from was herself. Then again, perhaps that was the problem. Could she handle making such an admission?

Frustrated with herself, Lizzy flopped back over onto her back. It was the truth—what choice did she really have? Putting her sentiments into words would not change them. She'd been so upset that he ignored her, it had seemed only natural to find fault with him in return, and then to delight in sharing grievances with Mr. Wickham. But it didn't stem from hate. Staring up at the ceiling, everything crystalized and left her breathless.

Slowly, painstakingly, Lizzy relived her rescue and the subsequent ride back to London, the way Darcy had held her tight against him the entire time, how once he had dropped his cheek to the top of her head. She was sure it had only been to get a better look at something behind him, but her traitorous heart still thrilled at the memory. She had been wrong about so many things, what was one more? No, there was no use in concealing it from herself, even if the rest of the world must never, ever know.

She was absolutely, unequivocally, hopelessly in love with Fitzwilliam Darcy.

TWENTY-TWO

Darcy

January 1808

"Do you remember, Darce, when I said that nothing could make Rosings a less pleasant place to visit?"

Darcy looked up at Richard's statement, blinking as he cleared his mind of a certain young lady. After multiple letters from his aunt, Lady Catherine, Darcy and Georgiana had reluctantly traveled to her estate in Kent for Christmas. Richard's recent arrival had gone a long way in making the remaining days of the visit bearable for Darcy. "Vaguely."

Richard gave a grim smile. "Remind me not to tempt fate in the future, will you?"

Both men instinctively looked across the room, where their aunt was deep in conversation with her utterly ridiculous new parson, Mr. Collins. "I can see why she chose him," Darcy remarked. He and Richard were well-practiced in ignoring their aunt's lectures. Collins, on the other hand, was leaned forward so far and nodding so vigorously he was in danger of falling off his chair.

"Can you imagine being married to a man who puts so much importance on what another woman says?" Richard returned in the same low voice. "I feel sorry for his wife."

Darcy glanced again at Mrs. Collins, as he had done multiple times since the couple was admitted to the drawing room at Rosings Park. Something was familiar about her, although he was sure they had not met before. Mr. Collins had called twice during his stay, but this was the first time his wife had accompanied him. "Perhaps she is happier this way. I can imagine that Mr. Collins full attention might drive anyone to distraction." Or to drink, not that a parson's wife had that option.

Richard failed to smother his snort of laughter, and Lady Catherine's head snapped up. "What are you talking about, Darcy?" she demanded.

"We were recalling our rather disastrous attempt to climb the folly," Richard lied smoothly, turning towards his aunt without a hint of guilt on his face. Visits to Rosings Park offered all sorts of practice in giving half answers and misdirection when possible. Darcy abhorred lying on principle, but he could hardly berate Richard when the alternative was a lengthy tirade from Lady Catherine.

"That was a horrible idea," Lady Catherine said. "I am glad that Anne had no part of the excursion, but then she does have the soundest judgement I have ever seen in a young lady." She smiled patronizingly at her daughter.

Anne, who had instigated the entire scheme, if not participated in it, winked at Darcy when her mother looked away. Georgiana, sitting beside her cousin, smothered a smile. She was too young to have been present, but Darcy had told her the story.

"Not everyone is as well-regulated as Anne," Lady Catherine went on, glaring at Darcy, "which is why guidance is so crucial." She had been peeved with him since Darcy refused to discuss Mrs. Young's abrupt dismissal, seeming to think the fault lay with her niece or nephew rather than the shrew that had tried to swindle them. Darcy clenched his teeth.

"Have you seen the folly, Mrs. Collins?" Richard asked.

"Why would Mrs. Collins care to see the folly?" Lady Catherine responded, cutting across the other woman's reply.

"Perhaps she is fond of walking," Richard replied in the overly reasonable tone he often affected when speaking to his aunt. "The folly is a good destination, and you are always reminding us of the need to improve our health through regular exercise."

Mr. Collins bounced in his seat once before catching himself. "Yes, Lady Catherine is most wise on the matter of personal health, as she is on innumerable other subjects. I admit that I admire you gentlemen for having such good fortune as to grow up with such knowledge, so that it could truly become a part of you. I strive to take all of Lady Catherine's advice to heart and one day, with constant effort, I may be so lucky as you."

Darcy thought that Lady Catherine looked rather impressed with the speech, and instead of finding something to correct she turned to Mrs. Collins. "Are you a walker, Mrs. Collins?"

"I claim no natural inclination to walking," Mrs. Collins said, voice prim. "I believe that my time is better spent on the improvement of my mind and soul, as befits my station, and in the practice of music for others' enjoyment. Of course, if you believe walking is necessary to maintain a suitable degree of health then I will adapt my routine immediately. I do not foresee having difficulty with the activity, for my sister Elizabeth does have an inclination and is an excellent walker, and my younger sisters are proficient."

Good Lord, she was nearly as bad as her husband! Darcy studiously avoided looking at Richard.

"Anne would have been a marvelous walker if her health had allowed for it," Lady Catherine declared.

"It sounds as if you have a large number of sisters, Mrs. Collins," Richard observed, ignoring their aunt.

"Yes, four sisters," she replied. "I am the third of the five."

Five sisters, and Elizabeth an excellent walker. Darcy met Georgiana's eyes across the room. "What are their names, Mrs. Collins?" He thought of Elizabeth so often perhaps he was imagining the coincidence, but if not then it was remarkable indeed.

She looked surprised at his question but answered readily enough. "Jane is the eldest, then there is Elizabeth, Catherine, and Lydia."

"You must be Mary!" Georgiana exclaimed, then immediately clapped her hands over her mouth.

From the corner of his eye, Darcy saw Lady Catherine draw breath, frowning at her niece. Thinking only to draw her attention away, he said quickly, "Was your maiden name Bennet, Mrs. Collins?"

Definitely confused now, Mrs. Collins admitted that she had previously been known as Miss Mary Bennet.

"Miss Elizabeth and Miss Kitty," Richard said slowly, the realization dawning on his face.

"Yes," Darcy told his cousin, then turned back to the young lady before him. "Miss Darcy and I are well acquainted with two of your sisters."

"Georgiana, is that true?" Lady Catherine asked sharply.

"Oh yes," Georgiana replied, lighting up in the way she usually did when the Miss Bennets were mentioned or present. "Lizzy—Miss Elizabeth, I mean, and Miss Kitty are dear friends."

Lady Catherine scowled at Darcy; next to her Mr. Collins' jaw had gone slack.

Richard had seen the pending trouble as well. "Yes, the ladies are quite charming," he said. "They are staying with Lady Lichfield, and I know my mother expects Miss Elizabeth at her ball next month. She is a delightful dancer and most accomplished on the pianoforte—although she has told me herself she will never compare to Georgiana." He smiled at his cousin, who returned it shyly.

"I had no idea," Mr. Collins said dully, looking poleaxed, and Darcy wondered if he had meant to speak aloud.

Lady Catherine opened her mouth and was cut off again as a manservant appeared at the door. "Dinner is served, your ladyship."

*

Never before had Darcy been so relieved for the end of a meal. Lady Catherine had spent dinner interrogating Mrs. Collins on a great number of subjects, and it hadn't taken Darcy long to notice a theme. She was setting the Bennet family and especially Elizabeth and Kitty up as lesser young ladies, improper friends for Georgiana. Knowing his aunt as he did, Darcy could only imagine she found it preposterous that her highly-born, well-dowered niece was on such intimate terms with the sisters-in-law of her parson. She would be even more insistent that Georgiana have a companion now.

Both Richard and Georgiana inserted their own opinions throughout the conversation, the latter's involvement surprising Darcy. His sister had previously been known to go several meals at Rosings without saying a word, much less contradicting their overbearing aunt. It seemed Elizabeth had rubbed off on her more than he'd realized. Darcy himself had remained silent, not trusting himself to speak for fear he might not be able to stop once he opened his mouth. It was torture to hear Elizabeth criticized in such a way.

"Mr. Darcy, I am still all aflutter," Mr. Collins said as they settled themselves and Darcy accepted a glass of brandy from Richard. "To think, my own wife's sisters—my own cousins, indeed—are on such terms with a relative of Lady Catherine herself!

"I did not realize that Mrs. Collins was your cousin prior to becoming your wife," Richard said, and Darcy resolved to secure a bottle of the finest brandy for his cousin. He wouldn't have made it through the evening without him.

"Oh yes," Mr. Collins said. "I am to inherit Mr. Bennet's estate, you see, for it is entailed away from the female line. There was a disagreement subsisting between Mr. Bennet and my late honored father which always gave me much uneasiness, and since I had the misfortune to lose my father, I wished to heal the breach; but for some time I was kept back by my own doubts, fearing lest it might seem disrespectful to his memory for me to be on good terms with anyone with whom it had always pleased him to be at variance.

"It occurred to me, however, as I was studying to take my vows that as a clergyman it is my duty to promote and establish the blessing of peace in all families within the reach of my influence, and I could not preach such a message if I did not intend to heal the breach in my very own family. Since I also think it the right thing for every clergyman in easy circumstances to set the example of matrimony in his parish, I fixed upon securing one of my cousin's hands in marriage. By doing so, I hoped to mend the rift, give security to my dear cousins so they need not fear their father's eventual death will turn them out of their home, and of course to add very greatly to my happiness and comfort in life.

"I intended first to make an offer to Miss Jane Bennet, the eldest daughter and a young lady of incredible beauty. She had been quite ill, however, and her father was kind enough to point out that she may not be strong enough to, ah, fulfill all aspects of a wife's duties, assuming she even made a full recovery, which I thought to be very wise. I then decided that Miss Elizabeth would do almost as well, and was assured by everyone that she is the second most beautiful daughter as well as second in age. In the end, though, she could not be bothered to return home to her family when her father passed on my request to meet her. I believe she has begun to think of herself as quite grand, living in London as she has done, and so I suppose it is better this way."

This man had wanted to marry *his* Elizabeth? This bumbling, conceited, obsequious fool of a man paired with the lively, intelligent young lady that had become his personal angel a year ago in Hyde Park? It was too preposterous to even imagine. And to suggest she *could not be bothered* to return home! For heaven's sake, the lady had run away twice, hoping to *escape* London's grandeur.

Darcy looked up to find Richard watching him with a concerned expression. "You would do well, Mr. Collins," he managed to say through his clenched jaw, "to remember that you are not acquainted with the young lady in question. You also indicated, whether you meant to do so or not, that you do not respect or esteem your wife, which no gentleman *or* man of God should ever do. It reflects quite poorly on you."

Mr. Collins looked aptly taken aback, his self-contented expression turning to one of alarm. "Mr. Darcy, I do hope you will forgive me! Of course you are correct, and I cannot thank you enough for your insight! A *true* gentleman such as yourself is a great credit—"

He spoke on, but Darcy stood, placing his hastily emptied glass on the side table. "We should rejoin the ladies," he said, looking only at Richard. Perhaps he could ask Georgiana to play and avoid all other conversations. Unlikely, but perhaps.

"Are you well, Darce?" Richard asked in an undertone as they passed into the drawing room.

No. Not when Elizabeth is so thoroughly arraigned by both her relatives and my own. An idea had struck him, though, and he forced himself to focus on that. In the same low tone, Darcy replied, "It is of no matter. Pray tell, when is the ball that your mother is holding? Will you be present?"

Now Richard looked truly alarmed. "It is to be held the twelfth of February, and I hope to be present. You know as well as I do I only have so much control of my schedule. May I ask *why* you wish to know this?"

"You may, and I will even answer you, but not at the moment. I have an idea, but there is planning to be done. If I am able to arrange matters, I will need your help. Until then, I will say nothing." Ignoring his cousin's heightened alarm, Darcy made his way towards the instrument, where Georgiana had indeed taken a seat and was preparing to perform. She would like this idea as well; of that he was certain.

He must call on Lady Lichfield when they returned to London. Then, pending her agreement, he had an interesting letter to write.

*

15 January 1808

Mr. Bennet,

You do not know me, but you may have heard of me—or more likely, my sister Georgiana—from your daughter Elizabeth. My name is Fitzwilliam Darcy, and for the past year Miss Elizabeth has been the most beloved friend of my aforementioned sister. In that time, she has spoken so frequently of her sister Jane that Georgiana feels she is friends with Miss Bennet as well, despite never having met her.

Recently, it has become clear that Miss Elizabeth is out of spirits, and Georgiana is quite distressed. She is only twelve, and having lost both parents at a young age, I believe she relies on Miss Elizabeth perhaps more than she ought. She also lost her companion recently—but I digress. In all honesty, I have grown accustomed to Miss Elizabeth's humor and feel its loss as well.

My request is this: if it is agreeable to you and your daughter, I would like to send my carriage for Miss Bennet and bring her to Town as a surprise for Miss Elizabeth. Lady Lichfield has agreed to the scheme, as you will see in the enclosed letter in her own writing, and Miss Bennet would stay with her. She has also agreed to send a ladies' maid so that Miss Bennet has a chaperone for the journey. If I overreach myself, I sincerely apologize—I mean no disrespect. Should, however, you agree to the journey, there is a party hosted by my aunt, Lady Fitzwilliam, on 12th February that would work well for the surprise. I ask only that you respond at your convenience so I know what plans to make.

Respectfully yours,

Fitzwilliam Darcy

Twenty-Three

Lizzy

January – February 1808

She'd faked an illness through Christmas, avoiding celebrations with the Gardiners, who did not want to expose the baby, and all but the most instrumental events that Lady Lichfield arranged. It was easy to keep up the ruse, Lizzy reflected sourly as she sat picking through a piece on the pianoforte: she truly felt sick to her stomach a good deal of the time.

At least the long hours of self-imposed house arrest had improved her musical ability. She might never play like Georgiana, but for the first time in her life Lizzy felt proficient on the instrument. Maybe next she'd take up Latin. Anything to avoid thinking about her horrible judgement, her mistaken prejudices, and above all, Mr. Darcy.

Because it was adamantly clear that Mr. Darcy did not want anything to do with her. Where Georgiana had welcomed her back with concern but undeniable warmth, Mr. Darcy seemed to go out of his way to avoid any possible contact. If they were forced to interact, he kept the conversation short and precise. Although she'd never found him verbose or gregarious, Lizzy realized now how much she'd enjoyed crossing verbal swords with the gentleman.

Still, she could not blame him for his distance. It was remarkable that he had not banned her from the house so Georgiana would not be exposed to her ways. A man forced to rescue her from an utterly stupid situation of her own making not once, but *twice*, could be excused for not wishing to make polite conversation.

Lizzy just wished it didn't hurt so much. She'd been so caught up in her own reflections immediately following the incident that by the time she felt up to seeing *anyone*, Mr. Darcy had taken Georgiana to visit relatives Kent, where they remained through Twelfth Night. She had hoped, upon their return, that she might be able to thank Darcy for what he'd done. Instead, he'd come to call on Lady Lichfield only once, requesting a private audience and leaving swiftly when their meeting was done.

Visits to Darcy House provided no opportunities, either. While he was occasionally present when she called, they were never alone. Georgiana's new companion, Mrs. Annesley, arrived at the beginning of February, and she was far stricter about supervising any young ladies that might enter the house. That was only proper, after all, but Lizzy couldn't help wishing for a stolen half-minute in which she might be able to give relief to her feelings and thank the gentleman for correcting her stupidity. Since entering Darcy House still brought back her mortification, Lizzy had taken to inventing excuses to stay home on many of the days Kitty went to visit Georgiana.

It was on one of these days that Lady Lichfield entered the drawing room to find Lizzy at the pianoforte, contemplating the music in front of her listlessly. "How do you feel this morning, Lizzy?"

Lizzy lifted her shoulders in an unladylike shrug, one habit she stubbornly refused to correct. "Sufficiently well," she relied, returning her eyes to the music.

"I know you've found it difficult to interact with society since your father's letter." Lizzy looked up sharply and Lady Lichfield gave her a sad smile. "I know what heartache looks like, Elizabeth. You're not ill in any traditional sense of the word; you're despondent. I've a feeling there is more to it than I fully understand, but no matter the cause I am still concerned about you."

"I am," Lizzy repeated, "sufficiently well." She could not bear it if Lady Lichfield, always so poised and proper, discovered what she had done. Running away to Cheapside had been bad, but her latest mistake compounded the shame, because she should have known better. She *had* known better. The last year had given her a great deal of respect for her guardian, and *her* presence could not be avoided by refusing to make social calls.

"Have I ever told you how it is that I became the Countess of Lichfield when I began as a simple governess?" Lady Lichfield asked just as the door opened and a maid entered with a tea tray. "Thank you, Betty, you can put that here. Will you join me for refreshment, Lizzy?"

Realizing she had been ambushed, Lizzy quit the instrument and settled into the chair opposite Lady Lichfield's. Waiting until Betty had left the room and Lady Lichfield had poured the tea, she said simply, "You know you haven't told me. Is it a matter of significance?"

Lady Lichfield sipped her tea. "I believe it is—not so much my story, but how it affects someone else. I had not intended to say anything, but the past two months have made it clear that you are suffering. I think a greater understanding will help you find peace with yourself."

Intrigued despite herself and more than a little confused, Lizzy sat her tea cup down and raised her shoulders. "Who else did it affect?"

She received another sad smile in return, but nothing could have prepared her for the words that followed. "Thomas Bennet."

"My father?"

"Your father. Did you not wonder how you came to be in my care, when you have relatives that could have taken you in, at least for a while?"

"Of course I did," Lizzy said, thinking back to her father's announcement that she and Kitty were leaving to stay with a woman whose name she'd never heard. He hadn't even explained the nature of his acquaintance with the lady, and Lizzy had been too concerned with other matters to push the matter.

"Thomas indicated that you would not have any idea who I was, which I cannot say surprises me. After all—well, perhaps I should begin at the beginning, hmm?"

Lizzy nodded; Lady Lichfield took another sip of her tea and then folded her hands in her lap. "I met Thomas Bennet when I was five years old and he was eight. My parents had leased Netherfield Hall—you'll know of it?—and Mr. and Mrs. Bennet came to visit, bringing their sons with them. John, your father's older brother, was nearly twelve and could not be bothered to take note of me, but Thomas and I ran off and explored part of the attic. He discovered a tarnished old necklace and gave it to me. It was my first piece of jewelry."

Beginning to see where Lady Lichfield's story was going, Lizzy leaned forward, tea forgotten. Surely—?

"Yes," Lady Lichfield said, catching sight of the look on her face. "We became best friends. I would drag Thomas into all sorts of scrapes, and when the weather was poor or one of us was injured—usually me, to my mother's chagrin—we would find a quiet nook and he would read to me. He always had a book on him, even when we climbed trees! He had a way of turning the most boring books into something real, making an adventure out of a set of dates and facts on a page. My governess used to say she couldn't complain that I ran off to play instead of studying, because she'd never have taught me history on her own."

For a moment, Lizzy found herself back in Hyde Park almost exactly a year ago, laughing as Georgiana complained about studying. *Oh, don't think of it as facts. That's the fastest way to end up bored out of your mind. The secret to studying history is to think of it as a marvelous story.* Blinking to clear the memory, she looked up to find that Lady Lichfield had paused, watching her. "History is only boring if you forget it happened to people just like yourself."

"You sound very like your father," the lady said, "although something tells me you have climbed plenty of trees and torn or muddied more than your fair share of gowns."

Lizzy bit her lip. Her mother had often bemoaned the state of her clothing, while her father only laughed. Had he been remembering his childhood friend? "What happened next?" she asked. Despite the fact that she knew the outcome, her stomach knotted in anticipation.

"When I was fifteen, my parents allowed me to attend my first public assembly. We arrived when the first dance was in progress—my father was late for *everything*—and I remember being so worried that everyone would already be paired up for all of the dances. Thomas was home from Cambridge, and the second he saw me his face lit up. We danced the second dance of the evening, and I remember him saying it was a shame he had to change partners, because no one else could be bothered to talk of anything interesting."

Lady Lichfield paused, watching Lizzy for a moment before she said, "I think it was that evening that I realized I was in love with him, and I think in turn he realized I wasn't a little girl anymore. The time we spent together after that was certainly different than before."

"But—" Lizzy stopped, wondering how to articulate the questions on her mind. *Why didn't you marry him? Did he not care for you? Did you know my mother?* And most of all: *what happened?*

The lady went on without further prompting. "When I was sixteen, we had an absolutely horrible year. It started when John Bennet died in a riding accident. The old Mrs. Bennet was never the same after that and lasted only three months before succumbing to an illness; many people said she died of a broken heart, because John was her delight. Then, just a month later, my parents were travelling to London when their carriage overturned. The driver was thrown clear, but everyone else perished. Thomas was at school when it happened.

"There had always been a rift between my father and his older brother, and my uncle didn't see fit to make an exception for me. He collected me from Netherfield and, rather than taking me home with him as I had expected, drove me to Oxfordshire. His friend, the Earl of Lichfield, needed a governess for his young daughter. My uncle knew that my parents had educated me more than was expected for a female, and I believe he was very pleased with how matters were settled at such little inconvenience to himself.

"Luckily, Lady Sophia was a delightful girl, and I stayed with her for five years, becoming her companion when she no longer had need of a governess. Her eldest brother, Lord James, inherited the earldom the year Lady Sophia was presented at court. I assumed he would turn me out of the house. You can imagine my surprise when he made me an offer of marriage instead."

Clearly, she had accepted him, but so much was left unsaid. "Did you never hear from my father again?"

Lady Lichfield paused, and Lizzy wondered what memories filled her mind. "Not during the time I spent with Lady Sophia. Thomas wrote to me after James died, to give his condolences. That letter answered a good deal of questions I had carried for years. It seems that my uncle did not bother to tell any of my previous acquaintances where I could be found. Since all the females within those families had passed away prior to my departure, I could not reach out within the bounds of propriety. Thomas said it was quite a shock to read the announcement of my marriage in the newspaper, almost as if a ghost had come back to life."

"Did you know my mother?" Lizzy burst out, desperate to have a better understanding of her father's story in the intervening years.

"We were never more than acquaintances, but I knew of her. *Everyone* in Meryton knew your mother by sight. She was a beauty, very similar to how you describe your sister Jane. I know your father admired her, although I remember thinking they had nothing in common. Still, it wasn't altogether a shock to hear that they had married."

"They didn't," Lizzy said flatly, various emotions warring to win precedence. "Have anything in common, that is.

Lady Lichfield raised one slender eyebrow, transitioning from confidant to guardian with that single motion. "I disagree with you there, Elizabeth, and I will go one step farther: your father loved your mother, and I believe she loved him as well. A marriage does not always make sense to those outside of it, but that does not mean it is bad. There were many people who made wildly incorrect assumptions about my own marriage, and if I had viewed it with their perspective I would have thought them correct."

They sat in silence for a time, Lizzy turning the revelations over in her mind. "Why did you tell me this?" Lizzy asked at last, reaching out absentmindedly to her tea cup, then abandoning it when she realized the tea had gone cold.

"Because," Lady Lichfield said slowly, "I believe it explains your father's behavior over the last year, and if you consider what I have told you, I think you will agree with me. Beyond that, I value your company, Elizabeth, and it pains me to see you so out of spirits. I have wondered more than once if this past year has shown you that your father is only human. While I certainly won't argue that fact, I don't think it is fair for you to judge him without a clearer view of the truth."

Something in Lady Lichfield's countenance struck Elizabeth as strange, and she froze, trying to pinpoint the look or action that had caught her attention. *She still loves him,* flashed through her mind. Then Lizzy blinked and the lady looked as she always had, poised and elegant. If anything different had been there, it was gone now.

"Thank you," Lizzy said slowly, considering the woman across from her as if they were meeting for the first time. "I appreciate your candor, and I will think on what you have said. If—if you don't mind, though, I would like to be alone with my thoughts at the moment. May I have your leave to retire to my room?"

"Of course," Lady Lichfield said, standing and shaking out her own skirts. "Mrs. Simmons will be wishing to see me." She followed Lizzy from the room, turning the opposite direction and heading down the hall in search of the housekeeper.

Elizabeth climbed the stairs to her room slowly, mind whirling. Until Lady Lichfield mentioned it, she'd never considered how she viewed her father. Her mother had been a silly, fanciful creature, undoubtedly human—Lizzy had known that for years. But her father? How had she thought of him, before her world tipped upside down?

Her ally. Her friend. The person who could always be counted on to take her opinion seriously, to explain something instead of telling her young ladies shouldn't be concerned with politics or war tactics or experimental crops. The smile across the room when she found something humorous, letting her know he had seen it as well. Of course *she had been devastated when her image of him was forced to change.*

Lizzy threw herself down on her bed. Nell would fuss later, since she had tried a new hairstyle on Elizabeth that morning and been quite pleased with the result, but Lizzy herself didn't care. What did hair matter, when the inside of her head was so abuzz with new ideas and considerations?

Staring up at the ceiling, Lizzy turned Lady Lichfield's story over and over in her mind until the connections began to make sense. She was still horribly ashamed of her own actions, and nothing could make Mr. Darcy think better of her, but for the first time since November Elizabeth didn't feel as though she'd been abandoned by her beloved father. Neither had she been entirely cut off from everyone she'd previously known and forced to work for a living.

Perhaps life wasn't *quite* as hopeless as she'd thought.

Twenty-Four

Darcy

February 1808

Darcy arrived at the Fitzwilliams' London residence far earlier than he usually would for a ball. The rather harried butler told him that Richard was in the library, then left Darcy to find his own way past musicians setting up and maids putting the finishing touches on decorations for the evening.

"I wondered when I'd be seeing you," Richard said, looking up as Darcy entered. "Is your grand scheme still set to move ahead tonight?"

"It is," Darcy said, keeping his face impassive. "Mr. Bennet, Miss Bennet, and Miss Lydia arrived at Darcy House just before I left. Miss Bennet will be preparing for the ball there. She and Mr. Bennet should arrive when the dance is in full swing, and Miss Kitty has agreed to spend the evening with Georgiana. It will be a surprise for her as well—apparently she and Miss Lydia are as close as Miss Bennet and Miss Elizabeth. Mrs.

Annesley will ensure they behave themselves." Georgiana's new companion had been delighted by the scheme.

"And when will you be offering for Miss Elizabeth?"

Halfway through adjusting his cravat, Darcy froze and turned to face his cousin. "I beg your pardon?"

Richard leaned back on the nearest bookcase and crossed his arms. "Come off it, Darce. First you're charmed by a lady you straight out told me ought to inspire your disproval, then you nearly strangled that fool of a parson Collins when he mentioned wanting to marry her, and now this. I've only been around the you occasionally for the last year, who's to say what I've missed? What would *you* think, were you in my position?"

Nothing that I'll admit to. "You didn't see Georgiana, after Father died. You don't know what it was like in that house. After everything Miss Elizabeth has done for my sister, how can I not wish to repay her in kind? It has taken little enough time and next to no money to arrange."

Richard rolled his eyes. "Very well, you did everything for Georgiana's sake and never once thought about yourself. I'll save my 'I told you so' for when I wish you happy."

Darcy scowled and turned back to finish adjusting his cravat. He would have happily offered for Elizabeth months ago, but he was determined to give her space after Wickham's perfidy. Arguing with his cousin would only be a waste of time and absolutely counterproductive to his peace of mind.

*

Unsurprisingly, the Bingleys were the first of Darcy's acquaintances to arrive. No doubt Miss Bingley thought she could integrate herself with his relatives and therefore secure his hand. Ever since he'd stopped paying court to Miss St. Clair, Caroline Bingley's attentions had increased tenfold. Darcy had considered asking Bingley to call off his sister on more than one occasion.

Lady Lichfield entered not long after, eyes seeking him out across the quickly filling room and giving him an almost imperceptible wink. Everything was in order on her end, then. He smiled in return.

Then Lady Lichfield stepped aside and his eyes lighted upon Elizabeth. She wore white, like almost all the other young ladies in the room, but everyone else disappeared as he beheld her. *His angel*. Her hair was pulled up and back and dotted with pearls, although one unruly curl had already come loose and was hanging by her left cheek. Darcy found it adorable.

She moved farther into the room so as not to block those arriving behind her, and Darcy lost track of her for several minutes. He was not overly concerned—Jane Bennet was not expected for at least an hour, and Lady Lichfield and Richard would both keep an eye on Elizabeth as well. In fact, Darcy decided it was probably better if he kept his distance. He didn't quite trust himself around Elizabeth since his revelations in December. The last thing he wanted to do was make her feel as if she owed him anything. Today was about Elizabeth's reunion with her sister, not any feelings he might have.

Darcy took up a position at the side of the room and watched Elizabeth dance both of the following two dances, looking even more lovely with bright eyes and another escaped curl framing her face. He could—no. No, he wouldn't he wouldn't ask her to dance and therefore remind her of what he considered 'the incident' tonight, when she was finally smiling again. She stared at the floor in a most un-Elizabeth-like way when he was present and had even stopped visiting in the past few weeks. Darcy highly doubted Georgiana was the reason she had chosen to stay away.

He was considering joining a card game to avoid temptation when Bingley appeared at his side. "Come, Darcy," he said, "I must have you dance. I hate to see you standing about by yourself in this stupid manner. You had much better dance."

Apparently, Darcy thought, *we've become good enough friends that Bingley is comfortable calling out my inadequacies. That or he's simply seen Bainbridge berate me often enough to think it a usual occurrence.*

The current dance ended and the crowd in front of them parted as the dancers moved off the floor, revealing Miss Bingley and Miss Elizabeth. The ladies were conversing with the air of cats sizing each other up before a fight, although their words alone seemed perfectly polite.

Miss Bingley caught sight of him first and turned so Miss Elizabeth was all but cut out of their circle. "Mr. Darcy, you are a perfect person to settle this debate, for I know you have put much thought into Georgiana's education." Luckily, Mr. Bingley's manners were far superior to his sister's and he shifted so Elizabeth was fully included. Refusing to move despite the awkwardness of their spacing, Miss Bingley went on, "Miss Eliza here is of the opinion that a lady is disingenuous if she does not make a specific point of voicing her own views even if she converses with someone far better informed than herself. Surely you would not wish Georgiana, and by extent well-bred young ladies as a whole, to turn to arguing with men on subjects ladies rarely consider? Why, think of the pleasant evenings that would be ruined!"

Absolutely awkward, rather boring, and unnaturally devoted to his sister. Miss St. Clair had seemed like the epitome of a well-bred young lady, and her disingenuity could very well have ruined any hope he'd fostered of a fulfilling domestic life. He knew that Miss Bingley referred to discussions over politics or current events, but with Miss St. Clair's words clear in his memory he could not even consider agreeing with her.

"I would hear Miss Elizabeth's stance on the matter," he said rather than answering directly, noting that her cheeks had taken on a brighter hue than could be contributed directly to the exercise of the evening. He'd been right to keep his distance; she had seemed perfectly composed while speaking with Miss Bingley alone.

"I believe it is a simple enough opinion," Elizabeth said, recovering herself. "I certainly do not claim that my views are superior—goodness knows I have made mistakes and misjudged people or situations, and I can only hope those I may have offended will accept my most sincere apologies. I cannot believe, however, that any good would come of building a relationship that is based on false information."

You don't owe me an apology, Elizabeth. Darcy thought about the poor woman who had written him after bearing Wickham's child and felt a wave of relief that the lady in front of him had at least escaped that fate. "On this point, I must side with Miss Elizabeth," he told Miss Bingley. "Disguise of any sort is my abhorrence. I have more far more respect for someone who shows a willingness to grow and adapt their opinions as more information is provided, than I do for a young lady who meekly agrees with every statement I utter. We are all only human, after all. What is to say *my* opinion is not incorrect?"

Elizabeth ducked her head, but Darcy thought he detected the hint of a smile. Had she heard his hidden reassurances? Miss Bingley looked dumbfounded.

Just then the musicians began to play the first notes of the next dance and Mr. Bingley hurriedly said, "I would ask an opinion as well. Mr. Darcy seems disinclined to dance while I believe his enjoyment of the evening would be enhanced by taking part in the exercise. What say you?"

Miss Bingley's eyes lit up, and she gave him a look he supposed was meant to be coquettish. Knowing she meant for him to dance with her and was not afraid to ask him directly, Darcy made a snap decision, praying he would not regret it later. "Oh, very well, Bingley," he said. "I will dance, if it makes you happy to see me do so. Miss Elizabeth, would you do me the honor?"

She looked up, clearly surprised, but placed her gloved hand on the arm he offered and followed him into the set. Only when they had taken their places and the dance began did she peer up at him and say, "What do you think, Mr. Darcy, should we arrange a signal so you can alert me when you need to escape from an overly pushy lady? At least Miss Bingley did not go to the same lengths as the lady at Vauxhall. Of course, if your intent was to avoid dancing altogether, we have already failed."

"Given time, I am sure Miss Bingley would prove just as persistent," Darcy responded. "To your second point, do not think me opposed to dancing. I had already considered securing your hand for a set, but did not want to cause any undue distress." He would not let her think she was only a convenient escape.

Elizabeth blushed, eyes dropping once again to the floor. Even in her embarrassment, though, she remained light and graceful on her feet. Oh, blast it all! She would tell him if the idea was repulsive to her.

"In fact, Miss Elizabeth, might I be so bold as to request your hand for the supper set?" She looked up, lips parting slightly in shock, and Darcy forced his gaze to stay focused on her eyes. "That is, of course, if no one has spoken for that dance already?"

"They have not," Elizabeth replied after a heart-rending silence. "I—yes, I will save that dance for you, Mr. Darcy." She raised her chin. "As previously stated, I am happy to help you keep from raising the expectations of those forward young ladies who make up such a large portion of this room."

No, damnation, I just want to dance with you, Darcy thought, but at that moment his attention was caught by a young lady entering the ballroom, an older gentleman by her side. As he watched, Lady Lichfield noticed them as well and started towards the pair. Miss Bennet had arrived.

Positioned as they were in the dance, Elizabeth could not possibly see her sister over the heads of the people around them. Darcy's stomach knotted in anticipation. How to point her out without suggesting he had prior knowledge of her arrival?

"Speaking of young ladies, I must beg your assistance on a different sort of matter. I know I do not pay as much attention as I ought, but a lady just entered and I feel as though I should know her name. Perhaps you could help me remember before I make yet another social blunder."

He saw her face crease into a frown, no doubt wondering his interest in a lady when he had just discussed avoiding them. The next steps in the dance would place Jane Bennet in their view. Placing one hand on Elizabeth's waist, he swung her around with slightly more vigor than required, ensuring she faced her sister directly.

Elizabeth froze, an involuntary sound escaping her lips as all the blood drained from her face. Beneath his hand she was trembling. "Jane?" she asked in a whisper, allowing him to move her out of the dance without seeming to notice. "Papa?" Turning away from the pair at the door, she looked up at him beseechingly through tear-filled eyes. Did she doubt what she saw?

Darcy moved his hand so it was on the small of her back rather than holding her waist and gave her a slight push towards the door. Seemingly no other encouragement was required; Elizabeth flew across the space between them, nearly running into a couple in her haste. Then her arms were around her sister and Darcy couldn't tell if they were laughing, crying, or both.

Once again, Bingley materialized at his side. "Who in the world—?" he asked, voice reverent, staring at Jane Bennet in awe.

Lady Lichfield caught Darcy's eye and subtly indicated he should join them.

"Unless I very much miss my guess," he told Bingley, moving towards the group at the door, "that is Elizabeth's sister, Miss Jane Bennet. Shall we see about an introduction?"

"I've never seen her like," Bingley breathed, following Darcy without taking his eyes off the newcomer. "She is perfection."

Elizabeth had just buried her face in the gentleman's chest and Darcy felt a sharp stab of jealousy as his arms closed tight around her. *You can't begrudge her father, surely*, he chided himself as they reached the group.

The man in question looked up and gently disentangled himself from his daughter. "I supposed one of you is Mr. Darcy?" he asked.

Elizabeth's eyebrows furrowed and she shot him a questioning look. *So much for keeping that secret.* Well, nothing could be done now. Darcy bowed. "That would be me, sir, and this is my friend Mr. Charles Bingley. I presume you are Mr. Bennet?"

"I am." The man turned to his younger daughter. "Lizzy, do you mean to introduce your sister, or are you leaving that to an old man far removed from his comfort zone?"

"Papa!" Elizabeth exclaimed. "You always managed in Meryton; this is not so different."

"I would still prefer to be in my library," he told her. "I have never been fond of balls. You can ask Cl—excuse me, Lady Lichfield—if you will not take my word."

Was it Darcy's imagination, or had Lady Lichfield colored? Wasn't her name Amelia? Had her maiden name started with "Cl"?

Elizabeth shook her head at her father, smiling, then turned to the gentlemen. "Mr. Fitzwilliam Darcy and Mr. Charles Bingley, may I present my eldest sister, Miss Jane Bennet, of Longbourn in Hertfordshire?"

Darcy and Bingley bowed. "I am honored to make your acquaintance, Miss Bennet," Darcy said.

"Honored indeed," Bingley added. "I cannot claim any great friendship with Miss Elizabeth, but even I have heard her speak of you multiple times. Now that we meet I see she has not exaggerated your beauty. I will not doubt her in the future."

Miss Bennet smiled and blushed; behind her back Darcy noted Mr. Bennet take in the scene with a raised eyebrow.

"Miss Elizabeth," Bingley said as the previous dance ended, "if she is willing, might I steal your sister away for a dance?"

Elizabeth's eyes flickered towards Darcy, and he knew she was remembering the scene in the garden with—what had that young lady's name been? Miss Carter? Looking back at Bingley, though, she smiled warmly. "Of course, Mr. Bingley. Oh, goodness, I forgot that I promised Major Fitzwilliam this dance, here he is now. If we hurry, we can be in the same set." Throwing yet another smile at her father, and a rather bemused look at Darcy, she accepted Richard's arm and walked away, introducing him to Jane as they went.

Lady Fitzwilliam bustled up to the remaining group, sparing a brief smile for her nephew, then linked her arm through Lady Lichfield's. "Amelia, I am in need of your assistance, do you mind?"

"Well, Mr. Darcy," Mr. Bennet said, his eyes on the lady's retreating back, "it appears that we are left to our own devices. Would you be so good as to show an old man to the card room? Perhaps then you could tell me more about yourself. I found Miss Darcy to be just as Lizzy described her, but she has written less about you."

Good lord. If the father was anything like the daughter, Darcy was in for an impressive interview, full of questions with multiple meanings. Then again, he couldn't blame Mr. Bennet. If someone ever arranged such a surprise for Georgiana, Darcy knew that *he* would put the gentleman through a thorough cross-examination. "Of course, Mr. Bennet," he replied. "It would be my pleasure."

Twenty-Five

Lizzy

February 1808

"My goodness, Lizzy, this is your room? It is lovely."

"It is," Lizzy said, spreading her arms and falling back onto the bed. She beamed up at her sister. "Now that you are here with me, I might be able to appreciate it fully."

There was a rap on the door and Nell entered. "Will you be needing help with your gown, Miss Lizzy?"

Elizabeth pushed herself off the bed. "I will, and so shall Jane. You'll notice that *she* is far too ladylike to rumple her clothing."

The maid shook her head, but her smile was clearly visible. "As long as you haven't drug the hem through mud, Miss Lizzy, I've no complaints."

Jane laughed. "I see that you haven't changed in essentials! But where do you manage to muddy your hems in London? Seriously, Lizzy, do you seek out puddles on purpose?"

They continued to chatter as Nell made quick work of removing their ball gowns, Lizzy noting with a shock that her dress was newer and of a finer material than Jane's. Strange, when before so many of her dresses had been hand-me-downs from her sister. Then clothing ceased to matter as both girls snuggled under the covers of Elizabeth's bed, facing each other as they had done so many nights at Longbourn.

"I can hardly believe you're here," Lizzy whispered. She'd found herself looking for Jane all evening, pinching herself to make sure her appearance wasn't a dream. Now, she simply stared at her sister, taking in every detail she could make out by the moonlight streaming through the window.

Jane laughed softly. "*I* can barely believe I'm here. Papa got a letter asking if he would be willing to let me come to Town as a surprise for you. Next thing I knew, Papa, Lydia, and I were all in the most fashionable carriage I've ever seen and my first matter of business when we arrived was to dress for a ball. It still seems like a fairy tale!"

"Lydia is here?" Lizzy exclaimed.

"Yes, did no one tell you? She is at Darcy House, with Kitty. I think Kitty nearly fainted when we came in. Miss Darcy must have been in on the secret, for she was delighted instead of surprised. I only saw her for a few minutes, but I like her very much. She is less reserved than you described, but then we met her at home, in the company of a dear friend. What?" Jane asked, smile morphing into concern. "You look—unsettled, Lizzy."

Elizabeth bit her lip. "Mr. Darcy did this, didn't he?"

"Did you not know? I assumed someone would have told you, once the surprise was out. To be fully honest, I thought he would tell you himself."

Lizzy shrugged with the shoulder not nestled into her pillow. "I guessed it was his doing, but I wasn't sure. If Lydia and Kitty are at Darcy House, though, it definitely is."

Jane giggled. "Well then, may I say I thought him very handsome and imposing?"

"Jane!" Elizabeth protested, blushing. "It's not like that."

"Lizzy, be serious. The man spent a month organizing an elaborate surprise for you. I also happened to notice that he danced with you twice, the second being the supper set. How exactly is it not *like that*?"

"It was a surprise for Kitty as well," Lizzy protested, knowing she sounded feeble. "Jane—oh, Jane, even if he could have liked me once, he's been present every time I've made a fool of myself this past year, and I've *truly* outdone myself. He would have every right to despise me. Just you wait, he'll have some noble reason for bringing you all to Town, and it will have nothing to do with his feelings for me. Maybe Aunt and Uncle

Gardiner are truly the ones who planned the surprise, and Mr. Darcy is just helping them."

"He knows *our* Uncle Gardiner?" Jane exclaimed. "A great gentleman like him, with an estate and a house in Grosvenor Square? How did that happen?"

"He is an investor in Uncle's business," Lizzy said. "They meet on a regular basis to discuss how some of the more experimental parts of the business are doing. I think he an Aunt Gardiner talk of Derbyshire—she grew up in the town nearest to his estate."

Jane refused to be sidetracked for long. "Well, that is certainly interesting news, but I highly doubt Aunt and Uncle are behind this. You didn't see how he looked at you, when you first caught sight of us."

"Don't be ridiculous."

"Fine. But the only dance he seemed to enjoy was the one I saw him dance with you."

Lizzy gave a short laugh. "That has an easy answer! He detests most of the young ladies that were in the ballroom and only dances with them because he is friends with their brothers. Speaking of which, dearest, you must tell me of your dance with Mr. Bingley! *That* gentleman looked besotted. What do you think of him?"

"He is just what a young man ought to be," Jane said, distracted at last. "Sensible, good-humored, lively; and I never saw such happy manners! —so much ease, with such perfect good breeding!"

"He is also handsome," Lizzy replied, "which a young man ought likewise to be, if he possibly can. His character is thereby complete." Stubbornly, her mind conjured up a scene in Bond Street where Caroline Bingley causally remarked that her brother was long over the lady he'd called an angel only a month before. It seemed impossible that anyone could treat Jane in such a way, but still— "Do not set your heart too quickly, though, Jane. Mr. Bingley is a wonderful gentleman, but there are many of those in London. You never know who you may meet tomorrow!"

"I believe you mean 'today,'" Jane said, yawning. "Forgive me, Lizzy, I'm exhausted. Can we continue this conversation in the morning?"

"Of course," Lizzy said, snuggling even farther into the bed clothes and giving her sister one last sleepy smile. "Sweet dreams, Janie."

Jane reached out and pushed the curls off of Elizabeth's cheek. "Sweet dreams, Lizzy."

*

Lizzy awoke early the next morning. For a moment she held perfectly still, sure the night before had been nothing more than a dream and dreading the return to reality. Then Jane mumbled something in her sleep and Lizzy hugged herself with happiness. It was real. *It was real.*

She slipped out of bed and dressed quietly, pulling on one of her simplest day dresses and pinning her hair out of her face. Jane might sleep for hours yet, but her father would be awake, and Elizabeth didn't intend to waste any of the time she'd been given.

Lizzy entered the breakfast room to find her father and Lady Lichfield present, both cradling cups of coffee in their hands. Breaking off what he had been saying previously, Mr. Bennet smiled at his daughter. "I wondered if we'd be seeing you soon, Lizzy. I've missed your company at home in the mornings."

At his words, all of Elizabeth's hurt feelings flooded back in. She turned away abruptly, going to the sideboard and giving far more attention to the offerings than was required. Lady Lichfield was a firm believer that offering the same breakfast every day prevented overeating, which meant Lizzy knew exactly what she wanted for her meal.

Lizzy let Lady Lichfield carry the stilted conversation through breakfast, answering direct questions but not volunteering information. A war waged silently in her mind. Finally, *finally*, her papa had arrived; she could at long last talk to him and *see* his eyes crinkle in laughter instead of receiving a return letter days later. Left to his own devices, though, would he have come? Or would another year have passed with vague promises that failed to coalesce? Having been hurt so badly by his seeming abandonment once before, Lizzy was loath to expose herself to future pain.

Mr. Bennet stood as Elizabeth swallowed her last bite of food. "Lizzy, I happened to observe a pleasant sort of wilderness not far from here. Could you be convinced to take a stroll with me?"

"You mean Hyde Park?" Lizzy asked with raised brows, standing as well. "Of course, sir, but you cannot convince me you are ignorant of the location."

Lady Lichfield fixed Elizabeth with a reprimanding look. "You know the rules," she said so quietly Lizzy doubted her father had heard.

Inclining her head slightly as she pushed in her chair, Lizzy indicated she'd heard and understood. *No running away*. Lady Lichfield must be worried that strong emotions would prompt her to act rashly—it had been over a year since she'd made her first ill-fated escape to the Gardiners'. Surely Darcy hadn't told of her more recent incident when he'd coordinated the surprise? No, that didn't make sense. He'd be honor-bound to offer for her then. Lady Lichfield was being cautious, nothing more.

Reluctantly, she followed her father outside. Mr. Bennet walked slower than Tom, but Lizzy matched his pace without complaint. Her father did not walk by habit, preferring to spend leisure time in his library. That he should choose to do so now told Lizzy he was hoping to speak with her, and once again she found herself torn. She longed to hear his explanation, but what could he possibly say that would make up for the past year?

They entered Hyde Park while Lizzy dithered and Mr. Bennet walked in silence, only occasionally pointing out something or interest or asking a trivial question. At last, he took a seat on a bench that faced the Serpentine. Lizzy recognized it as a favorite of

Kitty's and told her father so. Kitty would love to show him her drawings when she and Lydia returned from Darcy House.

Her father acknowledged the statement with a single nod. Then, seeming to rouse himself, he added, "Thank you Lizzy, I will ask her to show me the sketches. But I did not bring you out on this chilly morning to speak of accomplishments. You are upset with me, and rightfully so. I would hear you speak your mind."

Lizzy was quiet for a long moment, contemplating how to begin. No matter what her father said, she could not rail at him with unorganized anger. He was still her father; he still deserved her respect. He watched her in silence, waiting.

"I understand why you sent Kitty and me away," she said at last. "But why—*why*—did you ignore me? Why was I never allowed home, even for a fortnight? Didn't I make it abundantly clear that is what I wanted?" Her voice broke, and Elizabeth dug fingernails into her palms to regain her composure. "I have no other quarrel with you, but that has eaten away at me since the day we arrived and I was greeted by a stranger."

Mr. Bennet looked away, gazing out over the water. "I suppose I cannot keep it from you, after all I have put you through. Of all my daughters, Lizzy, you are the most like me. You know this, but you do not know what it has meant to me, all these years, to have your company. No, listen," he said, holding up a hand when she would have replied. "I was not just fond of your company. I cherished it, but the older you grew the guiltier I felt. To keep you cloistered in Hertfordshire, surrounded by silliness and small-minded people, ate away at my heart. It is not the life I wanted for you, but I could not be bothered to make the necessary changes, and it made me sour. When at last the illness required me to act, I was determined not to waste the opportunity. And then at last you were where I wanted you to be, with someone I had long wished was your mentor. It was perfect—all except the fact that I missed you, and you were unhappy."

He was silent for a while, but Elizabeth waited rather than filling it. She was not ready to forgive him, not yet. The pain had been too extensive for that. At last, Mr. Bennet turned back to her. "Do you want to come home, Lizzy? It is not what I want for you, especially now that I see all the ways you have grown since you have been in Town. But I will not keep the decision from you any longer."

Again, they fell into silence as Elizabeth considered. She thought about Lady Lichfield and Georgiana, about balls and walks—in Hyde Park *and* in her favorite country lanes. She considered the room she shared with Jane at Longbourn, and Lydia, the sister she really didn't know. Who would Elizabeth Bennet of Hertfordshire be now, were she to come into existence again? Lizzy was surprised to realize she couldn't say. Then she thought about Mr. Darcy, about the wonderful, over-the-top surprise that had brought her sister and father back to her, and she was struck by how much she would miss him, were she to leave, even if she would never be more to him than his sister's friend. How much she would miss all of it.

"No," Elizabeth said before she could second-guess herself, hoping her voice didn't waver. "No, I would like to stay here. Please, though, say that I can visit when I wish, and that you and my sisters might visit me as well."

Mr. Bennet nodded once. "Very well," he said simply, and Lizzy wondered if he was happy or disappointed. Then he gave her a sideways smile. "Does your decision have anything to Mr. Darcy?"

Lizzy turned and considered her father, pulling her pelisse tighter around her. For an insane moment, she almost expected Darcy to appear and scold her for not staying warm enough. Stranger things had happened, after all. "Yes, it does," she said slowly. "And with Miss Darcy, and Lady Lichfield, and little Fanny Gardiner; and with the fact that I have spent most of my year in London wishing I was anywhere else. I think I might like it here if I don't see it like a gilded cage, and I would be disappointed in myself if I ran away before I knew for sure."

Unexpectedly, Mr. Bennet leaned over and kissed his daughter's forehead. "I am so proud of you, my Lizzy." He stood and offered her a hand; she took it without hesitation. "Come, Jane may be awake by the time we return, and I would not dare keep you from her any longer. Although," he gave her the teasing look she remembered so well, "it might interest you to hear we will remain in London for the next three weeks."

"Truly?" Elizabeth asked, stopping to face him directly. "All of you?" Three weeks with Jane! To share more whispered conversations rather than letters that could never truly convey the same meaning?

"Truly. I need to speak with your sisters, but Jane may remain longer if Kitty is amenable to returning home. I know she and Lydia have missed each other as well, and I do not fear for Lydia's poor influence on her as I once did. A year of constant attention from Jane has done Lydia much good. Now come, I believe Claire has plans for all of you, and she will not forgive me if I delay them."

"Claire?" Lizzy asked, letting herself be propelled forward again.

To her absolute surprise, Mr. Bennet blushed. "Lady Lichfield to you. You have heard that we knew one another as children? She detested being called 'Amelia' and so I always referred to her by her second name. It is a habit I suppose I shall have to break."

My second name is Claire. Jane's is Amelia. Ideas tumbling through her mind, Lizzy bit her lip to keep from bombarding her father with questions that seemed too inappropriate to voice. It was going to be an interesting three weeks indeed.

Twenty-Six

Darcy

March 1808

Georgiana had insisted—Darcy suspected with a bit of prodding from the younger Bennets—that they absolutely could not allow Mr. Bennet, Kitty, and Lydia leave for Hertfordshire without having some sort of a formal event. Since the younger three girls were not yet out, they had settled on a dinner, after which Georgiana could play the piano and the other girls could dance with each other. Bingley would attend, and Major Fitzwilliam had been invited so there might be gentlemen to dance with as well.

Sadly, Richard was out of London on army duties, and Darcy could only imagine his services as a dance partner would be required. Dare he hope to dance with Elizabeth? Even Lydia's exuberance could be tolerated—for she was not so bad, if one was accustomed to a girl who always seemed to be talking, moving, or both—if he could clasp Elizabeth's hand in his and pretend that matters were different between them.

Enough, Darcy. It was morning yet. The Bennets would not arrive for hours, and there was business that required his attention. He knew full well that at least half an hour would disappear into thinking of Elizabeth over the course of the day, but he would never accomplish anything if he began by daydreaming. Attempting to put her from his mind, Darcy reached for his ever-present stack of correspondence and plucked the top letter from the pile.

Mr. Darcy,

I write to you with news of Mr. George Wickham. Please forgive me if I have contacted the wrong person, but I have no name to go by other than yours. Only by tracing the name "F. Darcy" left on several of his accounts was I able to discover your connection. It pains me to write this, as it must pain you to read what I have to relate. If it were me, though, I would wish to know rather than simply wondering.

George Wickham was killed two nights prior. There is some contention as to how he died, for the man that shot him claims Wickham tried to steal his horse. There is something strange about his manner, but in truth neither man was known to the inhabitants of our town for long. There are numerous conflicting statements, and I am no judge. Rest assured that the other man is being tried and justice will be done based on our findings.

My feelings rail against the next statement I must make, for it is of a crude matter when you face a loss, but my sensibilities demand I press on: Wickham left behind him debts totaling six hundred pounds, with myself and other merchants...

Darcy scanned the rest of the letter, which mostly gave supporting details of Wickham's debt and where payment could be sent, assuming Darcy was willing to pay and not overwrought at the news. *Overwrought.* The news of Wickham's death brought all sorts of feelings—regret, relief, guilt at both the relief and the thought he may have sent Wickham inadvertently to his death—but he was not overwrought. Fitzwilliam Darcy had mourned the loss of his childhood friend years ago. He never would have chosen this ending, but, well, the fact remained that the ladies he cared about were safer now that the reprobate was gone.

Feeling heartless, Darcy forced himself to re-read the letter. In death, he could choose to remember Wickham as the boy his father had loved, who had spent countless hours getting into all sorts of scrapes with

Darcy and charming his way out of trouble. Yes, Wickham was the man that Darcy blamed for his father's death, and he doubted that assessment would ever change. He would have ruined Elizabeth's life for his own gain. They had been friends once, though, as close as brothers.

Settling behind his desk, Darcy allowed himself a quarter hour of recollection on the fonder times, the closest he would likely ever come to holding a vigil for George Wickham. Then he readied a quill and put the memories aside. Richard needed to be appraised of the situation, and his hot-headed cousin would not appreciate any sort of sentiment.

*

The Bennet ladies—Jane, Elizabeth, Kitty, and Lydia—arrived in a flurry of ribbons and giggles. Lady Lichfield and Mr. Bennet followed them in, remarkably more sedate for all that they were smiling.

"You are a brave man, Mr. Darcy, to willingly host so many flighty young ladies in a single room," Mr. Bennet remarked once everyone had made their way to the drawing room.

"Georgiana must receive credit for the idea. She was most determined that we should have at least one dinner together before you, Miss Kitty, and Miss Lydia return to Hertfordshire." He nodded across the room to where Bingley stood, speaking with Miss Bennet and Lady Lichfield. "Mr. Bingley offered to help even out the ratio of the genders." Luckily Caroline Bingley had been previously engaged for the evening.

“A brave man,” Mr. Bennet said wryly, watching as Bingley beamed at his eldest daughter. He turned back to Darcy. “I have been thinking about our conversation the other evening on what it takes to maintain a manor house. Were you able to find the book I mentioned?”

They spoke for several minutes, with Darcy finding it increasingly difficult to focus on the conversation. Elizabeth had moved so she stood only a few feet away, her laughter washing over him at regular intervals. He was determined to not look as obviously besotted as Bingley—after all, Jane Bennet was clearly more receptive to his friend’s advances than he had ever seen Elizabeth. Giving a favorable impression to Mr. Bennet was also important, but—Elizabeth laughed again. What were they discussing?

“I find that it is necessary, after a particularly wet season, to burn down the house and start anew to ensure that it is properly dry. Do you not agree, Mr. Darcy?”

“Oh, yes, yes, I—” Darcy’s brain finally registered the words and he jerked his head towards Mr. Bennet, face flaming in mortification.

“I had heard,” Mr. Bennet said with some distinction, “that Darcy House boasts an impressive library, especially when one considers that it is not your primary residence. May I request a tour?”

Better to be embarrassed in private than in front of a crowd—especially one that contained Elizabeth. “Of course, Mr. Bennet. I would be delighted.”

"Don't let him steal your copy of *Tom Jones*," Elizabeth said, having overheard the last comment. "He has quite a collection of that book, 'borrowed' from gentlemen around the country." She winked at her father, but directed her words towards Darcy, turning to face him in a swirl of skirts. "If you were not needed to guard your books, I would recommend you show Papa the way and then return, for my father's way of inspecting a library is to make his way through the shelves in absolute silence, ignoring all questions and refusing to leave or take sustenance until he is satisfied."

"I believe you have mistaken me for Mr. Bingley," Darcy said, unable to hide his smile. "The sort of interaction you describe sounds heavenly."

Elizabeth gave a shout of laughter. "In that case, I will tell Mrs. Crew a tray is required. The tea might be cold by the time either of you notice it, but Mrs. Fournier's scones are delicious no matter their temperature."

Darcy wondered if Elizabeth had any idea how intimate her words sounded. She had often stepped in to direct the staff over the past year, when Georgiana's bashfulness or inexperience kept her silent. Darcy had never stopped to question a guest essentially acting as the lady of the house, especially since Elizabeth's easy manners kept the staff from feeling as though she overstepped her bounds. Had Caroline Bingley made such a presumption, he would have put a stop to the behavior immediately!

Catching Mr. Bennet's eye, Darcy knew the gentleman had added at least one more question to his list. Still, he could not resist teasing the lady. "Thank you, Miss Elizabeth, but I cannot rightfully neglect the rest of my guests for so long. If we have not returned in an hour, Crew should be sufficient to recall us from the world of books."

Elizabeth made a show of noting the time, then dropped a curtsey. "Enjoy your respite, sirs. We females shall carry on with our frivolity here."

Both gentlemen remained silent as Darcy led the way to the library. "Port, Mr. Bennet?" he asked once they had entered and the door was secured behind them.

"Yes, thank you," Mr. Bennet answered. He walked a loose circuit of the room while Darcy poured, pausing to pick up a book and examine it. Placing the glass near the other man, Darcy set his own glass down on the table used for examining maps and leaned back against it, drumming his fingers on the wood until he realized what he was doing and clasped his hands together to still them.

Mr. Bennet placed the book back on the shelf and turned to face the younger man. "You seem like an intelligent sort, so undoubtedly you have determined what I wish to discuss. You are more discreet than Mr. Bingley, but I have noticed how much time you spend watching my daughter. I will admit to some surprise. She comes from a lower station in life than the one you hold, even if you know her as the ward of a countess. You do not strike me as the kind of man to make rash decisions, and you know as well as I do that many of your peers would not consider such a connection. If I may be blunt, what are your intentions towards Elizabeth?"

Having expected the question, Darcy was prepared to answer. "At the moment, sir, I have none. That is not due to any opposition on my part, but because I am not sure she would welcome my attention. We have crossed verbal swords on many occasions over the past year and I believe Miss Elizabeth only recently came to regard me as a friend."

He took a deep breath and let it out shakily, wishing he could reach for his port without the gesture giving away the extent of his feelings. *In for a penny, in for a pound.* "However, I am hopeful that might change one day. While I believe it to be precipitous at the moment, I would like to ask your permission to court your daughter, seeing how you may not be in Town for the foreseeable future. I had considered the possibility of speaking with Mr. Gardiner, but I would prefer to have your direct approval. Whether or not this conversation ever matters will rely on Miss Elizabeth's inclinations."

Mr. Bennet studied Darcy in silence for a while, then picked up his glass and took a sip. Feeling safe to do the same, Darcy copied him, although his mouthful could only be referred to as a gulp.

"Your sister is very different from Elizabeth," Mr. Bennet noted at last, then lapsed back into silence.

Yes, this was definitely where his lady had learned her sparring skills. Darcy would have smiled at the revelation, had his stomach not been twisted in knots. "You cannot have missed how Georgiana greeted Miss Elizabeth today, or any other time they are together. I am very like my sister, Mr. Bennet. Left to our own devices, the pair of us make up a silent dinner table and a house of very proper ghosts. Miss Elizabeth and Miss Kitty have done both of us a world of good over the past year." *They have been our angels,* he added to himself. *She has been* my *angel.*

"She has little money—there is four thousand pounds to be distributed between the five girls after they marry, and Longbourn is entailed away from the female line."

"Yes, I have met your heir, as well as the former Miss Mary," Darcy said, fighting the urge to scowl at the memory of Mr. Collins. "He is my aunt's parson."

Mr. Bennet laughed. "So you have met Collins. Tell me, what did you think of him?"

This time, Darcy allowed himself a frown. "I could have tolerated him, had he not insulted El—*Miss* Elizabeth. Apparently the lady could not 'be bothered' to return home when he demanded a meeting and he found himself sadly misused."

He paused to collect himself, then went on. "As for money, I will also be blunt. You yourself pointed out that this is my second home. Pemberley is quite solvent. Georgiana's dowry is funded and neither of my properties require extensive repairs. I do not gamble, and I cannot imagine how some men manage to spend the money that they do on clothing. In short, Mr.

Bennet, I have no need of a wealthy bride, for I am perfectly in control of my finances. Money does not make life worth living, though. I would very much like a wife who does."

Mr. Bennet looked amused. "Very well, I suppose I have tortured you enough. Lady Lichfield speaks highly of you. Between that and your responses today, I am satisfied. You may court my Lizzy, even offer for her, but I reserve the right to give my final approval before you notify the papers. Before you rush off to stare at her some more, I would like to hear your opinion. Would it be prudent for me to have a similar conversation with Mr. Bingley? The man puts a devoted puppy to shame."

Darcy hesitated, trying to think clearly through the happiness threatening to overwhelm him. The reference to a puppy helped—it reminded him only too clearly of Miss Lucy Carter and her assessment of Mr. Bingley. "I believe, Mr. Bennet, that it would be wise to wait until your next visit to speak with Mr. Bingley. He is young and eager. Such a conversation might cause him to act rashly, and he has known Miss Bennet for less than a month."

Nodding, Mr. Bennet said, "Lizzy insinuated something of the same. Should I be concerned with his character? Perhaps have a conversation with him that trends in the opposite vein?"

"No," Darcy replied slowly, still considering. "There is nothing wrong with him any more than a puppy not yet trained to the rules of the hunt is at fault. Bingley wants only for time to steady him—already I have begun to notice restraint and forethought that was once beyond him. If you are still concerned for Miss Bennet, however, remember that she does not face him alone. Miss Elizabeth is well acquainted with Bingley's nature, and her love for her sister is clear. She is better placed than either of us to know Miss Bennet's feelings, and she will not knowingly give advice that might end in heartbreak."

Mr. Bennet quirked an eyebrow. "You will have to be careful, Mr. Darcy, or Lizzy will be running all your affairs only a fortnight after the wedding."

His heart skipped a beat. If only such an event could be brought about! "There is nothing that would make me happier."

Twenty-Seven

Lizzy

March 1808

Lydia, Kitty, and Mr. Bennet departed for Longbourn in late March, leaving Jane with Lizzy and Lady Lichfield. Lizzy had sent up a prayer for her father's peace of mind as they left, although both of her younger sisters had undoubtedly improved in the past year and a half. Instead of fretting about her sisters' behavior, Lizzy found herself looking forward to seeing the sort of young ladies they would become.

Still, as Lizzy walked down Bond Street with Georgiana several days later she had to admit the change was nice. After a month surrounded by her sisters—especially the vivacious Lydia—Lizzy found Georgiana's quiet enthusiasm refreshing. It was the younger girl's birthday, and Darcy had insisted on taking her to all the finest stores to pick out items suitable for a 'proper young lady' of thirteen. In turn, Georgiana had begged Lizzy's company, especially since Mrs. Annesley had gone to visit her ill sister.

The light was fading as Lizzy and Georgiana returned to the carriage, Mr. Darcy having excused himself to run one last errand. They arranged the day's packages as they waited for him, chattering excitedly about the day.

"There he is!" Georgiana exclaimed at last, looking out the open door. "I wonder what he had to do?"

The accident happened so fast she only made sense of it later. One moment, Mr. Darcy was crossing the street towards them, a smile on his face that told Lizzy he was pleased with himself. The next, a horse yanked away from its owner, prancing on the cobblestones as if preparing to rear. Jumping out of the way, Darcy's foot landed in something wet and he fell backwards, arms flying out to grab supports that didn't exist. He landed hard on the road, head snapping back with a thud.

The packages were forgotten. Georgiana collapsed into herself, sobbing uncontrollably in one corner of the carriage. Lizzy hung halfway out the door, trying to keep up with the conversation between the men huddled around Mr. Darcy on the street.

"Let's get him home," she heard the carriage driver say after an indeterminable amount of time. "No good letting him lie where a horse might kick him any second." He turned to a man out of Lizzy's view—the footman, perhaps? "Send for the doctor and have him meet us at Darcy House. We'll get the master home."

The second man must have acquiesced, because the driver stood and turned his attention to the carriage, waving Lizzy back so he could peer inside. "Let's put him on the rear seat," he said over his shoulder, but his eyes stayed on Georgiana, who had pulled her skirt up to cover her face. "We'll need someone to hold his head," he added in a quieter voice.

Lizzy looked at Georgiana as well, then back at the driver. "I'll do it," she said, voice sounding as if it came from a long way away.

"You sure, Miss Elizabeth? You're awful white, and it won't help Mr. Darcy if you faint when he needs to be held steady."

Elizabeth set her shoulders and stuck out her chin. "I'll do it."

"Go sit in that corner, then, opposite Miss Darcy. We'll get the master in."

Lizzy obeyed, clenching her teeth as she tried to stop herself from trembling. *You need to be steady. You need to be strong.* She glanced again at the girl across from her. *For both of them.* With Mrs. Annesley gone, someone would need to see to Georgiana as well.

The driver and his helpers loaded Mr. Darcy carefully into the carriage, positioning him so his head rested on Lizzy's lap. The footman returned just as they had finished and took up a position across from Darcy's legs, which hung off the end of the rear bench awkwardly. "I'll make sure he doesn't slide off, miss," he told Elizabeth, studiously not looking at Georgiana. Lizzy only nodded in return.

The carriage moved slowly forward and, glancing down, Lizzy watched Darcy's eyes flutter open. "Mr. Darcy!" she exclaimed.

He regarded her dully for a moment, then his eyes slid closed again. Only by stooping quickly could she make out the words he whispered. "My angel."

Lizzy sat back in shock, knocking her head against the carriage wall, and considered the man lying across her lap. He couldn't have meant anything by that. He didn't know what he was saying, let alone thinking. He would wake up tomorrow and laugh if she recounted his words. *God, please let him wake up. Please, please, please.*

The doctor met them at the door to Darcy House and watched as his patient was gently unloaded and carried inside. Relieved of her burden and resigned to the fact that she could not change his fate, Elizabeth turned her attentions to Georgiana. Making sure the girl's dress covered her adequately, she bundled her out of the carriage and half-carried her up the stairs to the house. Mrs. Crew had been watching Mr. Darcy be transported up the stairs, but at their entrance she bustled over to the ladies.

Lizzy kept Georgiana moving, for fear she would collapse if they stopped. "There are packages in the carriage that should be brought in, and I will need a tray of something calming in Miss Darcy's room." *Laudanum*, she mouthed to the housekeeper and caught the quick nod in reply. "Oh—and please send to Lady

Lichfield. I will stay here tonight to ensure Miss Darcy has company in Mrs. Annesley's absence."

"Very good, Miss Elizabeth," Mrs. Crew said. "I will see to the tray and packages immediately, and the blue room will be made up for your use."

"Thank you," Lizzy said, gritting her teeth at the additional effort required to move Georgiana up the stairs. Seeing her struggle, one of the footmen came forward and easily lifted the girl into his arms.

She let out a bloodcurdling shriek, and Elizabeth was impressed the man didn't drop her in surprise. "No! Lizzy! Lizzy! Fitzwilliam! *I want my brother!* Everyone always goes away! I won't let him. *I won't*!"

"Shhh," Lizzy interjected, managing to capture one of Georgiana's hands in her own as the footman continued up the stairs. "Shh, I'm here, Georgie. It's okay. You need to stay calm so you don't worry Mr. Darcy."

"Fitzwilliam?"

"Yes, you need to be quiet so Fitzwilliam can rest. Everything will be okay, Georgie. Breathe." Continuing in the same vein, Lizzy walked beside Georgiana to her room and sat next to her on the bed, waving the footman away. A maid entered as he left, setting a tray next to the bed. A quick inspection told Elizabeth it held lukewarm tea and a bottle of laudanum.

Masking her motions, Lizzy uncorked the bottle and poured a healthy dose into half a cup of tea. "Georgie, I need you to listen to me. Can you drink this? It will help you stay calm, and we can't have you upsetting Fitzwilliam. Will you do this for him? He won't rest if he is worried for you."

The girl reached out blindly and accepted the mug. "Drink it all," Lizzy told her firmly, and she complied, handing it back with a grimace and a whimper.

"Everyone goes away," Georgiana whispered, turning on her side and curling into a ball on the bed. "Everyone always goes away."

Lizzy said nothing. Instead, she sat on the side of the bed, running a hand over Georgiana's hair, until the girl had cried herself to sleep. "Happy birthday, Georgie," she whispered, then carefully stood and made her way out of the room.

Let him live, God. Please, please let him live.

*

Once again, she was lying on her back in the blue room, staring at the ceiling and trying to not think of Fitzwilliam—no, she needed to think of him as Mr. Darcy, whatever she had called him earlier. Perhaps she should have stayed with Georgiana, if only so neither of them was left alone. But no, the younger girl needed her sleep and the laudanum had accomplished its purpose. Lizzy refused to take the medication herself, and therefore would only disturb Georgiana. She was stuck, alone in the dark and kept wide awake by the worries streaming through her mind. He could *die*, and she would never have even thanked him. Would never have told him…

You could thank him now. Angry in her anguish, Lizzy sat up and wrapped her arms tightly around her middle. She *couldn't* go to Mr. Darcy now—or could she? What stood between them except for two doors and rules that had already been broken? Someone would be with him—Mr. or Mrs. Crew, most likely, but would they turn her away? What was it Fitzwilliam—*Mr. Darcy*—had said on that horrible night in December, when she asked about the servants gossiping? *They wouldn't dare. You are safe here.*

Making up her mind, Lizzy climbed out of bed and donned her borrowed dressing gown. If Fitzwilliam died before she thanked him, she would never forgive herself, propriety be damned. Besides, she thought hopefully, something might have changed in the last hour. *Anything* would be better than not knowing.

Slipping out of the blue room, she made her way quickly down the empty hall to the master's chambers. No one stood outside Mr. Darcy's door, and Lizzy hesitated as she reached it, realizing that entering his bedchamber was a far different story than being in his study without a chaperone. If word got out, she would be irrevocably ruined.

Does it matter, if he isn't in your life?

The answer came immediately: *No.*

Lizzy pushed on the door, which upon close inspection stood slightly ajar, and slipped into the room silently on her bare feet. The only light came from a single candle on the bedside table, but Lizzy could make out the figure lying motionless on the bed.

"Miss Elizabeth?" She jerked towards the murmured question. Darcy's valet stepped out of the darkness and became recognizable.

"Nelson," Lizzy replied, lifting her chin. Too late to turn back now; she would have to brazen her way through. "How is he?"

"No change, miss. Do you mean to sit with him?"

"Are you planning to fetch Crew to throw me out?"

Nelson's face remained impassive. "No, miss. I think you might do him more good than I can at the moment, and Miss Darcy isn't an option." Elizabeth doubted anyone in the house hadn't heard of Georgiana's hysterics and subsequent dose of laudanum. Her shrieks had certainly been loud enough to carry.

"I don't plan on staying long," Lizzy said, eyes straying again to the man on the bed.

"Stay as long as you like. I'll be in the corner, over there. Please let me know if you need anything." He retreated back into the darkness of the room.

Lizzy hesitated by the door, biting her lip. She *could* approach him. She *could* pass on her thanks, and then perhaps she would be able to sleep. Standing by the door for half the night wouldn't accomplish anything except wasting time.

Padding slowly across the space between them, Lizzy linked her hands together to keep them from shaking, reminded suddenly of the way Fitzwilliam drummed his fingers when stressed. How often she had wanted to reach out and stop the motion with her own hand! It had seemed horribly improper at the time and Lizzy choked back the sudden urge to laugh. How preposterous to consider as she stood in his bedchamber, clad only in a dressing gown and chemise!

Reaching the bedside, she stared down at Mr. Darcy's still face. Would she ever see his eyes again? How often had she searched a room for him, long before she admitted it to herself, looking for the reassurance of his presence? He was awkward and taciturn, but he was also steady. He had stepped in more than once when a lady had tried to cut her, even when she could have managed perfectly well on her own. Was she doomed to lose him now, before she could tell him how she felt?

Feeling tears begin to pool in her eyes, Lizzy forced them back and whispered, "I never thanked you saving my life, Fitzwilliam. You didn't have to do that, either time. I didn't deserve the effort you put in. So thank you, from the bottom of my heart."

She squeezed her eyes closed, pressing a hand to her face as if that would hold back the tears. *Leave. Get out of here before you lose it.* Blindly, Lizzy turned to go.

"Elizabeth?"

Lizzy's eyes flew open and she whirled around. Nothing had changed about the man on the bed, and for a moment she was sure she'd hallucinated the rough whisper. Then he blinked several times and turned his eyes to hers. Feeling the tears begin to spill freely down her cheeks, Elizabeth sank onto the stool someone had left by his bedside earlier in the evening. "Are you really awake?"

"Elizabeth." It wasn't a question this time. "There's nothing I wouldn't do for you. Surely, you must know that." He lifted a hand from where it lay on the bedclothes and she reached out automatically to meet it, only noticing when his fingers met hers how much she was trembling. He paused, blinking. "What happened? Where am I?"

"You fell," she answered, voice as shaky as her limbs. "You slipped and hit your head, and no one could wake you. The doctor didn't know if you'd ever regain consciousness. Georgiana will be so relieved. She was convinced she'd lost you too."

Reaching up to brush hair away from his eyes with the hand that didn't hold hers, Darcy froze. "Elizabeth, are we in my bedchamber?"

She flushed scarlet and dropped her gaze, relieved the lack of light hid some of her discomfiture. "Yes. I couldn't sleep. I had to see you. I had to apologize, in case—in case there wasn't another opportunity to express my gratitude."

Darcy reached out and took her other hand as well. "I do not want your gratitude, Elizabeth. I did not act as I did in order to be thanked, or even because I thought it the correct thing to do. Nothing could have stopped me from coming to your aid, because I could not live with myself if any harm befell you."

Lizzy opened her mouth to respond and found herself held silent by a mixture of embarrassment and terrifying delight. Instead, she gave a small, disbelieving shake of her head.

"Elizabeth." Darcy took a tighter grip on her hands. "I had not planned to say anything yet, and certainly not in a situation like this, but"—he broke off and looked around them again, then back to her face. "You are not the only one with things left unsaid. If what you say is true, then I cannot stay silent anymore. It is unthinkable to waste more time. You must allow me to tell you how ardently I admire and love you. Elizabeth, I beg you to do me the great honor of accepting my hand."

Still, she could not speak. *I am dreaming*, she thought distantly.

"You are too generous to trifle with me," Darcy went on after a pause, the tension clear in his voice. "If I have overstepped, imagined something which is perhaps not there, tell me so at once. I have never been more sure of something than I am about my feelings for you, but one word from you will silence me forever."

She *must* speak! "I thought you were dying!" Lizzy burst out, hiccupping on the last word. "Forgive me, sir, I am not blind to your struggle, but I can scarcely believe we are having this conversation. I thought—" she stopped abruptly as a sob threatened, then forced herself to continue. "I thought I had lost you. I could not rightfully come to you, but neither could I stay away. I am so worried this is only a dream."

Some of the tension left from Darcy's face, and he freed one of his hands to reach up and cup her cheek, brushing back the curls that had escaped her braid. "Say yes, darling, and they can never keep you away again."

Elizabeth leaned into his caress, feeling the last of the horrible terror drain from her body. "Yes, Fitzwilliam," she whispered. "Yes."

TWENTY-EIGHT

Darcy

March 1808

Y*es*. Had any word ever brought so much joy? Darcy tried to sit up, the awkwardness of his position directly conflicting with the elation coursing through him, and winced at the stab of pain in the back of his head.

"Here, allow me," Elizabeth said at once, dropping the hand she still held and standing. She leaned across him to grab another pillow and the intimacy of the position sent a flood of desire through him. She wore a dressing gown, slipping open at the front to reveal her chemise beneath, and her hair was pulled back in a simple braid with curls escaping to frame her face. *Good God.* Darcy desperately hoped his face did not give away these new thoughts. She was in his bedchamber!

Her face showed only concern as she slipped an arm beneath his head and gently raised it enough to place the second pillow beneath. Of course, in her innocence she may not consider what he found so apparent. "I would have not assumed you to have such a practiced bedside manner," Darcy murmured as she settled him back onto the pillows. At least now he wasn't fully prone!

Elizabeth glanced down at him, her face so close he could feel her breath as she exhaled. She blushed, the color visible even in the low light. "You might recall I have four sisters, and my mother was *not* a comforting nurse. Jane and I spent plenty of time tending to each other or the younger girls." She settled back onto the stool.

"Will you mind having yet another sister?" Darcy asked with a smile, reaching out to reclaim her hand.

"I will love calling Georgiana my sister. Goodness, she will have quite the surprise when she wakes up. She will be so relieved you are well, and I do hope she isn't mad at me."

Darcy frowned. "Why would she be unhappy?" Surely not because they were engaged! He couldn't think of anything his sister would like more.

Ducking her head, Elizabeth glanced sideways at him. "I may have doused her with a good deal of laudanum."

Drawing breath to laugh, Darcy found himself coughing instead. The teasing expression disappeared from Elizabeth's face immediately and she looked across the room at something he couldn't see. "Nelson, could you fetch Mr. Darcy a glass of water?"

The valet stood and crossed to the end of the bed, entering Darcy's field of vision. "Of course, Miss Elizabeth." He nodded to Darcy, looking clearly pleased. "It's good to see you awake, sir. Is there anything else you'll be needing?" To Darcy's surprise, the question seemed to be directed at Elizabeth.

"Please send word to the doctor that Mr. Darcy is awake," she said, glancing at him to see if he had anything to add. When he shook his head, she waved Nelson off with a smile.

"Your father warned me you would take over the household, but I don't think even he realized how fast the transition would occur," Darcy said when the door had closed behind the valet.

Elizabeth swung around to face him, aghast, then realized he was teasing. "Oh dear," she said with a laugh. "I dictated several things to Mrs. Crew this evening as well, and absolutely snapped at one of the newer maids. I do hope your household is willing to put up with me." Her blush returned in full force, gaze dropping to their joined hands.

"It sounds like quite an eventful evening," Darcy remarked. "Would you mind telling me what happened? The last thing I remember is coming out of—" he broke off. "I was coming back to the carriage."

Elizabeth's face turned pale and she renewed her grip on his hand. "I—yes, yes, I can tell you. I do not wish to think of it, but I would want to know if it was me." She tucked one bare foot beneath her on the stool as she began to speak and Darcy was momentarily distracted. Wasn't she cold? Should he offer her a blanket? He thought of their ride home together on Aeolus, when he had opened his coat and wrapped both of them in the garment. What he would give to hold her like that now!

"Are you well?" Elizabeth asked, and Darcy lamented his lack of attention. He must have made a face. Reassuring Elizabeth nothing was wrong, he focused on her words. She'd made it to the part where Georgiana had to be carried to her room when Nelson reappeared.

"Here is the water," he said, handing it to Elizabeth. Darcy noticed he made a show of not looking at her too closely. Between that and the professional way he handled Elizabeth's presence, Darcy made a note to raise the man's pay. With any luck, such tact would soon become a standard part of the valet's job. "A footman has been sent to notify the doctor," he added, retreating back into the shadows.

"Thank you, Nelson," Darcy said. He looked back at his lady. "It sounds like Georgiana and I are both lucky you were present."

"The praise should go to your staff. They managed superbly with very little input."

Darcy kissed her hand, reveling in the fact he could do so whenever he liked. "Perhaps, but I am glad you were there, even if I did not know the difference at the time. What is it?" he asked as a strange look crossed her face.

For a long moment Elizabeth sat in silence, appearing to consider her words. Finally, she looked up and said, "You did know I was there, if only for a moment. At least, I think you did, I am not sure I understood you correctly. When the carriage started to move, you opened your eyes for just a second. Like I said, your head was on my lap and I think I was the only one to notice. You said—"

She broke off, blushing, and Darcy imagined the scene she described. "My angel," he whispered.

Elizabeth's head snapped up, eyes wide in shock. "I thought you were hallucinating. I never imagined—" she stopped again, looking down at their joined hands. "I suppose I never imagined *this*, either. I'm not entirely convinced this is real."

"I could pinch you, if you'd like," Darcy said. *Or kiss you. Yes, definitely kiss you.* "I don't remember the scene you describe, but you have been my angel since the day we met in Hyde Park. I wasn't even sure *you* were real until we met again at Lady Haddington's ball."

Her eyebrows arched. "Yes, the ball where you commented that I was a child and 'by no means tempting enough to give up your single state.' I fear you have been proven wrong, Fitzwilliam, but I hardly believe you thought me an angel *then*."

How he loved hearing his name on her lips! "Then, and a good many times since. I beg you will not give my statement any more thought, and I hate the idea that it caused you pain. My words were meant for Bainbridge. It was the first event I attended after my father died and I did not wish to be present, let alone be teased about offering for a lady after sharing a single dance." He frowned. "Whatever my reasons, I should not have spoken as I did. When we discussed pride and amiability last summer I felt wholly justified in my reasoning—it did not even occur to me that you were commenting on my own behavior until later. That I caused you pain by presuming my own feelings more important or justified than yours is repulsive to me, and I must beg your forgiveness."

"I am glad to hear your sentiments, but you owe me no apologies. We are so altered from the people who attended that ball I will not hear of you dwelling on it. Consider instead how Mr. Bainbridge will never again have a reason to tease you so."

He would argue with her later, for he could not so easily set aside his reflections, but now was not the time. "Perhaps not, but he will make up for it in other ways. Bainbridge and Richard—Major Fitzwilliam—will fight over who can say 'I told you so' first."

Elizabeth laughed. "Yes, I fear Jane will have several things to say to me as well. How *will* we survive?"

"Run away with me." He'd meant it to be teasing, but his voice was husky, altogether too serious. Elizabeth's eyes locked onto his and they stared at each other for a breathless moment.

"I believe, Fitzwilliam, you had best stay in bed until the doctor arrives. And while I mean no insult to

Aeolus, I would prefer a carriage the next time we travel together."

Her teasing broke the spell and he could breathe again. "I am sure a carriage can be arranged."

There was a commotion at the door and Mrs. Crew entered. Even in the low light Darcy could see her eyes widen as she took in Elizabeth. "Well," she remarked, recovering herself quickly, "I see who we have to thank for calling you back to yourself." Darcy watched her gaze sweep over Elizabeth rather than shying away as Nelson had done and he wondered what the housekeeper was thinking. "If you don't mind, miss, the doctor has arrived and will want to examine Mr. Darcy privately."

Elizabeth climbed off her stool readily, but Darcy kept a firm grip on her hand. "Is it possible that Georgiana is lying awake like you were, waiting for news?" he asked.

"I was quite liberal with the laudanum and doubt she will wake before morning," Elizabeth said. "I will check on her, though. Mrs. Crew is correct, I should go."

"Only if you promise to come back," he whispered.

"You are scandalous, Mr. Darcy. I will be back as soon as can be."

He kissed her hand and let go of it reluctantly, watching her until she slipped out the door and disappeared from sight. Hopefully the doctor's inspection would not take too long. Darcy had a letter to write to Mr. Bennet and did not want to delay any longer than absolutely necessary.

*

As expected, Georgiana was nothing short of delighted at the news. He'd made his way to the breakfast room the day after his fall, determined not to stay in bed any longer than required, to find Georgiana and Elizabeth present. He hung back for a moment before they caught sight of him, taking in the scene with pleasure. Before long this could be his reality every morning!

Then Georgiana caught sight of him and jumped up, Elizabeth following suit. "Brother!" she hurtled herself across the room, stopping short just before she crashed into him. "Are you feeling better this morning?"

He pulled her into an embrace, locking eyes with Elizabeth over her shoulder. "I am very well." *Did you tell her?* he mouthed to Elizabeth.

She shook her head with a smile. "I am surprised the doctor allowed you out of bed so soon, Mr. Darcy."

Releasing his sister, Darcy crossed to Elizabeth. "He said there was no reason to stay in bed as long as I do not overtax myself. Besides, I had a very compelling reason to get up this morning." She blushed prettily as he took her hand and kissed it, then turned back so they both faced a wide-eyed Georgiana. "Georgie, I am sorry your birthday outing had such a horrible ending yesterday. Would it make up for it if I gave you a sister?"

For a moment, Georgiana was speechless, staring at the pair of them as incredulous delight spread over her face. Then she squealed with glee and ran forward again, not bothering to check herself before catching Elizabeth in a tight embrace. "Truly?" Georgiana asked, pulling back and looking from one face to the other. "Really, truly?"

"We may have to reconsider, seeing how repulsive you find the idea," Elizabeth said, biting her lip to stop her smile and earning a pout from Georgiana in return.

Then Georgiana was beaming again, jumping up and down on her toes. She reached out to clasp Elizabeth's free hand in both of hers. "Oh, I cannot imagine a better present! You are not teasing, truly?"

Darcy looked down at Elizabeth, heart skipping a beat at the smile she gave him. *She said yes!* "Shall we convince her, Elizabeth? I have a present for you, too." Her eyes widened in surprise as he put a hand in his pocket and pulled out the bracelet he'd purchased the day before. "I worried I was being a bit precipitous when I bought this yesterday, but it seems the timing was," he hesitated, "destined."

"That was the errand you had to run," Elizabeth whispered, the surprised pleasure on her face turning to horror. He fastened the bracelet around her wrist, then caught her hand and held it tight. She stared at the jewelry for a moment, then looked up at him and in that moment Darcy knew they understood each other perfectly: it could have been months before they reached their current understanding if not for the accident.

All hint of teasing gone, Elizabeth squeezed his hand in return and looked at Georgiana. "Truly," she said. "I do hope you are happy."

The comment brought forth such an effusion of joy from Georgiana that Darcy wondered if his sister meant to continue speaking all morning. He could hardly blame her, not when she gave voice to many of his own feelings.

"I have been thinking," Darcy said once they were all settled at the table and Georgiana had paused for breath, "about returning to Pemberley for the summer." He looked to Elizabeth, sitting at his left hand. "Someone once told me it is not possible to really walk in a London garden, and Pemberley's lanes are delightful in the summer." Strange, how he looked forward to returning now that *she* would be with him.

"Oh, you will love Pemberley!" Georgiana exclaimed.

Elizabeth laughed. "Caroline Bingley will be delighted. Jane and I met her last week and she said I absolutely must convince you to return home for the summer. After all," she looked at Darcy with wide eyes full of mirth, "where else could she possibly beg an invitation to visit?"

He couldn't be cross with Miss Bingley when Elizabeth looked at him like that. "Let her visit, if you can stand her. Perhaps we might invite Mr. Bingley as well, and of course Miss Bennet should not be left alone in London. Do you think Miss Bingley will find that arrangement acceptable?"

"Oh yes," Elizabeth said, laughing again. "Yes, that sounds delightful." Mr. Bingley was still devoted to Jane Bennet after a month's acquaintance, and if he was still courting her in the summer Darcy would wish the pair every happiness. Caroline Bingley, who had recently decided Georgiana would one day be the perfect bride for her brother, hated the interruption to her plans.

Elizabeth held his gaze and Darcy imagined the summer with her, full of sunsets and laughter and stolen kisses in Pemberley's gardens. How different it would be from the silence and stilted conversations of the past summer! *I really need to kiss her, when we can find a moment alone,* Darcy thought, staring down at his betrothed with unabashed pleasure. There would be mornings like this, filled with laughter instead of silence, and nights with Elizabeth alone.

Yes, this summer would be delightful indeed.

Epilogue

Elizabeth

December 1811

The carriage rolled to a stop at the gate of an imposing house. From her seat beside the window, Elizabeth Darcy pulled back the curtain to reveal heavy snowflakes fluttering down, giving the entire scene a magical air. The little girl sitting on her lap apparently agreed. "Pretty!" she exclaimed, clapping chubby hands and bouncing up and down.

The person across from Elizabeth peered out the window as well. "Bingley is here," Darcy remarked, lifting a hand in greeting as the man appeared in one of the front windows.

"Oh, good," Elizabeth said. "I cannot wait to see Jane again."

"Little Charles will have grown so much," Georgiana added. "I can't believe it's been a six-month since we saw them last."

“At least you won’t have to worry that Lydia and Kitty have changed,” Elizabeth said, shifting her daughter as she prepared to exit the carriage. Her youngest sisters had called on Darcy House yesterday, unable to wait for today’s gathering to see Georgiana again. “Did you talk about anything besides the ball?” Georgiana and Lydia would be coming out this year, and when Darcy had suggested throwing a ball in Georgiana’s honor, they had quickly decided it should be for both of them. Elizabeth knew Georgiana would appreciate sharing the spotlight as much as Lydia looked forward to the attention.

“Yes, and I did not tell you! Lydia says Kitty has a beau, although she hasn’t determined who it is yet. I’m supposed to convince Kitty to tell me.”

The door opened as Elizabeth laughed. Her husband exited first, turning back to take his daughter before helping the ladies down from the carriage. “Look, Margaret, who is that?” he asked the little girl in his arms as they walked up the front steps, indicating the drawing room window.

“Grandpapa!” she exclaimed.

“I think this will be the first time he’s heard her say that,” Elizabeth remarked. “Her vocabulary has certainly grown in the last few months.”

They were admitted swiftly and shown in to the drawing room. Georgiana went directly to the couch where Kitty and Lydia sat, but Elizabeth stood frozen in the doorway for a moment, taking in the scene. All her sisters except Mary were present, but that was to be expected. Then Jane hurried forward, arms extended, and Elizabeth moved forward eagerly to greet her sister.

"Where is little Charles?" Elizabeth asked once pleasantries had been exchanged, glancing around the room again. Mr. Bingley came up behind his wife, and Elizabeth noted with pleasure that he still looked as enamored with Jane as the day they had met.

"Asleep in the nursery, thank goodness," Jane replied. "He did not care for the journey and was not at all afraid to let us know his feelings." Darcy set Margaret down next to the ladies and Jane knelt to speak to her niece. "Hello there, Miss Maggie. Do *you* like carriage rides?"

Suddenly shy, Margaret pressed her face into her mother's skirts. Elizabeth laughed. "She was very excited to see everyone before we got here. Apparently you are more intimidating in person than in her memories."

"I do believe that's the first time anyone has called you 'intimidating,'" Mr. Bingley told his wife with a smile. "Delightful to see you again, Darcy, Elizabeth." He bowed gallantly to Margaret, who watched him with wide eyes. "Well met, Miss Darcy."

Margaret hid her face again and Elizabeth scooped her up. "Shall we say hello to Grandpapa?" she asked her daughter, settling her on one hip.

Margaret brightened, looking around the room with renewed interest. Mr. Bennet had visited Pemberley several times over the past year, and his granddaughter loved to sit on his lap and play with his beard. It was a good thing, Elizabeth thought wryly, that Mr. Bennet seemed to enjoy the experience as well.

Her father stood across the room next to his wife, the former Lady Lichfield, and both watched the Darcys approach them with smiles. Mrs. Bennet—known to Elizabeth for the last two years as 'Amelia'—had remained in London while her husband visited the countryside, and the reason why lay sleeping in her arms.

"Whozat?" Margaret asked as they reached the others, peering down curiously at the baby.

"That," Elizabeth said, "is someone I am very excited to meet. Can you say hello to your Uncle Tommy, Margaret?"

The toddler examined Thomas Bennet the Fourth intently, Elizabeth and Amelia watching her in turn. At last the frown cleared from her face. "'Ello, Uncle Tommy."

"Someone has been growing since I've seen her last," Mr. Bennet said, holding out his arms for his granddaughter. She brightened, the baby forgotten as she reached out for her favorite relative.

Elizabeth handed her over with a smile, kissing her father's cheek before settling into the chair beside her old guardian. "He's beautiful, Amelia. He's almost four months old now, correct?"

"Yes, he'll be four months at the end of the week," Amelia said, smiling down at her son. "I'm amazed at how fast he is growing, and I see him constantly. I can't believe how big Margaret is now. And to hear her talking! I can't think of her as a baby anymore."

"No, and I'm very glad for that," Elizabeth said, hand falling to the still barely noticeable swell of her belly. "I can't imagine two at once, even with the help of a good nurse."

"Did I ever tell you my mother was a twin? I have twin cousins as well, and there was more than one night I laid awake worrying that this little one would decide to come as part of a pair."

Elizabeth laughed softly, reaching out a gentle hand to brush over her half-brother's hair. "Perhaps he will be twice as troublesome to make up for it," she said.

Amelia raised an eyebrow, a motion that immediately made Elizabeth feel like she was sixteen again. "I've told you the scrapes your father and I got into as children," she said. "It will be a miracle if Tommy is *not* particularly troublesome."

"Goodness gracious!" Lydia exclaimed suddenly from the window, turning back to face the room with wide eyes. "Mary has just arrived!"

*

"Well, my dear, that was certainly an interesting evening," Darcy remarked, kissing the top of Elizabeth's head before he settled into the armchair on the opposite side of the fire. At Pemberley, they often met in the small sitting room between the master's and mistress's chambers to discuss the day before going to sleep. Since

Darcy House did not boast such a room, Elizabeth had created a similar space by the fire in her husband's room.

"Yes, and it will continue to be interesting all week," she replied. "Truly, though, I am glad to see Mary. I've often wondered how she is doing, but was never sure a letter would be welcomed. You know how Mr. Collins feels about me. I did not want to cause problems for my sister."

"Were you surprised that Mr. Collins did not come with his wife?"

Elizabeth laughed. "Not at all. From how you and Papa have described him, he is holed up in Kent assuring himself of his superiority and feeling very ill-used. It *was* most inconsiderate of Papa to marry again, and even more so for Tommy to be born a male."

Lady Catherine had refused to welcome Elizabeth into her home, and subsequently she had never met her pompous cousin. Their only form of contact had been two letters, the first a lengthy missive reprimanding Elizabeth for accepting Darcy's proposal when Lady Catherine insisted he was promised to her daughter Anne. Since she had not felt obliged to answer or to revoke her acceptance, nearly a year had passed in silence before another brief note arrived, stating that Mrs. Collins wished her sister to know she had a niece, a perfect olive-branch they had—of course—named Catherine. While the little girl had not accompanied her mother today, Elizabeth was glad to hear Mary's report that Catherine Collins was a quiet but healthy child.

"I, for one, am glad Mr. Collins remained in Kent," Darcy said. "Your father might be able to laugh off his peculiarities, but I have never been able to fully forgive the way he spoke of you." He paused, then shook his head. "I found it interesting that Anne has taken an interest in Catherine Collins. Poor healthy aside, Anne has always been a sensible person, and her influence might do little Catherine good."

"I am glad to hear it," Elizabeth said. "I should like to meet your cousin some day, especially since you seem convinced she will not begrudge me for stealing your hand"

Darcy laughed. "Far from it. I knew for years that Anne did not wish to marry me. She is happy at Rosings, and marrying me would have required her to leave." He smiled at his wife. "Rosings belongs to Anne, no matter how Lady Catherine acts, and she can overturn her mother's decisions. Perhaps I will write and request to visit this spring, if you feel up to the journey. Anne has expressed a desire to meet you as well."

Elizabeth smothered a yawn. "That sounds agreeable. I will mention the idea to Mary tomorrow. I believe she has grown more sensible, likely in response to her husband's utter lack of sense, and I would welcome a renewal of our relationship." She had never forgotten the worry that Mary might die thinking her sisters did not care for her. Today had been the first time since the illness at Longbourn that all five Bennet sisters found themselves in the same room, and

Elizabeth did not want to wait another half decade to repeat the experience.

"It was strange," Elizabeth remarked slowly, "to look around the room today and realize how much good came from the illness and my exile to London, even if it felt like the end of the world at the time. Jane and Charles never would have met, Kitty and Lydia would have remained silly and undisciplined, and my father and Amelia might never have re-found each other. It gave Mary an opportunity to grow without constantly being compared to the rest of us, and little Tommy never would have existed." She looked at her husband with laughing eyes. "Of course, you and Georgiana have had to endure the rest of us, but I suppose sacrifices must be made in all situations." She yawned again, not bothering to hide it this time.

Darcy stood and pulled her to her feet, kissing her thoroughly. "Georgiana and I have been the luckiest of all," he said when he leaned back at last. Elizabeth tucked her head down onto his shoulder, relaxing into the familiar hold and letting her eyes close. He wrapped strong arms around her. "There is no one else who could have made me as happy as you do." Placing another kiss on the top of her head, Darcy stooped and lifted her easily into his arms, smiling down at his wife as she snuggled in closer. "Come to bed, my angel."

Want to hear more from Jennifer Kay?

Check out the following titles on Amazon.

Full-length novels:

Before A Fall: A Pride and Prejudice Reimagining

A Lady's Pride: A Pride and Prejudice Reimagining

Short stories:

Darcy's Tempest: A Pride and Prejudice Short Story

What Happened in Lambton: A Pride and Prejudice Short Story

About the Author

Jennifer Kay started writing stories in Kindergarten. She rarely got past designing the cover, but the habit stayed with her, and before long the covers turned into short stories and the stories into novels. In college, Jen discovered Pride and Prejudice and it's safe to say life has never been the same. She has a minor in English but primarily writes as an escape from her day job in engineering—and yes, all her coworkers call her crazy. Jen lives a long way from Pemberley with her own Mr. Darcy and a very regal cat. She can be reached at jenkayauthor@gmail.com.

Printed in Great
Britain
by Amazon

31220477R00201